THE WHITE CHARIOT

A Jockey's Chronicle

Boniface Ossai

The White Chariot

Boniface Ossai

Paperback Edition First Published in the United Kingdom
in 2019 by aSys Publishing
eBook Edition First Published in the United Kingdom
in 2019 by aSys Publishing
Second Edition published in the United Kingdon in 2022 by
aSys Publishing

Cover and Illustrations: Adobe Stock

Illustrations: One Pixel (www.onepixel.com)

Disclaimer

This is a work of fiction. Names, characters, businesses, places,
events and incidents are either the products of the author's
imagination or used in a fictitious manner. Any resemblance to
actual persons, living or dead, or actual events
is purely coincidental.

ISBN: 978-1-913438-62-3

aSys Publishing

This book is dedicated in loving memory of my brother Felix Ossai. Felix will be deeply missed by the whole family.

This book wouldn't have been a success without the effort of my wife Nkem, who worked tirelessly to ensure the success of this book, not to forget my children Ikechukwu and Ifeanyichukwu.

Finally, a big thanks to my friend Mark Campbell for his immense contribution towards the success of this book.

CHAPTER

ONE

Ron Rogers drove his wife to the supermarket for shopping and while his wife urged him to walk her into the supermarket, he hesitated and excused himself. Though, not pleased with her husband's reluctance to walk her into the supermarket, Mariah went into the supermarket alone leaving him behind in the car. The moment his wife was out of sight, he alighted from his car and then walked across the road and straight into the Catholic Church opposite where his car was parked, as the church's bell chimes. Ron walked into the church, and interestingly, there wasn't anyone in the queue, he entered the reconciliation room and knelt behind the screen.

"Forgive me father for I've sinned," said Ron.

"How long has it been since your last confession?" asked the Priest.

"I think it was the day before my last racing contest," said Ron.

"Ok, won't you mind me asking you what race it's you're talking about?" asked the Priest.

"Horse race, father, I'm a jockey," replied Ron.

"And when was your last horse racing contest, if I may ask?" asked the Priest.

"About six months ago," said Ron.

The priest listened keenly to know what Ron was getting at with his confession as he tried to spiritually discern what questions should follow in the wake of Ron's confession. This is new to the priest, even when the priest knew of the power and mystery behind confessions, Ron's comment is another mystery in this mystery. His confession is like a mystery made in heaven, and the priest wants to know more.

"How do you feel about your being here today?" the priest asked further.

"I feel good, father, because it would give me the courage to run my race tomorrow," said Ron.

"Does it mean you only come for confession each time you want to race in a competition?" asked the Priest.

This bizarrely awkward confession is rather unravelling and less unnerving for the priest, but the fact that this ritual is more about a state of being, and didn't' really reflect the condition of the heart of this jockey touched a nerve. More worrying for the priest is that this jockey's confession is more about winning a race and less about contrition.

"Hmm, yes father," said Ron.

"Why don't you make your confession more regular, and not just only for horse racing?" asked the Priest.

"I intend doing so, father," said Ron.

"Your sins are forgiven," said the Priest.

"Amen, thank you father," said Ron.

"Go in peace," said the Priest.

"Thank you father," said Ron as he stood up and left.

After the confession, Ron walked back to his car where his wife Mariah was already waiting for him, and if there's one thing that irks Mariah, then that will be when she's left standing and waiting for someone aimlessly.

"Hey honey, where have you been? I've been waiting for you," said Mariah.

"Oh sorry, I dashed in for confession," Ron replied jocularly.

Sadly, the mention of the word 'confession' was a slip of tongue that can't be taken back, and this error will be one that will define his career going forward.

This news came to Mariah as a shock because she'd no knowledge that going for confession is now part of her husband's routine, it was as if she was hit by a ton of bricks and her disposition tells it all. She's livid because has lived with this man all her life and had no idea he goes to church behind her back.

"Seriously, confession, how long have you been doing this?" asked Mariah.

"Hmm, I'll say, each time I've a race," Ron replied with a smile.

"And I knew nothing about this, after over twenty years of marriage?" asked Mariah.

"Hmm, Mariah, horse racing is a mystery and that makes a part of me a mystery," said Ron. "You sound creepy," replied Mariah.

"There isn't anything creepy about this; I'm just living out the mystery of horse racing in my own fashion," said Ron.

"And do you've to go for confession before competing in a horse race?" Mariah curiously asked.

"Yeah, I needed to be clean to compete," said Ron.

"What do you mean by being clean, are you dirty or what?" asked Mariah.

"Ah… you seem not to understand, horse racing is more than a sport to me, it means much more," said Ron.

"Realising something as important as this about my husband after over twenty years of marriage isn't a joke, so make me understand," said Maria.

There's no need sparring over this matter, at least not without touching a nerve. With over a thousand questions running through her mind, yet the answer to the least of these questions remained far-fetched, and funnily, Ron's penchant for keeping the lid on makes the mystery remain a mystery. It's now bindingly obvious to Mariah that her husband isn't moonlighting, rather he just made horse racing to be an impeccable sport.

"Mariah, please don't make this more dramatic than it already is," said Ron.

"Why do you go for confession before your horse race? Tell me, I want to know," insists Mariah.

"I want my spirit and my soul to be clean, to enable me to connect with my horse," said Ron.

"Are you saying you needed to confess your sins to be able to ride on Anvil during competition?" asked Mariah.

Ron looked away saying there's a special bond between him and Anvil but that bond is sacred and he wants it to remain so. Mariah on the other hand thinks gibberish of all she just heard her husband say.

"You're sounding creepy and wacky, and I don't think other jockeys share your belief," said Mariah.

This mystery won't yield a goodly outcome, because it isn't Mariah's thing, and she isn't going easy on the sarcasm either. Ron is a different man, and his mystery is personal to him, he then urged his wife not to indulge in this matter any further.

"No, of course they don't, but that doesn't stop me from doing my own thing," said Ron.

"It's a shame that your wife and children don't really know you, and is there something you aren't telling me about yourself?" asked Mariah.

"That's all of it, the confession is the only thing you don't know about me," said Ron.

"You go to confession but you don't go to church, what an irony?" asked Mariah.

"Yeah," he said and smiled. Then maybe it's time we consider going to church as a family," said Ron.

"That won't work, now the kids are all grown up and we didn't at any time introduce them to church," said Mariah.

"I tried at a time, but you were bent on allowing them to be free from religion," said Ron.

"Ooh, that's the reason for your going for confessions behind our back?" asked Mariah.

Mariah's insistence is enough to cut the air with a knife, and sadly, Ron seems to have had enough of his wife's bickering at this point. He suddenly paused, just as he was about to turn on the ignition of his car, and then fixed his gaze on his wife, as a way of saying stop, 'I'm not doing this anymore.' It's obvious that his facial gesture didn't do the job because Mariah didn't stop talking.

"Enough of this, Mariah! Ron exclaimed, as he turns on the ignition of the car and then drove off.

"I just touched a nerve, didn't I?" asked Mariah, as it suddenly dawned on her that she has pushed Ron harder than expected. She then tried to keep things a bit civil, at least to allow a warm and friendly ambience return. Mariah's reaction did send a subliminal message that touched a nerve, but this didn't come as a surprise to Ron.

"Not at all, perhaps you should be more thoughtful," said Ron.

"When we get home, you'll need to tell me every other thing you've been keeping from me," Mariah muttered.

"There's nothing else, Mariah, that's all of it and this matter is closed," said Ron.

The next day is the state championship race, and while all the jockeys were in the dressing room getting ready for their race, Bianca walked into the common area of the dressing room to bid her dad good luck, but stumbled into Arnold.

"Hello Bianca, what are you doing in our dressing room?" asked Arnold.

"I've come to see my dad, and I want to wish him good luck," said Bianca.

Funnily, Edger stepped forward and was quite jocular, as he pressed on Bianca not to waste her good luck on her dad. In a rather bizarre tone, he urged her to wish him good luck instead.

"What about me, Bianca, aren't you wishing me success?" asked Edger.

Arnold laughed and reminded Bianca that neither Edger nor her dad will win the day's race irrespective of her wishes of good luck. Insisting Ron will need many rabbit foots to cross the finish line before him this time. "You seem to forget that today is Blue

Diamond's day, so you should be congratulating me and my horse in advance," said Arnold.

"Really?" asked Bianca.

"Yes of course! And why's everyone lionising Anvil?" asked Arnold.

Bianca didn't flinch, and her confidence in her dad's riding partner didn't wane, and she's convinced that even a magic wand won't take victory away from Anvil and hand it to Blue Diamond, as long as Anvil remained on the tracks. She stood her ground and without the fluttering sensation of butterflies in her stomach to reflect she's taken over by anxiety. "Don't worry, Blue Diamond will become the champion only after Anvil stops racing," said Bianca.

"I suppose you're aware that the fans think differently?" asked Arnold.

"We'll find out who's right between the fans and I within the hour," said Bianca.

"Ah...," he chuckles. You mean your trust for Anvil is unwavering?" asked Arnold.

"You've said nothing new, it's like, you telling me the sea is wet," said Bianca.

Arnold smiled, then pointed to a room. "Your dad is in there," he said.

"Can I go in? I don't know if he is decent," asked Bianca.

"Yes, you can, he's already dressed," said Arnold.

"Ok, thanks," said Bianca.

Bianca rushed to her dad in the dressing room, and met her dad who's already in his full racing gear "Err., Bianca, you're here?" said Ron.

"I've come to wish you success," said Bianca..

"Oh good," Ron said and kissed her forehead. "Where's your mum and sister?" asked Ron.

"They're in the stand waiting to see you retain your position as the champion," said Bianca.

"Anvil doesn't share her first place with any other horse," said Ron.

Bianca had to intimate her dad of the speculations making the rounds, and that's Anvil losing the first place to Blue Diamond. Ron smiled in his usual display of emotion, his view of horse racing isn't just altruistic, rather he has a panoramic view that includes not just what Anvil can do, but who Anvil is.

"Anvil isn't just a racing horse, she's much more than that, or what do you think?" asked Ron.

"Anvil will show the world she's a special horse today," said Bianca.

"Eh... it's time, go to the stand and I'll meet you on the other side to celebrate my victory," said Ron.

As Bianca turns to leave, she told her dad they are waiting on the other side with his favourite bottle of brandy.

"Hey, give daddy a hug," said Ron, and Bianca returned to give her dad a hug for a second time.

"Love you, dad," said Bianca.

"I love you, my angel," said Ron.

Ron is a jockey whose bluff other jockeys can't call, and as far as the horse racing association in the Dallas County is concerned, Ron is second to none and one to beat. This tightly knit horse racing association is bonded by the unity of their hearts, and this isn't a cliché of some sort, but a lifestyle. The effort of the horse racing fans of the Dallas County to keep this oneness of heart is one cloaked in a language crafted by the new chatter that held unwitting alliance of jockeys.

The stage is now set, and it's time for Ron Rogers to do what he does best.

TV Presenter: *Hello, I'm Chamberlin, your usual horse racing presenter. Today is another day in the history of horse racing in this County, as we can see, the temperature is perfect and the mood here is fantastic. Though, the spectators seem anxious about the outcome of today's horse racing contest, because there are speculations a new champion could emerge.*

Commentator: *ladies and gentlemen I'm Martin Presley and I'll be running your commentary today. Grand Prairie is about to witness another memorable contest, because this is the home of horse racing, and the spectators are ready for the surprises today's race may bring their way. This is based on the speculations that the world fastest horse Anvil could lose the champion's title to her arch rival, the Blue diamond.*

TV Presenter: *Martin, what do you think about these speculations?*

Commentator: *Chamberlin, in just a few minutes we'll have a winner and these speculations will be over. Though, I understand the rivalry between Anvil and Blue diamond but I must say Anvil isn't just a horse that can be easily beaten.*

TV presenter: *Ladies and gentlemen, viewers at home the contestants are coming out to their tracks as the race is about to begin.*

Commentator: *Oh, this is becoming emotional as the spectators give our champion mare a standing ovation as she strides to her track.*

Commentator: *Ladies and gentlemen the race has started, and Anvil is in third place, with Blue diamond taking the lead as usual, this is becoming more interesting as Anvil moves to second place speeding past Beauty now and right behind her arch rival, the Blue diamond. The spectators are anxious as the tempo of this racing contest reached its peak, we are now in the last fifty meters of this race and ladies and gentlemen Anvil just passed Blue diamond, as she increases strides to about a meter and a half longer each time she strides, and she is doing* *this effortlessly. Anvil is now leading with a reasonable distance and the race is about to be over, ladies and gentlemen Anvil has won the race. Anvil remains the horse racing champion in the County of Dallas.*

TV Presenter: *Although, this remains a surprise to a few horse racing fans who wants to see a new champion emerge after Anvil has won this race four consecutive times before today's race. As you can see, this is a sweet surprise because the speculation that a new winner will emerge today has been proved wrong, as Anvil and Ron Rogers remains the horse racing Champion of Dallas County.*

TV presenter: *Martin what do you think about Anvil's performance?*

Commentator: *Anvil always gets the job done with ease, she's a living legend that dominates the game and I must confess Anvil is a power racing machine that rides gloriously to the finish line.*

TV Presenter: *Ladies and gentlemen and viewers at home, it has been an interesting evening, thank you for watching.*

Ron Rogers is the best Jockey in the County of Dallas in the state of Texas in the United States, thanks to Anvil, his riding partner with whom he's mysteriously bonded. Anvil's ability to respond to every one of his commands makes this union a perfect one, and she's also able to read and react to Ron's emotions. Ron Rogers has a wife, Mariah, and two daughters, Monica and Bianca.

Anvil, the world fastest horse, is a Thoroughbred sparkling white, never arrogant racing horse with some traces of the Arabian breed blood line. Anvil is quite a magnificent horse in appearance, however, she has the ability to run different gaits, most especially the special training received from Ron Rogers made Anvil's ambling gait to be second to none.

Two weeks later, Ron needed to cool off after retaining his title, and felt going on holiday is the best way of doing that. Ron decided it's best to discuss his time-off after a pulsating horse racing season with his family members. Though, he has a place in mind, but Mariah might need a bit of convincing to bring her on board.

While he's in the stable spending quality time with Anvil, Mariah walked into the stable in her usual fashion, and it's glaringly obvious that he has to spit out his plans a bit earlier before it becomes too late.

"Mariah, I want to travel to Pennsylvania with you and Bianca," said Ron.

"Why me and Bianca, and what about Monica?" asked Mariah.

"I spoke with her already, and she wants to stay behind," said Ron.

"And where in Pennsylvania?" asked Mariah.

"Pittsburgh, and I'll want us to leave next week," said Ron.

"Is Bianca aware of this?" asked Mariah.

"Yes, after all, they're on holiday, and this is the best time for a father-daughter trip," said Ron.

"Though, it's a good idea to take time off after a horse racing competition," said Mariah.

"Monica will stay behind to take care of Anvil," said Ron.

"To take care of Anvil, is that why she's staying behind?"

"Of course not, staying behind was her choice, but it will be better for me because I wouldn't want Anvil to be cared for in someone else's stable," said Ron.

Mariah thinks differently, she's convinced that a holiday with her husband and Bianca alone will leave her on the back foot, and this can't be a proper holiday without Monica. She insists that staying in a different stable will do nothing to Anvil. She then left Ron and walked into the living room to fix what she considers a setback in this holiday. "Bianca, where's your sister?" asked Mariah.

"She's at the balcony," said Bianca.

Mariah moved swiftly to the balcony towards Monica. "Why aren't you joining us to Pennsylvania?" asked Mariah.

"I've some school work I'll need to prepare for, and **it** wouldn't do me any good running around with you and dad," she insists.

"I thought this would've been an opportunity for you to give yourself a break and enjoy some time off?" asked Mariah.

"I'm better off staying back, and we still have a lot of time to enjoy together," said Monica.

"Ok then, suit yourself," said Mariah.

A week later, Ron, Mariah and Bianca arrived in Pittsburgh, Pennsylvania on holiday, and for the first two days of their arrival, they remained cooped indoors and enjoyed only the live band and the green scenery around their hotel. It's now time to hit the city, so as to enjoy the fun the city offers. Not long after they woke up from sleep Bianca walked into her parents' hotel room, and Ron wants to know each person's holiday preference. Unsurprisingly, he has to start with his wife who wants Bianca to tag along.

"Mariah, what are your plans for today?" asked Ron.

"I'll be going shopping, and I hope you're coming with me?" asked Mariah.

"No, I'm going to the racecourse to see what's going on there," said Bianca.

In hindsight, the reason why Mariah was pestering Monica to come with them is now glaringly obvious because the crack is beginning to surface. Unlike Monica, Bianca isn't a regular lady who likes the girly, girly stuff, like going shopping. She likes horse racing, and prefers to hang around racecourses, and sadly, her mum is on her own in this holiday, and she now wondered how to cope with these two.

Mariah was irked by the fact that she was left alone and she didn't hold back her feelings as she reminded her husband they're on holiday, and this mustn't be about horse racing activities, she then suggested they do something different for a change.

"In as much as I'm only watching and not riding, it's holiday to me," said Ron.

"Bianca, let's go to the high street for some shopping," said Mariah.

"I want to go to the racecourse with dad," said Bianca.

This isn't nice, after all, they're on holiday but Ron and Bianca are still caught-up by their love for horses, and fun to these two is simply what happens in the racecourse. Mariah isn't happy as Ron continues to sound illusory, as he held onto the view that watching people ride isn't the same as riding horses, and this could precipitate into a bust-up that's quite unnecessary.

"You're a lady, don't you like shopping?" asked Mariah.

"I love shopping, just that I want to see what their racecourse looks like," said Bianca.

"Then, you like horses more than shopping," said Mariah.

"That's your conclusion, mum, not mine," said Bianca.

Bianca's lack of feminine cooperation wasn't well received by her mum, and her sidelong glance at her daughter was her own way of expressing her displeasure.

Two hours after ascertaining who wants to do what for the day, they all pursued their passion, and while Bianca and Ron were about an hour into their fun.

"Are you enjoying Pittsburgh at all?" asked Ron, as he and Bianca sat at the spectator's stand, eating pizza and watching jockeys train on the tracks.

"Of course yes, I'm glad you asked me to come with you, I'm just taking it all in. Why haven't we visited Tommy Jones, we've been here for days now?" asked Bianca.

"Hmm, visiting Tommy would've been a good idea," said Ron.

"Let's pay him a visit, I've longed to meet him," Bianca insists.

"Tommy Jones no longer live here, he left Pennsylvania some years back, and moved to Delaware," said Ron.

Err.., oh! Meeting the man that made my dad, would've been the best part of this holiday," Bianca exclaimed.

"You and Monica met him years back, when we visited Pennsylvania," said Ron.

"That was twelve years ago, I suppose, when I knew little about horse racing," replied Bianca.

Bianca's interest in the track is growing, and Ron is unwittingly fanning the flame of his daughter's passion for the racecourse. If left to Mariah alone, Bianca wouldn't go near the race tracks because her passion and interest isn't aligned with what she expects from her understanding of a regular lady.

"Do you want me to pay for a horse, so you can join the jockeys in training?" asked Ron.

"Are you buying a horse for me to ride?" asked Bianca.

"No, I'm just paying for about an hour ride, do you care?" asked Ron.

"Yeah, yes, I want to experience what it looks like to ride alongside the jockeys in Pittsburgh," said Bianca..

"When we finish eating, I'll pay for a two hours ride for you," said Ron.

Immediately she finished snacking on her Pizza, they approached a horse owner and urged him to give Bianca a two hour ride. Interestingly, Ron's reputation precedes him, and his goodwill rubbed off on his daughter because the horse owner gladly allowed Bianca an opportunity to ride as long as she wish to. After having fun on the tracks, they returned home, Bianca felt quite fulfilled, just that Ron was plagued by the needling feeling that he has left Mariah feeling quite isolated and decided to seek a compromise that would accommodate her in future outings.

Days later, Ron thought of something him, Mariah and Bianca would like, and a visit to Raystown is that thing. Bianca woke up and left her hotel room to join her parents.

"Morning dad," said Bianca.

"Hello pretty, how was your night?" said Ron.

"Morning mum," said Bianca.

"Morning Bianca, hope you slept well?" asked Mariah.

"Dad, what's the plan for today?" asked Bianca.

"Mariah, guess where we're going today," said Ron.

Mariah wasn't too keen to fall for this guessing game, and after all, the holiday so far, hasn't been much of a fun as much as she would've loved it to be. So far, Bianca and her dad have been doing their own thing, while Monica who's a fan of Mariah chose to stay behind.

"Where do you've in mind?" asked Mariah.

"We're going to Raystown!" Ron exclaimed.

"Why Raystown! What's special about it?" asked Mariah.

"Two days ago you protested that this holiday shouldn't be about horse racing and I'm trying to introduce something different," said Ron.

"Then why did you choose Raystown?" asked Mariah.

"Have you been there before?" asked Ron.

"No, I haven't," said Mariah.

"Then give me the privilege to entertain my wife and my precious daughter," said Ron.

Bianca wants to get more from this holiday, she's actually keen to get more of something odd, and out of the ordinary, and this time she wants to know if Raystown is a good tourist place that fits that description. More so, corrupt flattery isn't Mariah's thing, she likes results and hates stories, and this time it's up to Ron to rise above board.

"Yes, there's a museum and a lake in the region," said Ron.

Funnily, Bianca seems to like it, but Mariah don't want the holiday to be a burnout, and worries about exhaustion.

"How far is Raystown?" asked Mariah.

"Raystown is in Huntingdon County here in Pennsylvania, but don't worry about the distance, after all, we're on holiday," said Ron.

"Ok dad, let me go and get dressed, and I can't wait to get to Raystown," said Bianca.

It didn't take long before they set off for Raystown after having their breakfast, and it was quite some distance to travel but they eventually got there. Mariah has been looking around since their arrival, the topsy-turvy is over, and twenty minutes after their arrival she can't help but commend Ron for his choice of holiday destination.

"Ron this is a good place to visit, this lake region is serene and beautiful," said Mariah.

"Which one do you want us to visit first, the lake or the museums?" asked Ron.

Mariah suggested they visit the museums first before finally settling by the lake side, she needs to make this lake side experience to be one that's quite exhilarating.

"Dad, where are the museums?" asked Bianca.

Ron pointed in response, and said the one over there sponsors the arts and crafts community festival, and then pointed to another one and said that other one will give you the ride you will never forget.

"Dad, which one is best?" asked Bianca.

"Let's go for the latter," said Ron.

"Yes, that sounds more like it," Mariah concurred. Flanked on both sides by his wife and daughter, they then walked over to the museum, as Bianca clung unto her dad on the left, while Ron held hands with Mariah on the right. They strolled along the isles in the museums, as they spent time enjoying the eye popping sights of the artefacts on display inside the museum. Moments later they walked out of the museums, and headed for other possible fun awaiting them.

"Wow, this place is beautiful. Dad what's that?" asked Bianca.

"That's an old fashioned historic electricity trolley, and we'll be riding in that," said Ron.

"There are lots of people here having fun," said Mariah.

"Fortunately for us, today is the ice cream trolley day," said Ron.

"Ok, let's get some Ice Cream then," said Mariah.

After about an hour relishing her Vanilla Ice Cream, Bianca wants to have a ride.

"Dad, I want to ride in that," she said pointing to the old-fashioned historic electricity trolley. Unsurprisingly, Ron thinks the fun will be incomplete with Bianca enjoying the ride alone, he then suggested it's best they all enjoy the fun together as a family. At least there will be something to memorialise about this holiday.

"Ok let's all go for the ride," said Ron, he then stood up, held Mariah by hand and they went on to pay for a ride in the trolley.

It didn't take long, Mariah is laughing as they ride. "This is fun," she said.

"As you said earlier, it shouldn't only be about horse racing," he said.

Thirty minutes later they, they got off the ride and as they walked to the lake side, Ron stopped abruptly and told Mariah he'll join them in a minute, he then turned back.

"Ron, where are you headed?" asked Mariah.

Bianca seems to know her dad a bit more, particularly when he makes brisk moves as this one. "I know where he's going," said Bianca.

"Where's he headed then?" asked Mariah.

"He's going to get pizza, look over there that's an outlet for Pizza," said Bianca.

"Your dad never ceases to amaze me, let's join him, so I'll choose my own drink," said Mariah.

Immediately, Mariah and Bianca didn't hesitate as they rushed towards the stall, and joined Ron.

"Ah..., you're here?" said Ron.

"Yes of course! I want a drink this time," said Mariah.

"Which one then?" asked Ron.

"Get me anything, lemonade," said Mariah.

While she was still speaking, Mariah realised that the man standing by her side, seems intoxicated, and smelt like a brewery, and this made her quite uncomfortable, she then inched away quietly, and switched over to her husband's left hand side, even though her long side-glance didn't do much to send a message to her husband about the man standing by his side.

"Ok, Bianca, what about you?" asked Ron.

As usual she wants the same as her dad, and five minutes later, they're good to go. The boozie man that caused Mariah to move over is no other person than Captain Greg who earned the sobriquet from his days of working as a cowboy in the Old Texas, and looks like he lives in the Old Tervan boozing all day. Interestingly, the Dead man's fingers deal is his happy hour drink of choice for the road.

Mariah couldn't stop thinking of having Monica around, as they walked to the lake. "Hmm, Monica missed out, she would've loved the ride, the environment, just all of it," said Mariah.

"I really wanted her to come, I tried talking her into it, but she refused," said Bianca.

"She has a lot of holidays to enjoy in the future," said Ron, as they sat by the lake side.

"Dad, have you been here before?" asked Bianca.

"That was fifteen years ago, you were six years old then, I came for a horse racing competition," said Ron.

"Is it with Anvil?" asked Bianca.

Mariah still recollects that experience as she interjected and said it wasn't Anvil, and that the race was actually with Dona. Mariah then turned to Bianca. "You remember Dona don't you?" asked Mariah.

"Yes, I remember Dona, did you win the race?" asked Bianca.

"Yes of course, didn't you notice most of the jockeys in Pennsylvania know me," said Ron.

"Tell me about this lake, this place, just tell me everything," said Bianca. They chatted all along and laughing, as they eat their pizza.

"This is the biggest lake in Pennsylvania; it was built by the Army Corps of Engineers in 1973," said Ron.

"What about swimming in this lake, have you ever tried swimming in this lake before?" asked Bianca.

"This is turning into a lecture session. Bianca, allow your dad enjoy his pizza," said Mariah.

"This is her moment let her enjoy it," he said, and then turned to Bianca and said he hasn't but he has done mountain biking and boating. As they speak, Mariah noticed Bianca was sharing her pizza with the fishes, and she seemed not to like it. Obviously, what Mariah don't like, she surely talks about.

"Bianca, why're you throwing pieces of pizza into the water?" she asked.

"I'm feeding the fishes. Don't you see they're enjoying it?" she replied.

"How do you know they're enjoying it?" asked Mariah.

"Because they keep coming for more," said Bianca.

"I'm just worried because it will make the lake dirty; you know that this is a recreational lake," said Mariah. She sees this as an opportunity to further her parenting skill.

"Mum, you worry too much," said Bianca.

"Ok, just have your fun, and after all you're on holiday. They enjoyed themselves and returned to Pittsburgh later that day.

Old habits don't die they say, it's obvious that Ron could hardly stay away from the racecourse. Three days later, Ron had to return to his old ways, after all, he couldn't do without horses and race-course. He had to treat Mariah and Bianca with a visit to Frank Taylor's stables, as they spend time trying to enjoy what the stables in Pennsylvania have to offer.

As they approach, Frank was standing in front of his stable, holding a cigarette between his fingers with smoke billowing from his nostrils like a chimney. He was quite ecstatic to see this legendary jockey walking down the path to his stable. "Hmm, ooh my God! Ron, is that you?" asked Frank.

"Of course, Frank, it's me," he replied.

"Of all the stables in Pittsburgh, you've chosen to visit my stable," said Frank.

"Why're you sounding like this?" asked Ron.

"You're a celebrated horse rider, and everybody will relish the opportunity for a hand shake with you," said Frank.

"I felt I should check out your stable, possibly I might learn new things from you," said Ron.

"How are you enjoying your holidays in Pittsburgh? Friends told me you're around" said Frank.

"For a jockey like me, where else should I be in Pennsylvania if not Pittsburgh?" said Ron. This meeting seem not the ecstatic meeting Ron was expecting, as Frank told Ron he's moving to Delaware the coming month. This news wasn't well received by Ron, who quickly inquired to know why Frank is making such move even when the horse racing business is doing well in Pittsburgh.

Frank muttered as he hinted his guests that the governor is coming up with a policy that brings horse racing to its knees.

Mariah, whose family has earned a living from horse racing, knew what it means for a thriving business to relocate to some remote oblivion. She quickly interjected as she took exception to this much derided move of the governor, she then clings to her support of the horse racing sport. "Why would he do a thing like that? This is a source of income for many families," said Mariah.

"I heard about it but didn't know it's this serious," said Ron.

Frank is now struggling to transport all of his horses to Delaware, and he has put some up for sale, and quickly made his intentions known to Ron. "I'm selling some of my horses to make movement to Delaware easier," said Frank.

"Why're you selling off your horses? You can keep this one, she's beautiful," Ron advised.

"I'm not selling off the horses in my other stable, it's just these ones that are up for sale," said Frank.

Ron took a liking to a particular horse, the one he earlier advised Frank not to sell because she's beautiful but after Frank insisted on selling, Ron's keen interest in this particular horse grew. Now that Frank has made it obvious that this horse is also up for sale, Ron decided to inquire of its going rate. "How much are you selling her?" asked Ron. Mariah, who seems to be the police of her husband interests in horses, thinks Anvil alone is a hand full, she cuts into the conversation and asked her husband if they really need this horse.

"Don't worry Mariah, we might, and it'll be for leisure," said Ron.

"Though, I'm selling at a giveaway for just $8,500.00," said Frank.

Ron decided to give a counter offer "You know this wasn't planned, what if I give you $6,500.00 for her," he said.

"Ok, you can have her," said Frank.

"Let me see if my daughter likes her," said Ron. Mariah wasn't too keen for this holiday to suddenly become about horses, and her idea of beauty and the modesty during holidays doesn't include stables and horses, yet she'd to accommodate whatever comes her away as she finds herself in the company of Ron and Bianca. She's particularly keeping tab on Bianca as she's keen on taming her passion for the racecourse. Ron, then called Bianca who's already inside the stable taking a look at the horses.

"Don't turn Bianca into a jockey," muttered Mariah.

"Dad, you called me?" asked Bianca.

"This horse is for sale, do you like her?" asked Ron.

"Seriously" Bianca ran to the horse, and began to give her an emotional rub on her body and the horse began to respond by reciprocating the gesture.

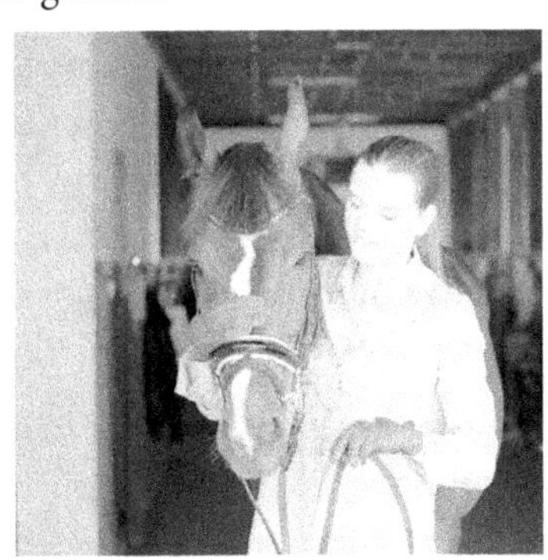

"She likes your daughter," said Frank.

"Yes, I can see that," replied Ron.

"Are you buying her for me?" Bianca muttered.

She seems to forget serendipity, and asked her dad if he brought her here to buy her a horse as a surprise gift.

"If you like her, then I'll get her for you," said Ron.

"Ooh, dad I like her, she's beautiful," she said and rushed and hugged her dad. "Thank you so much," said Bianca.

Now that his daughter likes the horse, Ron inquired of the horse's name from Frank, and funnily Frank was quite upfront and said the horse doesn't have a name yet.

Ron then turned to Bianca. "What name will you call her then?" asked Ron.

"I'll call her Fanny," said Bianca.

"Ha-ha, what a name! How did you come about that name?" said Frank, who finds the name to be one that creates quite a connection.

"That's the name of my best friend in school," said Bianca.

"Ok, that's good," said Ron.

Mariah looked on, but was quite handicapped by her inability stop this move without attracting unnecessary attention, at this point she couldn't save her daughter from her love for the racecourse. She's now convinced that this move by her husband will fan Bianca's interest for the racecourse, and all she could do at this point was to sound a note of caution. "You don't have to live in the stable with Fanny," said Mariah.

Days later, the holiday in Pennsylvania came to a wrap, and Ron, Mariah and Bianca returned from Pennsylvania where they went for holiday. Immediately they arrived, Bianca couldn't wait for them to enter the house before relating her holiday experience to her sister, and was quick to tell her sister of the fun she enjoyed.

"Hey Monica, you should've come with us, it was fun, and I missed you," said Bianca.

Monica was all ears as she was keen to hear of their experience, she then gave her little sister a hug and said she's glad to hear Bianca enjoyed herself.

"Ooh! You and this little sister talk, you've come again; you're only three years older than me," said Bianca.

"Those three years meant a lot, Bianca. Though, I missed you and I'm happy you enjoyed yourself," said Monica.

"Don't mind Bianca, instead of going for shopping with me, she was hanging around horses with your daddy," said Mariah. It's glaringly obvious that Monica didn't really expect any different from her sister despite her mum's disappointment and decided to abstain from that conversation.

"Hi mum, welcome," said Monica.

"Thank you, Monica, how're you doing?" asked Mariah.

"I'm fine mum, though I missed you guys, but I'm glad you're back," said Monica.

"How is Anvil, I hope you took good care of her?" asked Bianca.

Monica put Bianca's mind at ease as she reminded her Anvil is fine and well cared for, and while the conversation persists, Monica suddenly realised she hasn't seen her dad and quickly asked of his whereabouts.

"Dad is coming with Fanny," said Bianca.

"Which Fanny, I suppose you aren't referring to your friend?" asked Monica who seemed lost as to who Fanny was.

"No, Fanny is my horse," said Bianca.

"Monica, let's go inside the house, so you can continue with your questions," said Mariah.

"You mean dad bought a horse from Pennsylvania?" asked Monica, as they walked in to the house.

"Yes, she's a Pennsylvania thorough breed, dad bought her for me," said Bianca.

Monica turned back and saw Bianca running to the stable. "Where are you going, Bianca?" she asked.

"I want to see Anvil," she replied.

Moments later, while Monica was holding a conversation with her mum, she looked through the window and saw a Van driving towards the stable. "Mum, that must be dad," said Monica.

Monica rushed out to welcome her dad, and they hugged each other "My angel, how are you?" he asked as he kissed her on the forehead.

"I'm fine, dad, and what's in the van?" asked Monica.

"That's Fanny," said Ron.

"It didn't take long, before Bianca rushed out of the stable to welcome her horse, and when Fanny eventually came down from the van, Monica was quick to exercise her big sister's right. "Let me ride her around first," said Monica.

"That's my horse you're talking of riding," Bianca protested.

Ron intervened and said Fanny must have been stressed as a result of the travelling, and she may need to rest. Monica began rubbing Fanny emotionally, to create an emotional connection between her and Fanny. "Hello Fanny, how're you my friend, who named her Fanny?" asked Monica.

"I did," said Bianca.

"Oh my gosh! The name of your best friend is the name you gave our horse," exclaimed Monica.

"Is it bad?" asked Bianca.

Monica quickly reminded her sister, that her friend Fanny behaves weird sometimes. She then suggested that this choice of name might irk Fanny and perhaps a more conventional name will make some sense.

"I hope she likes it," said Monica.

A week after Ron's arrival from holiday, in one of his usual daily practice session at the park, Ron decided to answer to Kenny Walter's call. Funnily, while Ron wants to speak with Walter about what he had in mind, Walter has equally sent out a message to have a word with Ron.

"Ron, how are you doing?" asked Walter.

"I'm fine, Walter, I told Arnold I'll like to have a word with you," said Ron.

"How come we are both looking for each other? I just told them at the park that I would like to have a word with you," said Walter.

"You or me, who should go first?" asked Ron. It's now obvious that they both have something to say to each other, and it doesn't matter who speaks first, what matters is that each person will definitely have their turn to speak.

"Ok, you go first, before I tell you what I've in mind," said Walter.

"I bought a horse from Pittsburgh, Pennsylvania, for my daughter Bianca, and I want to register her as a member of the park," said Ron.

Walter wants to know what Ron has in his mind, buying a horse is one thing, but registering his daughter in the park to ride alongside professional jockeys is another. "Are you preparing Bianca to be a jockey?" asked Walter.

"No, it's just for her leisure," said Ron.

"But if you want her to be a jockey you can be her under-study, at least you're the best for now," Walter.

"She's studying to become a Veterinary Doctor," said Ron.

Walter didn't hold back as he probed Ron's intentions for Bianca, and said he knew Bianca has special interest in horses and horse racing, he then inquired of the name of the horse. The name of a horse matters a lot in the horse racing sport because it's of sentimental importance.

"She named her Fanny," said Ron.

"Fanny, what a name? Though, I like the uniqueness of the name" said Walter.

"I want her to be a member of the park so that she could come around whenever she feels like it," said Ron.

"It's ok; just let her know that it's sorted, but the sister Monica, she doesn't seem to be into horses?" asked Walter.

Ron quickly put the conversation into perspective, as he reminded Walter that Monica also love horses and horse racing, but the intensity of her passion for the sport isn't as pronounced as Bianca's. Now that Ron's need is addressed, it's now time for Walter to say what he has in his mind.

It's now Walter's turn to tell Ron why he sent for him, but just as Kenny Walter opened his mouth to speak, Justin, the receptionist at the park cuts into the conversation and informed Walter that Mayor Brown, the mayor of Dallas County is on the line. "He wants to speak with you, and he left the line open," said Justin.

"Ron, let me attend to the Mayor, and I'll get back to you," said Walter, who immediately returned to his office located within the park.

Immediately he stepped into his office, Kenny Walter picked up the phone to attend to Mayor John Brown who was on the other end of the phone.

"Hello Mr. Mayor, it's me, Kenny Walter," said Walter.

"Hello Walter, I was told you want to speak with me," said Mayor Brown.

"Of course, Mayor Brown, the horse racing association in this county wants to honour a member," said Walter.

"Honour a member? You're free and it's a good thing, I'm not stopping you," said Mayor Brown.

"Mayor Brown, the thing is, we're inviting you as our special guest of honour because the member we're honouring is a special horse," said Walter.

"A horse, you said?" asked Mayor Brown.

"Yes, a special horse," replied Walter.

"Ok, I'll be there to give you the support you need," said Mayor Brown.

"Thank you, I'll send you the invitation," said Walter.

"Ok, I look forward to that," said Mayor Brown.

Immediately he finished his conversation with the Mayor, Kenny Walter went in search of Ron Rogers so they could continue their conversation. He painstakingly looked around for Ron in the park and didn't find him, and decided to give him a phone call later.

"Hello Walter," said Ron.

"Yeah, Ron, we couldn't finish our conversation the other time," said Walter.

"Sorry, I left because an emergency came up," said Ron.

"That's not a problem; the thing is, the Horse Racing Association in this County wants to honour a member of the association," said Walter.

"That's good news, when will that be? And who's he or perhaps who's she?" Ron enthusiastically asked.

"Who else will it be, if not Anvil and Ron Rogers?" asked Walter.

"Err.., ooh, you must be joking?" said Ron.

"This isn't a joke, Ron. That's what my conversation with Mayor Brown was about," said Walter. Ron and his riding partner have always been in the limelight and the feat of this pair is something that has always graced the headlines but what the Dallas Horse Racing Association has chosen to do is much more than a mere formal recognition of the remarkable achievements of Ron and Anvil.

Ron smiled and said he's quite elated by the decision of the association to honour him, and he went on to say he will remain eternally grateful for this kind gesture.

"Ron, you deserve it, and that's why the association is doing this," said Walter.

"Thank you Walter, thank you," said Ron.

"No, thank you, I'll send the invitation across to you," said Walter.

Immediately after his phone conversation, Ron sauntered to the balcony where his wife and daughters were seated. He stood in the middle with smiles wreathed all over his face, and with a display of a grin that made his wife pause her conversation.

"Mariah, the association is honouring us," said Ron.

"I don't get you, what association are you talking about?" she asked.

"The Dallas County horse racing association, wants to give me the life time horse racing achievement award," said Ron.

"Oh my God! That's good, I would've said it's coming a bit late, but it wasn't," said Mariah.

"That's great, dad, you and Anvil deserves it, enjoy the spotlight," said Monica.

Bianca interjected and said she particularly likes the spotlight. After all, Ron's family will grace the stage with him, and Bianca now sees this occasion as one that's deserving of going for shopping. At least, it's another opportunity to show off. Mariah didn't hesitate to give her usual long side-glance before sounding a note of caution in her attempt to restrain her daughters appetite for the contents of their dad's pocket. She then urged her girls to go easy on their dad, and reminded them that this shouldn't be an opportunity to bankrupt their dad.

Funnily, Ron seemed upfront for it and insists his girls deserve to look special for the award ceremony, and they'll all be going shopping the next day.

"You're taking your daughters alone for shopping, what about me?" asked Mariah.

"Without you there can't be any shopping, you know that already," said Ron.

A month later, it's now time for Ron Rogers and his family to grace the spotlight, as the Dallas County Horse Racing Association honours Anvil and Ron Rogers.

Master of Ceremonies: Today, we're honouring a five-time horse racing champion in this County and the fastest horse on record. Though, without taking much of your time, I'm inviting the mayor of this great County to declare this occasion open.

Mayor Brown: I know every other Mayor in the United States thinks Mayor John Brown is a jockey, because of my unflinching support for the horse racing sport. I must confess that horse racing is our thing and the world thinks everybody in the County of Dallas is a jockey, and for this reason I'm proud to say I'm a jockey because it's a good thing. Who wouldn't like to be associated with Anvil and Ron Rogers, but before I declare this occasion open, I make a demand to the horse racing association that this County should win the next national horse racing championship before my departure from office. This occasion is therefore declared open.

Kenny Walter: The horse racing association has taken note of the Mayor's demand and we promise to bring next year's national horse racing championship trophy to this County. However, today in this county we are honouring one of our own, who had made headlines around the world, because of her spectacular performance in the sport of horse racing. Therefore, I gladly say to you ladies and gentlemen that Anvil and Ron should be honoured with a standing ovation as they take the stage.

Ron Rogers stepped onto the stage with Anvil looking sparkling white as ever, and he was accompanied by his wife and two daughters.

Ron Rogers: Thank you for this great gesture, I'm overwhelmed with joy as I stand before you the honourable people of Dallas, and every horse racing fan from around the world who have come to make this occasion worth-while. I'm receiving this award on behalf of Anvil, and I say to everyone present here that my family and I want to say thank you.

Master of Ceremonies: That was a great speech from Ron Rogers, though humbling as well, this is a special song for Ron and Anvil. Ladies and gentlemen let's enjoy the music "I was Born to be a Cowboy" by Red Steagall.

Weeks later, Ron thought it wise to organise a local outing to compensate Monica for staying back during the Pennsylvania trip. Ron woke up one of the mornings, and in his organic sportsman approach he walked to Monica's room and stood by the door. "Monica, are you up?" asked Ron.

"Morning dad, yes I'm up, come in the door is open," said Monica.

"Get ready, I'm taking you out," he said.

"Where are we going this morning?" Monica asked curiously.

"Just a father-daughter time out," said Ron.

Monica protested while still wrapped under her bed sheet, she was quite upfront as she reminded her dad he never cared to know if she'll like the idea of this surprise father-daughter stunt.

"If I say it, you'll like the idea," said Ron.

"Organically, it has always been the racecourse, except he has something else planned out Monica insist, but this time whatever he has planned for the day can't remain wrapped up his sleeve for too long, because he had to spit it out at some point.

"We are going to the Big Cedar Wilderness Trail," said Ron.

"Oh my gosh! Dad, you must be joking," said Monica.

"I guess you like the idea?" asked Ron.

"Sure, dad I love it, I've been dying to visit The Big Cedar Wilderness Trail one more time, I'll get dressed immediately," said Monica.

This father-daughter arrangement is about to get a kicking, as Bianca interestingly, overheard the conversation between her dad and Monica, and thinks sidelining her lacks the touch of a genius. "What about me, dad?" asked Bianca.

"Bianca, this trip is to compensate your sister for staying behind, when we visited Pennsylvania," said Ron.

"Dad, does it matter? I suppose you're already aware that this idea of segregation is invidious and will make mum and I mad," said Bianca.

While she registered her protest, Bianca then turned to Monica and asked if she could tag along with them. It's now obvious to Monica that not a cat in hell's chance will she find this trip to be fun, if she goes alone and leave her sister behind.

"You can come along, dad let her come with us if that'll make her happy," said Monica.

"Ok then, I'll go with the two of you," said Ron.

Not long after hatching out a plan for a walk in the woods, the girls were busy getting ready for their trip that Mariah walked into the living room, and was surprise to see everyone getting prepared for something. "Where are you all preparing to go?" she asked.

"Dad is taking me out," said Monica.

Bianca interjected "me too," she said.

"Where are you all going this morning?" Mariah queried further.

"We are visiting the Big Cedar Wilderness Trail," said Monica.

"And you're thinking of leaving me behind to baby sit Fanny and Anvil or what?" Mariah protested.

Ron stepped into the conversation as he tried to make his initial intention known to Mariah, he then turned to her and said this outing is to compensate Monica.

"It's no longer for Monica; it's now a family trip," said Mariah.

Mariah stuck to her gun, and overruled the earlier arrangement, this holiday is now a family outing, and without further objection, they all began to prepare for a family trip. "Let me get our bicycles into the car, I'll be back," said Ron.

Two and half hours later, they are already at the mountain top, but Mariah wants to be sure they are on the right path as she isn't too keen on relying on her husband's memory.

"Ron, are you sure we are going in the right direction?" asked Mariah.

"The last time we came here, we didn't take this route," said Ron.

Ron continued and said he heard a new trail head is now open to drivers, and he then picked up his address book to look up the map within for directions. Mariah isn't interested in the gamble, she quickly asked Ron what if he can't find the new trail head in the direction he's heading.

"Then we go back to the trail we are used to," said Ron.

Mariah isn't blessed with Ron's fisherman kind of patience, she insisted they retrace their steps immediately, and go back to what they're used to, instead of leaping into the dark. Ron concurred as he dropped the address book on the dashboard and then turned back, and minutes later they're at their desired destination.

"Dad, I love this place, the experience here is second to none," said Monica.

They eventually got to their first point of call, which is the picnic point. They sat down at the picnic area, and after making themselves comfortable, it's now time to rustle on some snacks. Ron then asked Monica to get the pizza and the drinks ready.

"Ok dad," said Monica. Who later brought out the snacks and pass them round.

Bianca decided to make her choice and requested for the burger and the diet coke, insisting she wants to give pizza a break.

"Your dad always assumes everyone likes pizza as he does," said Mariah.

"I don't know actually, I seem to like pizza the way dad does," said Monica.

They all got into the chatty, chatty mode as they eat their Pizza and burger, Ron was busy assessing the rest of the activities ahead of them and suddenly asked "Which of you girls want to go on the all wide double track?"

"Why are you asking?" asked Mariah.

"It's for walkers and joggers only, maybe mum will want to do the walking," said Monica.

Mariah seems to take an exception to Monica's comment. "Why, is it because mum is old and can't ride a bicycle?" asked Mariah.

"It's risky, mum," said Bianca. The response seem to leave Mariah on the back foot, and makes her more of a burden than a company, and this could send her kicking off because she hates being described as being old. "I know it's risky, and I've been coming here since before you were born, and I'm still fit. Your dad is fifty six and I'm fifty four years old," she insists.

"Your mum will ride with me, and you girls should follow so we ride together, it should be about fun," said Ron.

"We'll start from the beginners' level, to the intermediate then the advanced," said Monica.

Ron was keen to make sure everyone felt comfortable, and suggested they ride and assess the risk as they go. "We're here to enjoy the awe associated with the riding experience," he said.

Moments later, they all finished snacking, then Bianca began handing out to each person their helmets, and they set off.

Unsurprisingly, Ron has a plan and suggested they start with the dragon fly meant for beginners, then move to the death valley for the intermediates and finally to man bites dog which is the intermediate-advance.

"Dad, how come you remember all these?" asked Monica.

"Because dad is a sportsman, let's ride," said Ron. They had fun until evening, and returned home.

A month later, in one of the Saturday evenings, Ron received a phone call from Walter.

"Hello Ron," said Walter.

"How're you doing, Walter? I guess you were calling to know why I wasn't at the park today," said Ron.

"Yeah, because it's unlike you, if you aren't coming for training, what about coming around for drinks?" asked Walter.

Ron apologised to Walter, and said he understands the ritual but he have to sort out his back garden because it went off suddenly.

"And that can't wait for later?" asked Walter.

"No, not with Mariah, you're aware she doesn't take excuses for an answer," replied Ron.

Walter then steered the conversation away from the usual pleasantries, and suddenly got emotional.

"That aside, I think you should know about Edger," said Walter.

"Edger! What about him?" asked Ron.

Walter's voice cracked as he told Ron that Edger is dead. The news came as a big shock to Ron who felt Edger was beginning to recuperate and could join them on the tracks in no distant time.

"What! How did this happen and when?" asked Ron.

"The information just reached me a few minutes ago," said Ron.

Ron was suddenly grief stricken, and his voice cracked as he inquired further to know what happened. Ron had to remind Walter that it's general knowledge that Edger fractured his left leg, but wondered how this could lead to Edger's death.

"I just learnt the fracture got worse, and the doctors had no choice but to amputate the leg," said Walter.

Ron continued toeing his earlier position in the conversation as he insisted that amputation shouldn't kill Edger, and Ron knew Edger to be full of life and thinks the young man shouldn't die from an amputated limb.

"The whole thing got messy because the doctors erroneously amputated the good leg," said Walter.

"What! Is this some fairy-tale or what? Edger fractured his left limb, isn't that the limb the doctors amputated?" asked Ron.

"Not at all, they amputated the right limb and the decaying left limb killed him," said Walter. Ron suddenly became statue-still while still holding the phone to his ear, and remained flummoxed as to how a horse racing accident quickly precipitated into amputation, and then death.

"But why didn't we know of this all this while, or did you've any hint his limb was to be amputated?" asked Ron.

"Hmm, Edger hid this from us, it's demoralizing for him, talking about his too many misfortunes," said Walter.

"But we are his friends, it isn't helpful keeping a misfortune as bad as this from us, and does it mean there hasn't been contact with him?" asked Ron.

Walter reminded Ron that Edgar left Dallas for Detroit after the horse racing accident because he wanted his sister to nurse him back to health, sadly the accident was quite forgiving to have taken a life.

Ron have no choice but concurred with Walter that Edger has been bedevilled by too many strokes of bad luck, and what a sad end, Ron became emotional again and his voice began to crack further.

"Sorry about this, Ron, I'd love to come over," said Walter.

"Does it mean it's all over for Edger?" asked Ron.

Walter scoffed at the unpredictability of life. "What can I say, Ron? Edger just missed out on the earnestness and the beautifulness of horse racing," said Walter.

Minutes later, they ended the conversation and Ron walked into the living room where Mariah and the girls were seated watching the TV and Mariah noticed his facial expression is devoid of the slightest of joy.

"Honey, is anything the matter?" asked Mariah.

"No, it's just ..., no it's nothing," said Ron.

"What do you mean it's nothing? It's written all over your face, something isn't right, but if it's about the garden you can leave it for later," said Mariah.

"No, it isn't the garden, its Edger," said Ron.

"Edger, what about him? You told me the other time he's in Detroit," she said.

"Edger is dead, Walter just gave me the info," said Ron.

"What? How come and what happened?" asked Monica.

"The doctors in Detroit made a mistake, a costly one and it killed him," said Ron.

"We all knew he had a horse racing accident and fractured his left limb, apparently that shouldn't kill him," said Mariah.

This news broke Ron's family, and Mariah began shedding tears immediately, this was particularly quite shocking and painful because Ron's family took a liking to Edger whom they consider to be a fine gentleman. This time Ron has a lot of explaining to do, and Mariah wants to know how this happened, but even as he answered the barrage of questions coming from his wife, Ron seem to be dressing up in a hurry.

"The doctors amputated the right limb, the good one," said Ron.

"Oh my God, this is horrifying and sickening, and where are you off to?" asked Mariah.

"I think I should be at the park, I need to meet up with Walter," said Ron.

Mariah was still sobbing, while Monica and Bianca remain in shock over Edger's death. "What a sad death," she said.

It didn't take long before Ron hurriedly left for the park to join the gathering of fellow jockeys grieving and mourning the loss of one of their own. Later, that evening while Mariah and the girls were still in the living room, Ron returned home.

Immediately, the entrance door opens and shut. "Mum, dad is back," said Bianca.

"How did it go?" asked Mariah.

"Edger is dead, his death doesn't sit well with me," he said.

"Hmm, what can I say, we can't turn things around, we'll have to live with this unfortunate loss," said Mariah.

"What a tear- jerking story," said Ron.

Ron was able to manage the shock as the clock ticks away, and it didn't take long before they began to reminisce Edger's life time. Bianca asked about Edger's horse, and wants to know if the horse racing association will take it over to memorialise him. From Ron's understanding, the horse is Edger's only surviving memento, it's still in the stable, and thinks Edger's relations should decide what happens to the horse.

"Oh, what a nice gentleman, I liked him for his pointy perfection," said Monica.

Bianca who thinks more like a jockey, interjected and said Edger will be greatly missed by the tightly knit and clannish horse racing community. Each of Ron Rogers' family member seems to be expressing their thoughts about this fine soul that has just passed.

"I like him particularly for his ingenuity and resourcefulness," said Ron.

Monica turned to her mum, and told her of how Bianca use to fancy Edger, and funnily, Mariah quipped and wasn't quite pleased to hear of this, not just because it is Edger, but because he's a jockey. She fears, her daughter is drifting into becoming a jockey.

"No mum, it's nothing, he cheekily made a passing comment at me and we both laughed afterwards, but that's all Monica saw," said Bianca.

"It wasn't a pervy remark, so there isn't any need to be leery," said Monica.

Despite successfully disabusing her mind that there's nothing funny between Edger and Bianca, Mariah issued her subtle note of caution as she reminded her daughter that Edger is gone now, his departure is untimely and a painful one, but she doesn't want her hanging around Jockeys before she ends up in horse racing.

"There's nothing between us, I'm not in love with him, I just liked him because him and dad were besties, though not like dad and Walter," said Bianca.

"Walter was grooming him to replace your dad when he eventually steps down," said Mariah.

"Edger was an easy-going guy, suave and an epitome of modernity," said Monica.

Ron now supported Monica's view of Edger, as he reminded them of his experience of Edger's demeanour. "Yeah, you're right Monica, the other day Jockeys made jests of him in the dressing room, describing him as mop haired, and he went along with the banter laughing hysterically even though he wasn't comfortable about the whole repartee" said Ron.

A week later, Bianca returns to school, and interestingly, none of her roommates saw her arrive. She quickly dropped her stuff and rushed off to class for lectures. Later that day, Lisa walked into the hostel room "Oh Bianca is back already, and when did she return?" she asked.

"She came in this evening; didn't you see her?" asked Kristin.

"I left the hostel this morning, and what makes you think I saw her?" replied Lisa..

"She attended the last lecture; just that she came in through the back door," said Kristin.

"I knew she would be here within the week, but never knew it will be today," said Lisa.

Kristin had to make the job easy for Lisa as she said she knew Bianca would be here, because she intimated her she was on her way. While the conversation persists, Bianca and her best friend,

Fanny walked in, and interestingly, Bianca was all smiles. "Hey girls, what's up?" she asked.

"What's up girls?" said Fanny.

Lisa turned to Bianca after the girls finished exchanging pleasantries, and said she was just talking about her. She then asked to know about Bianca's Pennsylvania holiday experience.

"Oh good, I missed you girls!" Bianca exclaimed.

The girls all went on holiday, but Bianca's online buzz seem to be the loudest, and have attracted interest from her peers. Having Bianca in close proximity, Kristin's itchy ears can't wait any longer. "Why don't you tell us all about it?" asked Kristin.

"Why the interest about my holiday, at least you girls also travelled during the vacation?" asked Bianca.

Lisa didn't hesitate reminding Bianca their questions wasn't disingenuous, after all, she precipitated their interest and now they want to know why she's always sounding so excited each time they speak.

"Yes of course, and there's a reason for my excitement," said Bianca.

"Then what's the reason? Let it out," said Lisa.

"We had so much fun, we travelled to Raystown, to other places, and there were lots of activities, but guess what, I've gotten a pet," said Bianca.

The trip to Pennsylvania isn't news as these friends keep each other updated about what fun they enjoy per time during their vacation. This surprise, surprise, didn't go down well with Fanny, Bianca's best friend, who picked offence that Bianca never mentioned having a new pet since she arrived that day. She then questioned if Bianca's holiday was a boorish one and wasn't quite as fun as she purports it to be.

"Sorry about that, it was meant to be a surprise," replied Bianca.

"Then what's the name of your cat?" asked Lisa.

"What makes you think my pet must be a cat?" asked Bianca.

"Is it a Salamander?" asked Kristin.

"No," said Bianca.

"A dog?" said Fanny.

"No," said Bianca.

"I know for sure it can't be a snake," said Fanny.

This guessing game is beginning to lose its flavour, and Lisa's patience has grown thing, she wasn't keen to play this any further as she turned to Bianca and asked her spit it out and stop freaking them out.

Instead of saying what her pet was, Bianca rushed to her bag and brought out the photograph of a horse. "This is my pet," she said.

Fanny wasn't particularly thrilled with her best friend's choice of pet, as the girls passed the photograph around. "A horse, how can this be your pet?" asked Fanny.

"She is from a horse racing family, so what do you expect?" asked Lisa.

Bianca was still holding the photograph in her hand when she stood up, and attempted to paste the photograph on the wall by her bed-side. "I named her Fanny," said Bianca.

Fanny frowned immediately. "What, why would you do a thing like that, like she is my twin sister or what?" asked Fanny.

"You don't have to be mad at me, I expect that you'll feel honoured or even blush at the thought of it," said Bianca.

"Honoured for what, sharing my name with a horse? Stop taunting me with your menacing mindset," said Fanny.

The mood suddenly went cold, particularly when Bianca's best friend turned on her over her choice of name for her pet, and she insists it's moronic to name a horse after her.

"Naming my most prized possession after my best friend isn't idiotic, and why aren't you ecstatic about this?" asked Bianca.

It's now important to restore the friendly ambience and Bianca suddenly got support from Lisa who insists Bianca is right to name her horse Fanny, for there isn't any way a friend will express her love other than in this manner.

"This is kind of nice though, it makes some sense," said Kristin.

For today this horse is what I hold dear the most, and each time I call her Fanny I remember you. Moreover, even after schooling your name will always be on my lips," said Bianca.

Fanny was touched as her friends shed more light in support of Bianca. "You're now making this emotional for me, I'm sorry for my earlier reaction, though I thought this to be one of your mischiefs," said Fanny.

"No, this is from sincerity of heart," said Bianca.

"Girls, enough of this, let's talk about something else," said Lisa.

Bianca rushed to her bag and brought out some cans of fruit drinks and handed one each to her friends. "This is a new product and it tastes nice, I brought some of it for you girls to have a taste," she said.

After having a sip, Lisa was quite impressed. "Oh this tastes nice, I hope we'll be able to find this in town," said Lisa.

"Maybe we'll have to look for it," said Fanny who then turned to Kristin and asked why she wasn't drinking.

"You girls know I always like it....," said Kristin.

Bianca, Fanny and Lisa interjected and chorused "Cold."

"Yes, cold, why the hilarity?" said Kristin.

Ron and Anvil's achievements seemed to cut across geographical boundaries, and their feat has graced the headlines in nations around the world, and most horse racing associations wants to be associated with this pair. Months later, Ron Rogers was honoured by the Samaritans' Horse Racing Association.

The President of the Samaritans Horse Racing Association of England, Garry Winter honours Ron Rogers and his family during a Dressage contest in England.

Garry Winter: Today we're honouring a champion in horse racing. Though, he hasn't won a Dressage contest in England, but so far Anvil is the fastest horse on record, the horse that best understands the emotions of its rider than any known horse ever, whether living or dead. Ladies and gentlemen please join me to welcome Ron Rogers of Dallas County for the world all time best performance award.

The crowd cheered and welcomed Ron Rogers with his wife, Mariah, and children Monica and Bianca with a standing ovation as they climbed the stage to receive their award. The song titled "I was Born to be a Cowboy" by Red Steagall began to play.

Ron: Ladies and gentlemen, my family and I want to thank you for this great honour, but I must emphasize that I'm receiving this award on behalf of Anvil, who has made all the achievements mentioned here today possible. Unfortunately, Anvil isn't here but I'll say thank you on her behalf.

Mariah: My children and I want to thank you for this honour, we are grateful to you the people of England, thank you, and we love you so much. (They stepped down from the stage).

Garry Winter: Once again Ron, thank you for honouring our invitation, we are proud to have you in our midst, but the next time we'll be having you in England, we'll want to see Anvil take part in a horse racing contest here on this ground (Laughed).

CHAPTER

TWO

The National Horse Racing Championship Competition

Kenny Walter and Ron Rogers were at the Lone Star Park discussing the National championship competition. Walter excused himself for a minute then rushed into his office and returned bearing the forms for the National Championship Competition. Walter handed the form to Ron. "I know you don't participate in the National Championship, but take this, it'll be expiring next week," said Walter.

"Ah, the form for the National championship," said Ron.

Kenny Walter was quite pre-emptive as he subtly encouraged his friend to fill out the form and hand it back to him, and possibly right away. Ron asked about the enrolment fee, since Kenny Walter advised that he fill the forms and hand them back to him immediately. Walter wasn't keen on payment, he's willing to pay the fees on their behalf and be reimbursed later, all he's is concerned about is getting his jockeys enrolled. The expiry date for submission of the form is on the horizon and Walter is keen to register the jockeys he considers to be the best in his association.

"You can pay at the bank and send evidence of payment to me later," said Walter.

"My bank is just a stone throw, I can walk in and make payment right away if that would be ok," said Ron.

Walter tapped Ron on the shoulder and suggested he fill the forms and pay later, he then later handed a copy of the same form to Arnold and asked him to please fill it and hand it back right away. Arnold collected the form, and fixed his gaze on Ron, and jocularly said this contest is more between Anvil and Blue diamond. Unfortunately, only one horse will represent this county.

"Yeah, everyone knows Anvil and Blue diamond are the best horses," said Walter.

"Ron, you're quiet about this," said Arnold.

Even when Arnold was blabbing about the performance of his horse, Ron remained silent, and funnily, his silence isn't golden. Ron wasn't keen to respond to Arnold's comment, he went rather silent for a moment then opened his mouth in protest, "I know every other horse wants to beat Anvil, and it's putting my horse under pressure," said Ron.

Arnold turned to Walter and commended him for his role as the President of the horse racing association in this county, Walter on his part has a promise to keep and that's the promise he made to the Mayor and the horse racing association.

Days later, Bianca took Anvil for a ride at the park, and funnily, her mum has been looking around for her, to help her out with domestic chores.

"Bianca, where have you been?" asked Mariah.

"We went for a ride at the park," said Bianca.

Mariah wasn't particularly thrilled that Bianca left her house chores undone and went horse-riding, more annoying is the fact that she's riding Anvil and not fanny.

"Daddy took Fanny to see the Vet for her routine check up," said Bianca.

"But you're riding at an excessive speed," said Mariah.

"I'm riding at an average speed; this can't be compared with dad's racing speed during competition," said Bianca.

Mariah didn't hesitate to sound a strong note of caution as she reminded Bianca not to say a thing like that. She pointed out to Bianca that her comparism is flawed because it's quite inappropriate and unfitting because her dad's speed happens only on the tracks designed to accommodate such speed.

"Sorry mum, you know I love riding with Anvil," said Bianca.

"You've to remember you're a lady and scars from horse related injuries wouldn't look good on this pretty face of yours," Mariah insists.

Bianca moved the goal post to a very uncomfortable dimension that got her mum kicking off, even as she tried to assuage her mum's fears by reminding her not to be put off by her riding speed because she could one day become a jockey, she seemed to have just gotten her mum spooked and it's obvious that she couldn't stomach this silliness any longer.

"Bianca, you're training to become a Veterinary Doctor, and not a jockey," said Mariah.

"Which means I'll be working with horses," said Bianca.

Mariah had to use every opportunity at her disposal to let her daughter know that working with horses doesn't necessarily mean becoming a jockey. Bianca isn't letting go as she's always out to let her mum know that she should be aware that it's her love for Anvil that informed her decision to study Veterinary medicine, and more so, now that Fanny is here that decision couldn't be any better.

"Don't worry, when your daddy gets old, you will inherit Anvil," said Mariah.

"I'm going to be Anvil's personal doctor," said Bianca.

Mariah then asked Bianca to take Anvil to the stable and join her in the kitchen, but instead of doing that right away she spent some time chatting Anvil up and giving her a friendly rub and promised to be with her mum in five minutes time.

Ten minutes later, Mariah returned to the stable with a frown and was furious with Bianca for not joining her in five minutes and reminded her she has been expecting her to hlp her out in the kitchen.

"Mum, I'm coming, and I just want to feed Anvil," said Bianca.

Mariah reminded Bianca who always seemed carried away in her own world each time she's in the stable with Anvil, that she asked for five minutes, and that's about ten minutes ago.

"Ok mum, I'm coming right away," said Bianca.

Mariah wasn't moving an inch until Bianca makes a move out of the stable, she insists Anvil can feed herself and urged Bianca to at least give her some help before returning school.

"Ok, I'll give you all the help you need before leaving for school," promised Bianca.

"Let's go, if I give you the chance you will sleep in the stable next to Anvil," said Mariah.

Bianca couldn't hold her mum off any further, not after having an ear full of her mum's nagging. She then dropped the straw in her hand and followed her mum, and jokingly reminded her mum that Anvil is under her special care, as they walked to the kitchen.

Days later, Bill Shannon the owner of "the racers" betting house stopped by the stable on his way to his office and walked up to Ron who is in the stable cleaning Anvil and Fanny up.

Immediately Bill Shannon walked in, he said hello to Ron with his hand stretched out for a hand shake. "Hmm, good morning, you're welcome," said Ron who immediately became jocular and asked his guest what he's doing in his stable this early morning.

"I'm going to my office, but felt I should stop by, how is Anvil?" asked Bill Shannon.

"Anvil is good, and I've got Brandy in the house, should we go inside?" asked Ron.

"It'll be too early for brandy, and I still have a lot to do in the office," said Bill Shannon.

"Ok, then maybe next time," said Ron.

Bill Shannon is a man on a mission, and a glass of Brandy is the least thing on his mind, business first, and drinks later. He's here on business ground, as he opened his brief-case and hands Ron an envelope containing money. "Ron, the national championship starts next month," said Bill Shannon.

"What's this for?" asked Ron.

"Use it to take good care of Anvil; you know we're banking on you and Anvil," said Bill Shannon.

Ron insists the championship is still far away, and said he can take care of Anvil and also take care of himself. Bill Shannon wasn't flinching and he was quite upfront with his proposal as he chose to say it as it is. "Ron, let me put this straight; this money is meant to secure my business with you," he said.

Ron was quite disinterested, and his reply to Bill was one of a man on the fence, as he insists and pressed Bill Shannon to keep his money, and when the time comes, he'll decide which firm to work with.

"I know you and Anvil are a priority for every betting shop, and we don't want to lose you," said Bill Shannon.

"Then, what do you want me to do?" asked Ron.

Bill Shannon tried to maintain a friendly ambience even as he told Ron he's only making the first move, before others. "I've worked with you before, Bill, but I don't know the reason for the hurry," said Ron. "We want to get to you before others, now you know why," said Bill Shannon.

"We want to get to you before others, now you know why," Bill Shannon.

Ron promised Bill he'll take his proposal under advisement, but then handed the envelope back to Bill. Funnily, Bill refused the envelope and asked Ron to keep it, and then begged to take his leave while still promising to stay in touch.

"But you don't have to leave your envelop behind, what if it doesn't work out between us?" asked Ron.

"I pray it will, just give it some thought, please," said Bill Shannon as he walked to his car.

Mariah's keen interest in what brought Bill to her house this early, meant she's itching to know more about this visit as she immediately joined Ron in the stable moments after Bill Shannon left.

"What's he doing here this early?" asked Mariah.

Ron was lost as to who Mariah was referring to, and asked who it was she's talking about "Him, Bill," said Mariah.

Ron didn't talk much, as his focus was still on his horse, all he said to Mariah was that Bill came to inform him of the championship. Unfortunately, Ron's response didn't carry much information as Mariah would want to hear, it's like saying the sea is wet, after all, everyone knows the sea is wet.

"What championship are you talking about?" asked Mariah.

"Mariah, the national championship will start next month," said Ron.

Mariah knew what another competition means to her family, she's keen to know the selection process and this is different because her husband has always taken part in the County championship. Selection process for the national championship might mean a change in her diary, and Ron had to take his time to talk through the process with Mariah.

Mariah isn't daft, she knew what it meant to compete at the national level, yet she allowed Ron to talk her through the process once again. "We'll compete at the County level, the winner of the County championship will represent the County at the state championship, and the winner in the State championship will represent the state of Texas at the National level," said Ron.

Mariah isn't perturbed by the outcome of the championship, she's confident Anvil could easily win this championship with her present record. As far as the United States is concerned Anvil is the fastest horse on record.

"Anvil has been a source of livelihood for this family," said Mariah.

"I really can't explain what life would've been like without Anvil," said Ron. While their conversation persists Mariah observed as her husband climbed on Anvil and then asked where he's going with the horse. Ron just strides the horse a few steps further then turned around and told Mariah he's taking Anvil for a ride, for training at the Lone Star Park. Mariah was enjoying the company and she wants this conversation to continue, but not for her sportsman of a husband who just can't do without his routine training with his beloved horse.

"Is it a must that you should train every day?" asked Mariah.

"Anvil and I need to always stay fit," said Ron.

"Ok, don't stay long," said Mariah.

Ron stopped and asked Mariah what she wants him to get for her on his way back, and after all, she's still his baby. Mariah laughed, as she told her husband anything nice will do, at least he knows what she likes and how she like it.

It didn't take long before Ron and Anvil arrived for training at the Lone Star Park, and met Arnold, his friend and rival who's also a jockey. Arnold and his horse, the Blue Diamond, have only one mission, and that's to beat Ron and Anvil. Success to Arnold means only one thing, and that's crossing the finish line before Anvil, a feat he has only dreamt of yet unsuccessful.

"Hey Ron, good to see you today," said Arnold.

"Yeah, you're early today," said Ron.

For all it's worth, despite the feelings of butterflies in his stomach, this rivalry has no animosity attached to it, and it's just sport nothing more. Arnold felt he should do more practice, to see if he could beat Ron and Anvil in the next championship. Ron understands too well that he doesn't have to engage in a duel to prove he's a man, but playing weak man's game by turning the cheek is his strength.

"Why me and Anvil, and why not just train to win?" asked Ron.

"I'm assured of the first position if I'm able to beat you and Anvil," said Arnold.

"Ok, train harder, maybe you will," said Ron.

"Ok, how's Anvil?" asked Arnold.

"Ah, Anvil is fine, I suppose you want to use the national championship to make your mark?" asked Ron.

"Yeah, I know it's in June, that's the day I'll cross the finish line before you" said Arnold.

"A month from now, June 25th to be precise," said Ron.

Arnold became cheeky and said he needed to train harder to come first, he gazed at Ron for a while, then speed off with Blue Diamond.

The moment Arnold Speed off with Blue Diamond, Ron then focused on his horse, and began giving command to Anvil, and Anvil was responding through actions as they raced through the tracks, Common Anvil, give me a "jog." After hundred meters race, Ron changed the command, "Anvil, give me rein back," he changed the command after another hundred meters. Give me a halt, Anvil. Finally, Ron gave Anvil the commands for a rigorous race, Anvil, give me the "ambling gaits." After spending time on the tracks, Ron walked into the bar in the park and cooled off with a jug of beer.

Weeks later, the holiday is over and it's now time for Bianca to leave for school, but she has to get her concerns off her chest before she leaves.

"Err.., Bianca, you're set to leave for school?" asked Mariah.

Bianca, at first walked back and forth then stopped and said she wants to say something to her mum and dad about Anvil. Now that Bianca is returning to school, Ron just realised he's about to lose the extra pair of hands he had in taking care of the horses, he unwittingly confessed to his daughter that her presence is usually some sort of relief for him.

"How dad, what sort of relief are you talking about?" asked Bianca.

"You care for Anvil even more than I do, and Anvil knows that," said Ron.

"Ron, are you saying the rest of us cared less about Anvil?" asked Mariah.

"No, Mariah, what I'm saying is, there's a special bond between Anvil and Bianca," said Ron.

Mariah sulked, but even Anvil knew who her best friend is, but making it look like aside Bianca every other person is a waste of space irked Mariah, she then turned to Bianca and inquired from her what it was she wants to talk to them about.

"I want Anvil to retire after the National Championship," said Bianca.

"Why, how did this thought come about?" asked Ron.

"Dad, Anvil has won so many tournaments, and she's getting old," said Bianca.

Bianca's assertion is just the obvious truth glaring before everyone's eyes, she isn't just pensive by insisting it's time to give Anvil a break. This suggestion doesn't seem to be down to serendipity, and funnily, Ron has news for his family, and said Anvil's retirement, means his retirement.

"Why? You can get another horse and continue your career, what about Fanny?" asked Mariah.

"Anvil and I have a special bond and our souls are tightly knitted, one can't continue without the other," said Ron.

"Anvil is presently the fastest horse in the United States," said Bianca.

"I know about that," said Ron. He isn't taken over by some sort of egotistical individualism, rather Ron seem to be sure to erase every atom of misinformation effect, that would mean his intention not to race again is well understood. Currently, his inability to race without Anvil, and the fact that one can't continue the sport without the other is his altruistic view about the future.

"Definitely, you will win this national championship, and you will make a lot of money to start a new business," said Bianca.

Mariah was quite upfront in her support for her husband, as she turned to Ron and said retiring from horse racing wouldn't be a bad idea, and it could actually be an opportunity to start something new if he retires.

"Bianca, thank you," said Ron.

"For what?" asked Bianca.

"For your suggestions, at least Anvil will be my personal horse after my retirement from racing," said Ron.

Bianca smiled and asked her dad never to worry, after all, as a Vet doctor she'll take good care of Anvil for him when Anvil will be nothing but just for leisure and no longer for sports.

"Come here," said Ron, he then stood up from his seat, hugged and kissed Bianca on her forehead, and then thanked her, "I love you," he said. After their little pep talk, Bianca said goodbye and left for school.

Two weeks before the national horse racing championship contest kicks off at the County level, Ron received a call from the Golddy Bets. This time it's Vivian from Golddy Bets that's on the line.

"Hello Vivian, how're you?" asked Ron.

"Are you free, Donny wants to speak with you?" said Vivian.

"You mean Donny McDonald?" asked Ron.

Hearing Vivian mention Donny's name means the horse racing fans has just woken up to this county's interest in the National Championship, and the buzz has began, funnily, where best to start if not with Ron Rogers and Anvil.

"Yeah, Donny McDonald," said Vivian.

"Ok, put Donny on the line," said Ron.

"Hello Ron, good to hear from you," said Donny.

"Yeah Donny, it's been a while, and how're you doing?" asked Ron.

"I'm fine, Ron, the national horse racing championship will kick off in two weeks time, so I felt we should talk about it," said Donny.

"Ok, I'm listening," said Ron.

Donny is a player in the betting industry and currying favours from Anvil that's most loved by the fans, isn't a misstep. "At least you remember we took good care of you in the last championship, and we equally want to work with you in the coming championship," said Donny.

Ron didn't hesitate to let Donny know he would've loved to work with his betting house, but he's already engaged.

"Ron, I don't understand what you're talking about, who engaged you?" Donny asked curiously.

"Donny, I'm engaged and if there's a change in plan I'll let you know," said Ron.

"But you should've known we would want to work with Anvil," replied Donny.

"I'm sorry, but let's leave it for now," said Ron.

With the fans in this county of Dallas warming up to see who represents them at the state and national level, the days seemed to have gone too fast, and it's now time for the contestants to slug it out on the tracks. The National Championship is by the corner, and preparation means the horses are fit to race. The Veterinary doctor visited Ron's Stable to give Anvil a medical check-up before the national championship begins.

"How's she?" asked Ron.

"She's fine, but she should be due for retirement soon?" said the Vet.

"Yeah, my family and I just discussed about that, but that'll be after the national championship," said Ron.

The Vet's advice is completely in sync with Bianca's earlier advice to her parents, and funnily, the Vet deemed Anvil fit for the race but urged Ron not to put her through so much stress. "Ok, I'll do just that," said Ron.

The Vet though made it plain that it doesn't mean Anvil shouldn't practice, but he shouldn't let Anvil be over stressed. "Anvil's safety is my priority, and whatever happens to Anvil affects me," said Ron.

The Vet seem to steer the conversation away from the present into Ron's horse racing future, as he urged Ron to start looking out for Anvil's replacement, since Anvil will retire after the national championship as he said. Ron interjected as he objected to the idea of shopping for a new racing partner, and insists he wouldn't need a new horse because he'd rather retire with Anvil.

"Why? But you're still fit to continue racing, and after all, you've got Fanny," said the Vet.

Ron quickly disabused the Vet's mind because he noticed the Vet has his focus on Fanny, and subtly reminded him Fanny is his daughter's horse, and the thing is, he can't race with any other horse but Anvil. Funnily, Ron suddenly seemed to be upfront with volunteering unsolicited information about his future.

"Ron, you're beginning to sound as someone under an oath," said the Vet.

"Of course not, just that we've a special bond, and we're soul tied," said Ron.

"We'll continue this conversation after the championship. Just take good care of Anvil," said the Vet.

The championship is now about a week away, the girls are back in school but Mariah needed some attention from her husband, and she had to free up the needed space required for some scintillating time with her husband. Mariah rose from bed while Ron was still asleep, and rushed to the stable to feed Anvil and Fanny with some hay, she came back and prepared a quick breakfast for herself and Ron.

"Wake up, Ron," she said tapping him on the shoulder.

"Oh Mariah!" exclaimed Ron.

"Your breakfast is ready," said Mariah.

"This early! Leave it on the table for later, I'm coming," he said. Mariah's insistence means Ron has no choice but to get up from the bed, he then enters the bathroom to wash his face and mouth. It's quite compelling that you can't unlearn certain things even where you learn them from a mile away. This time, Mariah is bent on doing things her way because Ron could be taken over by his preparation for the national championship.

"No, you're eating in the bedroom because you've got work to do?" said Mariah.

"Let me attend to Anvil, I'll be back," said Ron.

"Anvil has eaten, I've done that already," said Mariah.

"Ok then let me eat, but why the surprise?" asked Ron.

This isn't a regular day, and Ron is serendipitously not in a train bound to nowhere, he's at home and the girls are back at school, and funnily Mariah needs her husband's company, and Ron can't be on the back foot.

"But I've always been here," said Ron.

"No, it's either the girls or Anvil takes either your attention or mine," said Mariah.

"You're right, so this surprise has worked out perfectly then. Ah Mariah, give me a minute because I love this surprise," said Ron, and they eventually spent time together in each other's arms.

Days before the national horse racing championship begin at the county level, Bill Shannon and Kenny Walter visits Ron Rogers, but met Mariah who pointed them to the back garden where Ron sat in a sedentary position enjoying the cool of the evening.

"Hey Ron, we were in the house, but Mariah said you're here," said Walter.

"Yeah, I'd to enjoy the breeze out here, Bill, how're you?" said Ron.

"Ron, Bill came to me, and he told me he spoke with you some time ago," said Walter.

Ron continued but turned his attention to Walter while his conversation with his guests persist, this time Ron was actually unequivocal that Bill came to him some time ago but he told him it was too early to make a decision concerning his request.

Bill had to take his time to address Ron's concerns, and said they've spoken for sure but he'd to bring Kenny Walter along to help convince him.

Ron wasn't quite impressed with Bill Shannon for bringing Kenny Walter as a mouth piece. He suddenly stopped what he was doing and turned to Bill, and asked if he brought Walter because he's the president of the horse racers association in the county.

Kenny wouldn't want to spoil his friendship with Ron, he had to quickly put things straight, and said Bill came to him not because he's the president of the horse racing association, rather, he came because he's close friend of Ron.

"I know you'll say that, Walter. I consider you as a friend as well," said Ron.

"Then, I prefer the friend option," said Walter.

"Ron, I just want to work with you, and both of us will benefit from this," said Bill.

"Ron, what do you think?" asked Walter.

"The last championship you refused to work with me," said Bill.

"Ok, accepted," said Ron, he then extends his hand to Bill for a handshake.

"Good to hear this, thank you, thank you for doing this for me," said Walter.

Bill was quite ecstatic, with smile wreathed all over his face, he then exclaimed, saying this is good news, and he needed to celebrate this. Ron Rogers and Kenny Walter looked on as Bill Shannon rushed to his car, and came back bearing a bottle of champagne in his hand.

CHAPTER

THREE

The Racing Contest

The next day, which obviously is just a day away from the championship competition at the County level, Bianca visits Monica in her hostel at school to inform her of her intention to travel home to support her dad. Funnily, Monica was quick to dispense of all pleasantries before nagging her sister with the 'little sister' phrase.

"Hey little sister, where were you yesterday when I came to your class?" asked Monica.

"You mean you checked on me?" asked Bianca.

"Yeah, I love to know about how my little sister is coping with academic work," said Monica.

"My almighty big sister! For your information, little sister is fine, and as for yesterday, I was in the library," said Bianca.

"Nothing serious, I was passing by, and decided to check on you," said Monica.

Bianca walked into the kitchen and found nothing to eat, she then asked Monica if she has got something edible because she's quite hungry, she then proceeded to open the refrigerator to see if she could find something.

"I don't have any cooked food in the house. Just look in the fridge and eat whatever you can find," said Monica. Bianca took bread and chocolate spread out of the refrigerator then sat down to hold a conversation with her sister.

"Monica, I'll be going home tomorrow to give dad support," said Bianca.

"What for, is it for the National championship?" asked Monica.

"Yeah, I'll be going to Dallas tomorrow," said Bianca.

"Your exam is coming up next week, and I don't think it's a good idea," said Monica.

"But I'll come back immediately after the competition," said Bianca.

Monica wasn't quite forthcoming with Bianca's proposal for a trip back home because she's convinced her parents won't encourage her to come home either. The pair disagreed and Bianca was miffed by Monica's opposition, she then turned on her sister, accusing her of insensitivity and for sounding as if giving their dad the support he needs isn't important.

"It's important to me as well, but dad will not be happy if we perform poorly in our exams," said Monica.

"Let me give dad a call, to know how he feels about it," said Bianca. The only way out of this deadlock will mean putting a call across to their dad. She immediately reached for her phone and put a phone call across to her dad, and after their formal exchange of pleasantries, Bianca went straight to the point. "Your mum is with me, we want to buy a befitting Tack for Anvil, for the championship," said Ron.

"I'm thinking of coming home to give you support during the race," said Bianca.

"But your exam is coming up next week?" said Ron.

As it's always the practice, Bianca reminded her dad he'll need to be encouraged by his family during the race, and not just leaving the cheering for the fans alone.

"Yeah, but don't worry, I've seen your heart, and how's your sister?" asked Ron. Interestingly, the phone was on speaker and Monica interjected and said hello to her dad. She then asked about her mum.

"Your mum is here," Ron said, and he then handed the phone over to Mariah so her daughters could speak with her.

"How are you, mum?" asked Monica.

"I'm fine, Monica, I know your sister is there with you," said Mariah.

"Yes mum, I'm here, I'd wanted to come home for the championship but dad said I should stay back because of my exams," Bianca interjected.

"Don't worry, if you miss this you won't miss the other contests, I've to go, we're shopping for Anvil," said Mariah.

"Bye, mum," said Monica.

Ron and Mariah continued their shopping for Tack. Shopping for Anvil is a ritual for Ron because Anvil never uses the same accessories for more than one championship contest.

"Ron, what do you think about this?" she picked up a white horse Tack, "I like this Tack," said Mariah.

"Ah, Mariah this is a western style bridle, I like the design, where did you pick it from?" asked Ron.

"Over there," she said, and pointed to a row of shelves, and they walked to that direction.

"I'll take these horse bits, saddles and saddle pad, I want them all in white colours," said Ron.

"Because everything about you and Anvil must be white, isn't it?" asked Mariah.

"Yes Mariah, this time, but look at that," Ron said as he points to a horse boot. Mariah was lost as to what Ron was talking about because there are a number of items on display in the direction he's pointing.

"Those horse boots, please remove them from the shelve and bring them over here," said Ron.

"These ones?" asked Mariah.

"Yes, bring them here. Let's have a good look at them, just that I like the design," said Ron.

Mariah looked on in excitement and jocularly told her husband she enjoys watching him prepare for a horse racing contest.

"Why do you say that?"asked Ron.

Mariah laughed again and reminded her husband he prepares as a king going to receive his crown. They continued their shopping experience, and twenty minutes later, they walked in lockstep to the till and paid for their shopping.

The day of the National Horse racing championship competition at the county level is here, moments before Ron and Anvil come out to take their position on the start line.

Mariah rushed to Ron and kissed him..., "I wish you luck," she said.

"Oh Mariah, what would I do without you? Thank you," said Ron.

Mariah looked into her husband's eyes for a while, she then kissed him again. "Ok, go and get your trophy," she said.

Today's race belongs to Anvil, who cares about tomorrow? Army of rivals lining up to beat Anvil can continue but she's got today. Serendipitously, Arnold will never forgive himself if he fails to go all out to cross the finish line before Anvil, and at this point,

Arnold cared less about what Ron thinks about today's race, he's here to make a record for himself and his horse.

"Thank you," said Ron.

The TV presenter and the commentator took over the broadcast.

TV Presenter: Hello, I'm Chamberlin, Premier of Grand Prairie. Tonight's Dallas County story is about a sporting fairy tale that has captured the imaginations of horse racing enthusiasts around the world. In today's story, Anvil the world fastest horse is taking the stage to compete for the national championship for the first time.

The Commentary: Ladies and gentlemen, I'm Martin Presley, today's race in Grand Prairie will be a chance to see Anvil, the five time Dallas County horse racing champion and the fastest horse on record compete for the national championship in the United States. However, from what we have learnt from Arnold, Blue diamond will make this competition a stiff one for Anvil.

TV Presenter: Martin, you just mentioned Blue diamond, why do you think Blue diamond will be a challenge for Anvil?

Martin: Arnold told us that Blue diamond isn't here to accompany Anvil to the finish line but to win the race.

TV Presenter: You mean the rivalry between Anvil and Blue diamond continues, despite the fact that Blue diamond have never succeeded in beating Anvil.

Martin Presley: Yes, Chamberlin, let's see how the race unfolds, all I know is that Anvil can't be beaten.

TV Presenter: Thank you, Martin let's see how the jockeys and their horses perform today.

All the horses are lined up at the start-up line and a minute later, the umpire fires the gun.

Commentary: Ladies and Gentlemen the race has started, and in a moment we're going to have a winner, surprisingly Blue diamond has taken the lead halfway into the race.

But wait a minute, Anvil is putting up show as she speeds past Blue diamond, we're now into the last twenty meters of the race, Anvil is now having a comfortable lead over Blue diamond.

Anvil has just crossed the finish line, she has won as expected, and if I must tell you, Anvil is a combination of character and tenacity.

TV presenter: Anvil just proved to be the champion that she is, the County of Dallas has just gotten a new champion to represent the County at the state level for the national championship competition. However, Blue Diamond tried to outmatch Anvil but failed.

Minutes after crossing the finish line, while Ron was still celebrating their victory, Anvil collapsed and the Vet rushed to attend to her.

Commentator: Wait a minute, Anvil is down, and a Veterinary doctor has just rushed to her side, but we don't know what the problem could be. The spectators are all looking forward to seeing Anvil on her feet again.

Mariah was on her way to congratulate Ron, when Anvil collapsed, she then ran faster toward her husband who fell to the ground the moment Anvil slumped to the ground. Ron got up immediately, but Anvil didn't. "Ron, Ron, are you ok, and how's she?" asked Mariah.

"I don't know, but it isn't good, Mariah," said Ron.

Mariah tried to calm her husband as the Vet rushed to the scene to give Anvil some attention. She held Ron as she advised that the Vet is here, let him take a look at Anvil.

Walter rushed down to the scene from the pavilion where he was standing. "How is Anvil?" asked Ron.

"It's not good, Kenny, Anvil seems hurt," Ron replied, while sobbing.

"Let me get more Vets to check her out, just stay put and watch Anvil, I'll be back," said Walter. Ron drew Kenny Walter back to himself, and said he can't, he can't do it, and he just can't continue to watch Anvil suffer. Kenny Walter looked on in confusion as Ron wept like a baby.

"What do you mean you can't?" asked Walter.

Mariah interjected and advised her husband not to give up hope, and said it's best to allow the Vet to continue checking Anvil out and see if she can make it.

"Kenny, I can't stand watching my horse suffer, maybe someone should do the watching for me, while I look away," said Ron.

TV Presenter: The spectators are still anxious about what the problem with Anvil is, because Anvil has been down for about thirty minutes, the area has been cordoned off by the police as the Vet continues to give medical attention to Anvil.

TV Presenter: (Turned to the commentator), what do you think the problem could be, Martin? The spectators and our viewers at home are all agitated.

Commentator: Yeah, Chamberlin, I'm apprehensive about Anvil's condition, our champion needs to be on her feet, because a champion isn't celebrated while on the ground.

TV Presenter: Wait a minute, Martin, Ron Rogers seem to be crying, the situation looks worse than we think. What's going on?

The Vet tried to resuscitate Anvil, but all efforts failed. He'd to pronounce Anvil dead at the Scene.

"Sorry, I don't think Anvil can make it. Anvil's heart is really failing," said the Vet.

"What do you mean? I don't understand what you're talking about," said Ron.

"I mean Anvil won't make it, I'm sorry," said the Vet.

"What! Oh my God, Anvil," Mariah screamed and cried the more.

Ron suddenly seems to be suffering from a loss of hearing, and he's also losing track of time, and needed Mariah to confirm what the Vet just said. Sadly, Anvil's feat and achievements is all about to go up in smoke without a possible miracle, her heroic days are now likened to a train bound to nowhere, and for all it's worth, this can't be vanity.

"Mariah, what did he say" Ron stood up and walked back to Anvil and turned to Mariah, "will she make it?" asked Ron.

"He said Anvil might not make it," said Mariah, and not long, Anvil breathes her last.

"Anvil has stopped breathing," Ron exclaimed, he then turned to the Vet and pleaded with him to please do something.

"Calm down, Ron," said Walter.

"Somebody help me please, anybody, please help me," Ron cried out for help to save his riding partner.

The Vet checked to see if Anvil is still alive. "I'm so sorry, Ron, Anvil is dead," said the Vet.

Ron and Mariah wept as Anvil lay dead, and Arnold was on hand to comfort Ron, while Walter comforts Mariah. It didn't take long, news of Anvils' death reached the commentator and the TV presenter.

TV Presenter: Viewers, today is a very sad day as far as horse racing is concerned in this county. From the news reaching us, we are sad to inform you that Anvil, the winner of today's horse racing championship contest is dead.

TV Presenter: Martin, what do you've to say about this sad news?

The commentator: What do you think Chamberlin? I'm very sad about this news because the world fastest horse shouldn't die in this manner. This would've been her moment to win the national championship, but that dream just fades away like a shadow, and aborted. Anvil was a special horse, a racing champion the world never got to see in action.

TV Presenter: Thank you Martin, we're ending this broadcast on a very sad note, we say rest in peace, Anvil.

That night, there was utter silence in all the racecourses in the County of Dallas. After all, their legend is gone, and all people could hear was nothing but a silent whisper of goodbye carried by the calm breeze that blows through the streets of Dallas, and there wasn't a single soul that didn't feel the sense of eeriness in the air.

The ambience suddenly went sour, as the television captured Ron's raw display of emotion, and that left viewers reeling from within. Walter had to drive Ron and Mariah home because Ron was quite shaken and this made him shudder, as such, he can't drive in his current state. For the first time, Ron had to return home after a racing contest empty-handed, and without Anvil.

Walter stayed with Ron for a while to comfort him over his loss, and decided to return to the park to take care of things, but before he leaves he asked to know if Ron has informed his daughters about the incident.

Ron realised their phones have been off, and he really doesn't know if his daughters have been trying to reach him, at least to know the outcome of the race. Walter urged Ron to put himself together, and reminded him Mariah needs him because she's devastated as well, and his daughters will equally need him when they hear of this.

"Thank you Walter, you've been a friend," said Ron.

After spending time with Ron, Walter went back to Mariah on his way out.

"Mariah, please you need to be strong and I understand how great a loss this is," said Walter.

Mariah thanked Walter for everything, telling him he has really been there for them but Walter went on to ask whether her daughters have been intimated of the incident. "I asked Ron and he said he doesn't think so," said Walter.

Mariah realised she and her husband have been so consumed by their loss and forgets that this loss equally affects the girls. He urged them to give the girls a phone call and intimate them of what has happened.

"I told Ron about this and I feel I should say the same to you," said Walter.

"What's it you want to tell me about?" asked Mariah.

"You and Ron need to pull yourselves together for your daughters' sake because when they get to hear this, somebody needs to calm them down," said Walter.

It's common knowledge that most residents in Grand Prairie know Bianca with Anvil as two peas in a pod, and while Ron sulk's over his loss, there's every possibility Bianca will weep much more than her dad.

"Yes, you're right, Walter," said Mariah.

Walter left, after promising to keep an eye on Ron and his family.

Minutes after Walter left, Mariah walked back to the stable where Ron was, but he immediately inquires from Mariah if Monica and Bianca are aware of the incident.

"The girls, its good they hear about this from us than hearing about it from the news," said Ron.

Mariah then asked Ron if the girls called because she's certain they would want to know about the outcome of the day's race. Ron himself couldn't confirm if his daughters have been trying to reach him because his phone has been switched off. Serendipitously, Mariah's phone has also been off, but she immediately reached for her phone and gave Monica a call right away.

Instead of calling Bianca, Mariah thought it wise to first call Monica who's studying in the same University in the state of Oklahoma to inform them of Anvil's death.

"Hello mum, how're you doing and how was the national championship race? I've tried reaching you and dad," said Monica.

"Sorry, our phones have been off, and how's your sister, is she ok?" asked Mariah.

Monica replied her mum, saying Bianca is fine and they were together the previous night. After all, they never knew their hunch was playing pranks on them with the situation at home, as Monica told her mum they hope to celebrate their dad's victory when they return home after their exams. Mariah interjected and said maybe Monica and her sister will come home sooner than planned.

"Why, mum, is anything the matter?" asked Monica.

Mariah decided to break the news as succinctly as possible and then said Anvil is dead and she's sorry, tears rolled down her cheek, and her voice cracked.

"What! Mum, what are you talking about?" screamed Monica.

"I'm sorry, Anvil died a few hours ago," said Mariah.

Monica protested on the phone and said no, Anvil can't just die, she insisted, yet asked to know how the death happened. Monica was still holding the phone to her ear as she spoke with her mum, she then stood up shut her door and wept.

"Calm down Monica, ok I'll call you in a few minutes time when you get hold of yourself," said Mariah.

After about ten minutes, Mariah called Monica again, to continue their earlier conversation but Monica was still sobbing and told her mum she's still in shock.

"Calm down, I'm still in shock myself," said Mariah.

Monica asked how Anvil's death happened, her mum wasn't in a mood to talk but had to find strength as she subtly hinted her daughter that Anvil collapsed after winning a race.

"What's the cause of the collapse?" asked Monica.

Mariah herself is lost as to the cause of Anvil's collapse, she insisted she doesn't know, yet suggested they wait for the result of the post mortem. She tried to disabuse Monica's mind, and stated that one thing for sure is that her dad gives Anvil the best of care.

"Have you told Bianca about this?" asked Monica.

Bianca's special relationship with Anvil might mean such news could precipitate into something grim, and she might hurt herself if she isn't managed properly when she knows about this.

"I know how close Bianca is to Anvil, but she needs to know," said Monica.

Mariah's interest in managing everything meant she equally had to manage the news of Anvil's death, she then urged Monica to bring Bianca home, so she can tell her about it at home. Monica wasn't quite convinced the bond between her sister and Anvil should be enough reason to bring her home just to inform her of Anvil's demise, rather she'll painstakingly inform her sister of the sad news,

"Monica, are you sure you can handle the situation?" asked Mariah.

"Of course yes, her hostel is just a stone throw from mine, and I'll be with her in ten minutes time," promised Monica.

Immediately after her conversation with her mum, Monica made herself decent and minutes later she's with Bianca in her hostel room.

"Hey Monica, you never told me you're coming," said Bianca.

Monica smiled and then jocularly banter her sister, asking if she would need to take permission from her little sister before coming to see her. In her usual protest Bianca, asked Monica if she's never tired of reminding her she's the little sister.

"No, allow me to enjoy the privilege of being the big sister," said Monica.

Bianca used her hand to feel the texture of Monica's dress as she dismissed her sister's banter, yet showed keen interest in her sister's dress. "I like this frock you're wearing, will you pass it on to me?" asked Bianca.

"You can have it, but that'll be tomorrow," said Monica.

"Seriously! Ooh, that's why I love my sister," Bianca said and gave Monica a bear hug.

"You can come and pick it up tomorrow," said Monica.

"Ok thank you, but have you been able to get mum and dad on phone, because their phone has been switched off?" asked Bianca.

This is quite a thorny conversation for Monica, as she went quiet for a while, and spoke in a low tone, and she opened her mouth then told Bianca that something happened at home. It wasn't unsurprising that Bianca suddenly became statue-still, as she's now keen to know what it was that happened back home, and funnily Monica stood up immediately and shuts door.

"What's it, what happened, Monica? Tell me," asked Bianca.

"It's Anvil," said Monica.

Bianca began to fret and she's now unable to contain herself until she knows exactly what it is that has happened to Anvil "What happened to Anvil, and is Anvil ok ?" she asked.

"Anvil is dead," said Monica.

"No! Anvil, no," Bianca screamed, and fell to the floor and screamed again, while Monica rushed to console her.

"It's ok, Bianca, and you don't have to hurt yourself," said Monica.

Monica finds it an arduous task keeping Bianca calm, after breaking the news to her, because Bianca now wants to know what happened, and who killed Anvil.

"Anvil collapsed after a race," said Monica.

Monica's explanations seem not to be making enough sense to Bianca who suddenly stood up from the floor, then reached for her bag and began packing her bag, as she continued saying she can't stay in school any longer, and insisting she's going to Grand Prairie to see Anvil.

"Stop, Anvil is dead, and I told mum we'll come a day after tomorrow," said Monica.

Bianca turned on her sister, as she tried painting Monica as stone hearted. "Why're you doing this? You don't seem to care about Anvil," Bianca protested.

"I've been crying before I came here," said Monica as tears rolled down her cheek.

Bianca became emotional towards her sister, and it now dawned on her that she has turned on her sister for no obvious reason, it didn't take long before she apologised for telling her sister she doesn't care, yet pleaded with Monica to let her travel home that same day.

"Bianca, please do this for me, I beg you, we'll go home the day after tomorrow," Monica pleads.

"Ok, but don't dare extend it," said Bianca.

"Mum's phone is back on if you wish to speak to her," said Monica.

Now that Anvil has obviously bitten the dust, all that Bianca now has left is her Fanny. "How's Fanny, did mum tell you about her?" she asked.

"No, but Fanny should be fine, and you'll get to see her a day after tomorrow," said Monica. Anvil was quite a beacon of hope to all other horses and jockeys in this County, it's now arguably obvious that all of that is about to change. Thankfully, people shine the brightest during their darkest hour but a sudden darkness has just befallen Ron, and his ability to swim this murky water still remains to be seen.

CHAPTER

FOUR

A day after Anvil's death, it became obvious to Mariah that Ron has been struggling to hold it together.

"Ron, you've to stop crying, Anvil is dead and you know I loved Anvil as well," said Mariah.

"I know Anvil is dead, but how can I cope without Anvil?" said Ron.

Ron is suddenly taken over by a sickness of the mind, and Mariah is now finding it difficult to get her husband back and around, she urged him to stop locking himself inside the room, reminding him he has a family.

"Mariah, I know I've been a mess but I'm just grieving in my own way," said Ron. Mariah emphasised and urged her husband to start eating, as she reminded him he hasn't been eating properly.

"I know, ok get me something to eat," said Ron. Mariah went straight into the kitchen and brought him some food.

Ron was seated on the floor of the stable when Mariah brought him some food, and as he ate his food even though he'd no appetite for food, Mariah then reminded him Kenny Walter called earlier, and said Ron should come and pick a horse of his choice he can continue racing with.

"If it isn't Anvil, then I can't continue racing," said Ron.

"You don't have to shut yourself out because Anvil is dead, what about Fanny don't you love her as well? You can race with her," said Mariah.

"Mariah, I promise you, I'll be alright," Ron said and pulled Mariah's head close and kissed her forehead.

Mariah held her husband, while giving his hand a slight squeeze, and then spoke in a soft tone that Kenny Walter will be coming in later that day to speak with him. She urged him not to shut Walter out.

Walter wanted Arnold to join him on a visit to the Vet to discuss about the need for a thorough post mortem. Immediately Arnold saw Walter approaching in the park, they exchanged pleasantries but Arnold didn't hesitate to ask Walter what he was doing in the park that morning.

"It's you I've come to see," said Walter.

"How do you know you'll find me here?" asked Arnold.

"Where else will you find a jockey, if not at the Lone Star Park," said Walter.

"Ok, you've seen me, though I'm thinking of going to Ron's house after training.

"That's why I'm here, and I want you to come with me," said Walter.

"Err.., to where?" asked Arnold.

Walter was upfront in asking Arnold to come with him, so they could make post mortem arrangements for Anvil.

"That's necessary, because Anvil isn't just any horse, Anvil is a special horse," said Arnold.

Walter then asked Arnold to jump into the car, so they could get going. Arnold, hesitated for while, he then opted to meet Walter at the Vet's office because he'd to take Blue diamond home to the stable. "How's Blue diamond?" asked Walter.

"Blue diamond is fine," said Arnold.

"I hope you know," said Walter, who suddenly wants to engage in a conversation with Arnold.

"Know what, what are you talking about, Walter?" asked Arnold.

Walter unblinkingly break the ice to Arnold, saying now that Anvil is dead the pressure will be on Blue diamond, and Arnold soon came to the realisation that his horse the Blue diamond has always come second behind Anvil.

Sadly, Anvil is dead, Blue diamond will become the fastest horse in this County, though not the fastest horse on record. Arnold understands that this isn't corrupt flattery, and it's time to braze himself up for the spotlight, and the challenges that come with it.

An hour later Arnold caught up with Kenny Walter in front of the Pathologist office, but Arnold suddenly developed cold feet and became hesitant.

"Walter, sorry, I can't go in there with you," said Arnold.

"Why, Arnold?" asked Walter.

"Making arrangement for Anvil's post mortem is like talking about Blue diamond's post mortem, and it kind of freaks me out and make my skin crawl," said Arnold.

"It's also not easy for me, Arnold, but we just have to be strong for Ron," said Walter.

"Please, Walter, I really wanted to do this with you, but I just can't," said Arnold.

Walter reasoned with Arnold for a while and decided to go in alone, but then turned around and asked Arnold to wait for him in the car, he then turned around again before walking into the pathologist office.

"Hey, good morning, how're you doing?" asked Walter.

"I'm fine, Walter, what are you doing here?" asked the pathologist.

While the conversation between the pair persists, Kenny Walter looked on as the pathologist cuts into another animal whose cause of death is being investigated by the pathologist. Funnily, watching as an animal is being butchered makes Walter's skin crawl because the sight wasn't quite pleasant. Yet he'd to stay around to discuss the business that brought him to the pathologist.

"Is it bad coming around to see how you're doing?" asked Walter.

"I don't think so, Walter, the only time I see you here is when one of your horses die, particularly when you're with Arnold," said the Pathologist.

"Hmm, you may be right," said Walter.

The pathologist steered the conversation into the calamity of the previous day, as he told Walter he watched the race and saw what happened to Anvil, and it was a very sad moment for him and his family. Walter smiled and said it meant the pathologist is already aware of the reason for his visit.

"Of course, yes! My wife hasn't eaten since yesterday; it was as if she lost a child," said the Pathologist.

"I know a lot of people felt that way, and Anvil isn't just any horse. Anvil is a special horse," said Walter.

Funnily, the pathologist seems to be the one needing help as he opened up to Walter that his wife has refused to eat since yesterday, and this loss is even affecting his home. Walter then urged the pathologist to establish the cause of death for Anvil, to see if the association can prevent a reoccurrence of this kind of tragedy.

The pathologist then handed Walter the request for post mortem form to fill, but Walter seem not to be in a mood for delays, as he turned to the Pathologist and asked when the result for the post mortem will be out.

Within a week the pathologist replied, he then urged Walter to bring Anvil's body to him later in today. Walter didn't hesitate to state his concern as he reminded the pathologist that his last post mortem result was delayed, and pleaded with him to make this result available on time. "Why the urgency?" asked the pathologist.

Walter didn't obfuscate his worry as he hinted that this incident happened in full glare and was captured live on the television and the world will want to know the cause of death and what the association was doing to avoid a future occurrence of such ugly incident. In fact he dreads the hollow feeling in the fans following Anvil departure.

"Yes you're right, even my wife will want to know what happened and what measures you're putting in place to forestall future occurrence," said the pathologist.

After making arrangements with the Pathologist Walter had to pay Ron a second visit to let him know he had arranged for a post mortem for Anvil. Mariah happened to be the first to come and receive Kenny Walter immediately he alighted from the car, and immediately they finished exchanging pleasantries, Walter proceeded to ask her about Ron's whereabouts and how he's doing.

Mariah looked at Walter and began to sob, she felt bad because everyone is asking to know how Ron is doing, and none have asked how she herself is doing. "Oh Mariah, sorry about that," said Walter.

"I loved Anvil and I'm devastated as well, because Anvil was family," said Mariah.

"Yes, I know," replied Walter.

"Have they established the cause of death?" asked Mariah.

The cause of death isn't what matters most to Ron, he just wants to be with Anvil, and if there's anything Ron desired, that should be wings, so he could soar with Anvil.

"No, we're still waiting for the post mortem result," said Walter.

Mariah thanked Walter for his support and after spending some time with Mariah, Walter then walked up to Ron and found him in the stable looking lost and poorly kept. "How are you, Ron?" asked Walter.

"I'm fine, though, I'm trying hard to hold it together but it all seem to be falling apart," Ron said and began crying.

"I know, Ron, just keep holding it together, and you'll be fine," said Walter.

"Where do I go from here and how do I go on?" asked Ron.

"We've gone to the pathologist and I've instructed him to carry out post mortem," said Walter.

Ron wasn't too keen for a post mortem, after all, his riding partner is gone, and whatever the pathologist have to say at this point makes no sense to him because it won't bring his beloved horse back to him. Ron stressed that Anvil is dead, and post mortem can't bring her back.

Walter on the other hand thinks otherwise because he has this feeling that Ron can live again, as he imagines the bloom hope in every heart.

Horse racing fans protest the death of Anvil carrying placards that reads various requests. They have vowed there won't be peace in Lone Star Park unless Anvil gets justice.

Protest organizer: Ladies and gentlemen, the horse racing sport or the equestrian sport in this County has been dealt a big blow with the death of Anvil, the world fastest horse on record. We hereby put forward our demands to the authorities in charge of horse racing in this county to investigate the following.

Whether Anvil got the required medical examination before the race.

To evaluate the speed at which Anvil was running in relation to the incident.

To review the racecourse to see if the racecourse is responsible for the incident.

We request that the post mortem result if any has been ordered be read openly.

Finally, it's important to review the Vet's effort to save Anvil and to find out if Anvil would've been saved if the Vet had done more.

Immediately after the protest organiser finished speaking, and putting forward their demands, Kenny Walter quickly took the stage to address this protest that's fast becoming a carbuncle. Life is more like footsteps in the sand, and it's all about making the best of each moment, Anvil has left the stage leaving fans wanting more of her feats.

Kenny Walter: Ladies and gentlemen, this is the County of Dallas, and we're a horse loving people in a horse loving County, and in a horse loving state. Yesterday was a sad day in this county, because one of our own died yesterday. I must tell you, Anvil isn't just any horse, Anvil is the world fastest horse and unfortunately Anvil's death was captured live on television. However, as the president of the horse racing association in this county, I wish to inform you that an autopsy has been ordered, and all your demands will be answered by the coroners' report because I wouldn't want to see the horse racing community in this county suffer a similar loss.

Interestingly, Mayor Brown was on hand to apply his charm of political suasion to the situation, and funnily, he has always branded himself the people's mayor, and it's now time to put some of his political skills to use.

Mayor Brown: Ladies and gentlemen I want to thank you for carrying out your protest in a peaceful manner, and for expressing your love for Anvil, the world fastest horse on record. Horse racing is our tradition, and that's what the state of Texas is known for but as you all know I was on ground yesterday to give Ron Rogers and Anvil a hand shake after winning their race before the sad incident took place. However, as the Mayor of this county, I've heard your demands and we promise you we'll do the right thing to make sure this never happen again.

Two days after Anvil's demise, Monica and Bianca returned home as planned, but Bianca suddenly became overwhelmed as she stepped into the house and immediately began to cry as she sets eyes on her mum. Emotions ran high almost immediately, as Mariah held tightly onto Bianca and shedding tears as well. Monica joined the party in show of raw emotion, because this family's hero has just gone with the wind, and Mariah just kept saying it happened so quickly, and she just can't explain what went wrong.

"How quickly did this happen?" asked Bianca.

"I can't explain, all I can say is that Anvil has left us," said Mariah.

"What about Fanny, is she alright?" asked Bianca.

"Err..., Fanny is good, she's very fine, Mariah replied.

For all its worth, Monica had to inquire to know how the race itself went before the unfortunate incident occurred and asked if Anvil did win the race.

Mariah responded and said Anvil actually won the race with a reasonable margin but collapsed minutes after the contest. Typical of Bianca, she wasn't particularly pleased with Monica for her interest in the outcome of the race, and as far as Bianca is concerned Anvil's death should be the only worry, nothing more.

"I don't know what you're thinking Bianca, but you aren't the only one mourning Anvils' death," said Monica.

Monica could feel her dad's absence around the house, she then asked her mum about her dad. Mariah didn't hesitate to let her daughters know their dad has been devastated, and he's locked up in the stable. The girls suddenly became exasperated on hearing their dad is locked up somewhere.

"Mum, who locked him up?" asked Bianca.

"He locked himself up, and he hasn't eaten since morning," said Mariah.

Monica stood up and immediately excused herself and held Bianca by the hand, leaving her mum behind. "Let's meet dad, we'll be back," she said.

Bianca and Monica walked into the stable and met their dad who's sat on the floor of the stable looking hurty and poorly kept. Immediately his girls walked in, he lifted his head and nodded as a way of saying welcome to them. Monica stood confused in front of their dad for a while, and this time Ron opened his mouth to speak. "You came, how're you?" asked Ron.

"We're fine, dad, but why're you sitting on the floor of the stable," asked Monica.

"Nothing, I just don't feel good, I need to mourn Anvil in my own way," said Ron.

Monica couldn't help but to remind her despairing dad that being incredibly isolated isn't the best way to mourn, she squatted and held her dad by the hand fearing her dad is losing it. Ron, on his part insists he seeks nothing but a complete tranquillity, because the most beautiful music sometimes is silence, and the stable is the best place to make that happen.

"Why, dad?" asked Monica.

"Anvil has been through thick and thin with me," said Ron.

Monica tried pulling her dad to get him off the floor, he resisted a bit but she insisted he doesn't have to sit on the floor of the stable. Ron isn't only looking lost, he looked so much like a man hit by a fast-moving truck, and it's obvious he hasn't visited the shower in the last twenty-four hours, yet Monica inquired if he has taken a shower.

"No, I haven't, but I'll do that later," said Ron.

"A clean shave wouldn't be a bad idea," said Monica.

Bianca interjected and said she doesn't think her dad has eaten either,

"Let's go inside, dad," she said.

"Go in to the house, I'm coming behind you," he said.

Monica made it clear to her dad that he should be sure that they aren't leaving this stable without him. Ron hesitated for a while but eventually gave in and got up, and he then held Monica and Bianca close to himself as they walked into the house. "Ok, you girls won," he said.

As they strolled from the stable into the house, Ron looked a little less smog, as he lightens up. "Dad, I'm setting the table it's time for lunch," said Monica, she then turned to Bianca. "Please get the table ready while I enter the kitchen."

Bianca suddenly left her dad with Monica, and ran back to the stable to see Fanny. I'll join in a few minutes, I need to see Fanny.

Moments after they entered the house, Ron continued to dawdle as he kept insisting he isn't hungry, and thinks he might eat later. Mariah cuts in to the conversation from her own sedentary position, and reminded Ron he should know already that his daughters won't take a no for an answer.

"No, dad, we haven't eaten either and we aren't eating without you, so I suggest you awaken your appetite," said Monica.

"Let me take my bath and join you at the table," said Ron.

A few minutes later Ron left the bathroom after taking his bath, and he then joined Monica and Bianca at the table. Funnily, Monica was quick on her feet as she was able to get food ready by the time her dad finished taking his bath.

"Mum, where are you," asked Monica.

"I'm in the bedroom trying to rest my head a little," said Mariah.

"Mum, have you eaten?" asked Bianca.

Mariah calmly tried avoiding joining her family at the table, as she's equally dealing with Anvil's death in her own way, though strangely, she muttered and said she's has taken a cup of tea, and she's ok for now.

"Just tea?" asked Monica.

"Yes, but I'm fine," said Mariah.

Monica left the table and walked to her mum in the bedroom, and told her a mere cup of tea isn't enough. Monica urged her mum join them at the table. "You and dad need to stay strong," she said.

"My daughter, you're just like your dad, never taking a no for an answer," Mariah said, she then got up from bed and joined them at the table.

After having their lunch they all sat in the living room having a conversation.

Mariah became jocular with Ron, and said he's looking much brighter, and thanked her daughters for making their dad come around.

"Tell me about it," said Ron.

"Does it mean that if your daughters hadn't come, you wouldn't have left the stable?" asked Mariah.

Ron jocularly laid bare the miserableness of his and Mariah's emotional state, and told her she's sounding as if she has been trying to comfort him, after all, they were both emotional wrecks since the incident, and thank God for the girls.

"Dad, have they established the cause of Anvil's death?" asked Bianca.

"No, but Kenny Walter has ordered a post mortem, and the pathologist promised to get the result ready within the week," said Mariah.

"Was Anvil given a medical check up, and certified fit before the race?" asked Monica.

"Yes of course! I would never go into a race without considering the health of my horse," said Ron.

Bianca was quite upfront in her suggestion because her intention was to make someone pay for Anvil's death, as she suggested they take legal action against the Veterinary doctor. Unsurprisingly, her mum thinks otherwise, at least, cool heads should prevail in times such as this. She then suggested it will be too quick, and urged her girls to wait for the result of the post mortem.

"What's this I heard about horse racing fans protesting the death of Anvil?" asked Bianca.

Mariah took a swipe at the protesters, because she seem to take the protest more personal as she stressed her disappointment saying, instead of sympathizing with them the protesters were trying to cause confusion. She felt quite betrayed by the protesting fans and said, after all, Anvil and Ron never promised the fans a Rose garden.

"They're only expressing their love for Anvil, strangely in their own way, and funnily, hell hath no fury like animal rights advocates protesting the death of a loved animal like Anvil.

"Dad, you're right, people grieve in different ways," said Bianca.

Mariah knew her girls' visit is a brief one, and confirmed she's aware their exam is close, and asked when they're you returning to school.

"That'll be the day after tomorrow," said Bianca.

Moments later, Mariah and the girls were in the kitchen doing the dishes, and Monica reminded her mum she isn't supposed to be in the kitchen, because it's obvious she has more than an extra pair of hand helping out.

"I'm only trying to help out here," said Mariah.

"We're home, and we are doing the cooking, so I don't think there's any job for you in the kitchen," Monica insists.

Mariah continued dawdling in the kitchen and know-towing her daughters and then stressing she needed to give helping hand to keep her mind off Anvil. Sadly, her daughters aren't impressed with her emotional state. Monica had to voice her concerns and reminded her mum that the way she's acting will make them to be worried about her when they eventually return to school.

"It's not me you should be worried about, it's your dad," said Mariah.

"Why dad, and not you?" asked Monica.

Mariah who seems to know her husband too well unblinkingly told her daughters their dad's laughter is a masked one, and feared Ron will go back to what he was, and that he only lightened up to make them happy.

"You mean dad was just fake-laughing?" asked Bianca.

"Call it whatever, he's the one you should pay attention to, I can manage myself," said Mariah. Days later, while Kenny Walter was in the Lone Star Park office,

John walked into Kenny's the office, "Good morning, Walter," said John.

"Hello John, how was your night?" asked Walter.

"Err.., my night was fine, Walter, the President of Dallas animal rights advocate was here to see you," said John.

Kenny Walter immediately smelt trouble because he knew what a visit by Florina Banks would mean, he wished John had mentioned that name in error, but sadly, John got it right and it was Florina who came calling.

For all it's worth, this visit alone is a threat even when no words were spoken, this thinly veiled threat meant nothing to this grieving family but a lot to do with the horse racing association.

"You mean, Florina Banks?" asked Walter.

"Of course yes, she was here two hours ago, and she promised to repeat the visit next week," said John.

"Did she tell you why she was here?" asked Walter.

"No, she didn't," said John.

Walter was glad they missed each other, and he doesn't have to face this treacherous animal right advocate scorned by Anvil's death, and he softly told John he knew she was here over Anvil's death, yet promised to give her a call. The news of Florina's visit left a sudden permafrown on Walter's face, but while their conversation persists the phone rang, and guess who? It was Mayor Brown on the phone, John picked up the phone.

"Good morning, this is Mayor Brown, is Kenny Walter in the office?" asked Mayor Brown.

"Good morning Mr. Mayor, and yes, Kenny Walter is in, let me put him on the line," John said and handed the phone to Kenny Walter.

"Hello Mr. Mayor, this is Kenny Walter on the line," said Walter.

"Yeah Kenny, how are you?" asked Mayor Brown.

"I'm fine, Mr. Mayor," said Walter.

Mayor Brown quickly dispensed of all pleasantries and inquired into the status of the investigation into the cause of Anvil's death, he wants to know what the pathologist said in his report.

Walter was upfront with a response as he told the Mayor the result is yet to be out, but he couldn't get is head around the Mayor's sudden and keen interest in this matter and promised he'll be visiting the Pathologist in two days time to pick up the result.

Funnily, Walter couldn't help as Mayor Brown became increasingly assertive and questioning why the report has taken so long because the result should be out by now.

"The pathologist gave me a week, and a day after tomorrow will make it a week, but why the sudden interest in this matter?" asked Walter.

"Have you forgotten I addressed protesters and promised them the death of Anvil will be looked into?" asked Mayor Brown.

"Yes you're right, and I'm a witness to that, and sorry for questioning your interest in the cause of Anvil's death," said Walter.

"To add insult to injury, Florina Banks just left my office and I don't want to be her reason for gracing the headlines this time," said Mayor Brown.

This whole Anvil's saga is fast turning into a rabbit hole with no end in sight, and the Mayor is worried that Florin Banks is after his tail. Walter now understands what the fuss about the pathologists report was all about and said Florina Banks has turned herself into a domestic hero after publicly speaking about her affinity for horses, yet wished her tawdry attempt to entrap him will end in futility. "I suppose she understands the ramifications of her heroic posture," said Walter.

Walter came clean particularly now that the cards are on the table, and hinted the mayor that Florina Banks was also in his office but he was glad they missed each other. "What did you tell her?" asked Walter. "I promised her I'll get to the bottom of Anvil's death, and sincerely I intend to do that," said Mayor Brown.

Walter is keen to do a proper investigation because he knew Florina Banks considers him a low hanging fruit and will focus her energy on him, than she will do to the mayor.

"Then let's get to the bottom of this, at least for Anvil," said Mayor Brown.

Walter and the Mayor came to some sort of understanding, and insists that a good post mortem is the right step in the right direction, because Anvil isn't just any other horse, she deserves this.

After spending time with their parents Monica and Bianca have succeeded in restoring the warm and friendly ambience within the home, but it's now time for them to return to school and prepare for their exams.

Girls, I suppose you're ready to leave for school?" asked Ron.

Yes dad, it's time to go back to school and please take good care of Fanny," said Bianca.

Ron didn't hesitate to address Bianca's demand as he said his present state of mind hasn't stopped him from giving Fanny the best of care.

"Dad, please make sure you eat and try to stay strong," said Bianca.

"I'll, just that Anvil isn't just any horse but a special horse, and I need time to grieve her loss," said Ron.

Bianca sat by her dad's side and held his hand, she then pleaded with him to understand that his actions could affect their concentration as they prepare for their exams. Monica interjected as she added her voice to her sister's and urged her dad to stay strong, and at least he knew what that would mean for them and their exams.

"Mum, we're leaving. Please make sure you stay strong, for yourself and for us," said Monica.

"Ok girls, I'll call you, don't worry, just make sure you concentrate on your exams," said Mariah.

Thank you mum," said Bianca. They stood up, gave their mum some hugs and went to their dad and hugged him equally and then made their way out of the house. As they walked some distance away from the house, Bianca unsurprisingly, turned back and gave her mum a shout-out, asking her to please take care of Fanny in case her dad couldn't.

Mariah who was standing in the balcony and looking at her daughters as they walk down the road, replied Bianca saying her dad has been doing a good job on Fanny, and she doesn't have to worry.

Days later, Walter visited the pathologist to get Anvil's post mortem result, and serendipitously met him this time cutting through a pussy cat, whose death is being investigated, while eating cookies at the same time. This obviously made Walter's skin crawl, and this time he's covered with goose pimples.

"Walter! You're here for the post mortem result as agreed?" asked the pathologist.

"Yeah, it's necessary, I suppose you saw the protest?" asked Walter.

Pathologist seems to have a good understanding of Walter's troubles, as he concurred he saw the protest, after all, he has been bootstrapping because his family was also impacted. "Yes, I saw the protest, my wife was among the protesters," said the pathologist.

"Seriously, your wife, you're sure of this?" Walter queried.

The pathologist described how his wife slept in a different room all alone, as she wept all night like a baby the day Anvil died, and she still sobs occasionally. Funnily, efforts to calm his wife down failed, until he bought her a bunch of red rose flowers and a framed picture of Anvil. He then hands out the envelope containing the post mortem result to Walter. Anvil's death was felt by all, the pauper, the high and mighty, and the county of Dallas knows it, in times like this there's no aristocracy.

"What's the cause of death?" asked Walter.

"Cardiac failure, you know that to be the common causes of death for thoroughbred horses," said the pathologist.

"Oh, no, another cardiac failure!" exclaimed Walter.

"I'm sorry about that, but a lot thoroughbred horses suffer this," the pathologist insists.

"Ok, we'll see what we can do to reduce these deaths, I've to go," said Walter.

Two days later, Mayor Brown has a press statement to make and journalists are all waiting to get their paws into him, the Mayor turned to his Personal Assistant. "Jonathan, is my speech ready? You know the press conference is holding in the next hour?" said the mayor.

"Yes, it's ready," said Jonathan, who stood up immediately and hands the speech to him.

"Good, let me study the speech to be sure the contents aren't misplaced," said the mayor. Typically, press conferences such as this will bring about the ultimate validation of his ego, and politics. While the mayor scanned through the speech, Jonathan alerted him that Kenny Walter is on hand to see him.

"Oh, please ask him to come in," said Mayor Brown.

Moments later, Walter is with the mayor and exchanging pleasantries.

"Walter, you're welcome, I'll be holding a press conference in the next hour, do you've the report?" asked the mayor.

"Were you expecting me?" asked Walter.

Mayor Brown is a half-glass full kind of man, who will stop at nothing but make lemonade when presented with a lemon. Though, he wasn't expecting Walter but since he's here, the mayor would stop at nothing but include the content of the pathologist report in his speech.

"Ok, that isn't a bad idea, this is a copy of the report," Walter said and hands a copy of the report over to the Mayor.

"What's the cause of death?" asked Mayor Brown.

"Cardiac failure," replied Walter.

Mayor Brown spent a few minutes going through the pathologist report, and asked if this cardiac failure is a human error or mere serendipity.

"No, it isn't, cardiac failure is a common cause of death in thoroughbred horses," said Walter.

"What do we do to avoid the reoccurrence of cases such as this?" asked Mayor Brown.

Walter suggested an increase in the number of medical checkups for horses, maybe that'll help detect early signs of any cardiac related illness.

Mayor Brown took notes as Kenny Walter makes his suggestions, saying these suggestions will form part of his speech. "Ok, this isn't a bad idea, and at least, it'll be a face-saving speech even for the horse racing association," said Mayor Brown.

The mayor is quite happy to include the pathologist report in his speech, at least this speech will stop Florina Banks and her animal rights team prodding him as they run around his office. He turned to Walter to please ensure he do as has just suggested to keep these horses safe. "I'm the one being pilloried by Florina Banks, so I won't do anything to mess the horse racing sport up," said Walter.

"The earnestness of horse racing makes it a beautiful sport, let's not jeopardize it," said Mayor Brown.

"Yes, I'll, because our reputation is tied to how these horses are treated," said Walter.

Later that same day, Walter brought the post mortem result to Ron, but met up with him in the stable where he spends most of his time.

"Ron, how're you and Mariah doing?" asked Walter.

"As you can see we are fine," said Ron.

Grand Prairie is a tightly knit community and everyone knows everyone "I saw your girls during the weekend, where are they?" asked Walter.

"They returned to school three days ago," said Ron.

Walter asked Ron how he's coping, and Ron on the other hand was quick to say he's fine, and funnily, Mariah was nearby and didn't hesitate to refute Ron's claim of being fine.

"No, he isn't, he only pretended to be fine when Monica and Bianca were here," said Mariah.

Though, Ron pantheith for something quite unexplained, it's now quite obvious to him and to all that Anvil is dead, and even the Yellow Rose in Texas felt Anvil's passing. Kind words are nice, they're like a spring day, and a little courtesy costs nothing. Sadly, Ron's courtesy is just a mask over the hollowness inside this man's heart, and this has nothing to do with penitence.

Ron dismissed every concern expressed by Mariah, and assured Walter he'll be fine. Walter steered the conversation into the result of the post mortem, and told him Anvil's post mortem result is out. Mariah interjected immediately, and asked what the cause of death was.

Ron was spooked by Mariah's request to disclose the content of the report because it will make him to relieve the experience of Anvils' death again and again. He wants to maintain the sanctity of Anvil's memory and hates to hear Anvil discussed in past tense. "Walter, no, please don't talk about that now," said Ron.

Ron insists he'll come for the post mortem result when he's ready, he then urged Walter to keep the report with him. Mariah's tack in her bid to manage the awkward situation helped as she urged Walter to keep the report in his office, and Ron will come for it when he's able to cope with the content of the report.

"Walter, I'm sorry, just do that for me and I'll come for it later, when I'm fine," said Ron.

"Ok then," said Walter, he then stayed with Ron for about thirty minutes and left.

CHAPTER

FIVE

The Racing contest in the dream world

The death of Anvil has left Ron suffering from bouts of clinical depression, and he has unwittingly withdrawn from his family and friends. He locks himself up in the stable most of the time where he stays to grieve the loss of his best friend.

One month after the death of Anvil, and in a bizarre twist of fate, Ron was in a sleep at night and had a dream. In that dream, Ron saw Anvil on a racecourse and ran towards Anvil. "Hey Anvil, is that you?" asked Ron.

"Of course it's me," said Anvil. In real life Anvil was a mere horse and doesn't speak, but Ron was taken aback to hear his beloved horse speaking audibly. Ron couldn't help himself but reminded Anvil she's dead, and how come she's speaking but despite his barrage of questions Ron was quite ecstatic to see his beloved horse again.

"You were crying when I died, saying I've left you, so I've to come back for you," said Anvil.

"Oh, you come back for me?" asked Ron.

Anvil was quite up front as she reminded Ron, she has been watching him from the heavens, and noticed he has refused to race with any other horse. "Yeah, I can't, your soul and mine are tied together, I can't continue racing without you," said Ron.

"What about your racing career?" asked Anvil.

"That's over for now?" Ron replied tearfully.

"But you're only the Dallas County champion, what about being the champion for the state of Texas, and even becoming the national champion?" asked Anvil.

This is the understatement of the mystery Ron had lived, he tearfully reminded Anvil, "I'm a champion and no other horse can help me continue being a champion except you," said Ron.

Anvil has been Ron's riding partner for a reasonably long time, and could see through Ron's pains, yet she laid it bare to him that his actions are hurting Mariah and others who equally love him.

"Yes you're right, but how come you're a white chariot instead of being a white horse?" asked Ron.

"When I died I changed to a chariot, but for your sake, I can go back to being a horse," said Anvil.

"Why're you doing that?" asked Ron.

"I want to help you win the national championship, but this will be in the dream only," said Anvil.

Ron was quite elated to hear of an opportunity to ride with Anvil but he's still confused as to how this whole race in the dream world will work. This isn't out of the ordinary, it's a hell of a ride for him, and he's quite upfront for the challenge.

"I'll come to you every night, in your dream, so we can take part in the competitions," said Anvil.

Ron was glad to have another chance to ride with Anvil in a competition. The duo will take to the stage again but this time in the dream. Anvil changed from a chariot to a horse and asked Ron climb on so they could go for practice. Ron excitingly grabbed the offer with both hands, and quickly climbed and they rode off for practice.

After spending the entire night practicing in the racecourse in the dream, Ron woke up from his sleep the next morning, and funnily, it was all a dream. Sadly, Ron couldn't get over the dream he'd the night before, and this leaves him in a bind. That morning, while Ron prepares to leave the house for the stable, he helped himself with a cup of coffee which is his usual routine, he spent some time looking through the window as flakes of snow falls at his back garden while holding his cup of coffee in one hand. He suddenly opened his mouth and turned around towards Mariah.

"Mariah, I'd a dream last night," said Ron.

"What kind of dream is it?" asked Mariah.

"Anvil came to me last night, she was a white chariot," said Ron.

"But Anvil is a horse and not a Chariot," Mariah insists.

Ron decided to let out more about his encounter with Anvil and described in a quite appealing manner, telling his wife about how Anvil asked him to climb on so they can go for practice.

Mariah didn't see anything out of the blue about Ron's dream, and after all, jockeys usually see themselves in their dream riding their horses, it's not new. Unsurprisingly, Ron thinks Mariah is mistaken about this particular dream because it feels real, and it's about finishing what he started with Anvil.

"This dream is different Mariah, Anvil talked about helping me win a national championship," said Ron. Mariah has been impacted by the emotional strain precipitated by Anvil's demise, she didn't hesitate to slap down the dream as mere blab. She then gave a subtle reminder to her husband, urging him not to take this dream to heart to avoid worsening his already poor state of mind.

Ron walked to Mariah and looked right into her eyes, and insists this isn't just a social call, it's more than a dream and there's more to this. "How do you know?" asked Mariah.

"Anvil, said tomorrow night is the contest at the County level," said Ron.

Mariah felt this conversation has taken a sudden twist into what could best be described as creepy, she immediately withdrew herself from her husband, and began walking away. "Ron, stop taking this dream to heart, because you've not been yourself lately," she insists.

After the back and forth between this couple they decided not to talk about this subject the rest of that day until they went to bed for the night. Funnily, Anvil visited that night as promised, and Ron competed at the county level for the national horse racing championship. The next morning Ron woke up from sleep and realised it was a dream as usual, and while he still lay on the bed he turned over to Mariah, facing her.

"We won," said Ron.

"Won what?" asked Mariah.

"Anvil and I, we won the county championship last night," said Ron.

Mariah was lost as to what Ron was about because she didn't take the conversation of the previous day to heart, and it took Mariah sometime to realise the conversation of the previous day is just back on the table. "What championship are you talking about? Anvil is dead for God's sake, and what's wrong with you?" asked Mariah.

"Yeah, you're right Anvil is dead, and I never said Anvil is alive," said Ron.

"Then where does all this come from?" asked Mariah.

Ron reminded Mariah that he already told her that Anvil came to him two nights ago, and promised to come back.

"Yes, but in a dream," said Mariah.

"That night Anvil promised to help me win the national championship," said Ron.

Mariah just couldn't get her head around this thing about racing in the dream, her husband was already suffering from clinical depression and withdrawn, this dream is now a new twist thrown into the mix. This depression has gone suffuse, she thought to herself. "How can you compete in a dream, how'll you touch and hold your trophy even if you win?" she asked.

"I don't know, I just don't know, but we won the county championship, Mariah. Mayor Brown was there, I mean the late Mayor Brown Senior. I shook his hand," Ron insists.

"You mean the former mayor, Philip Brown was there, and you shook his hand, how real is this?" asked Mariah.

Ron wasn't flinching, and for sure wasn't wavering about how real his dream was, and sadly, Mariah can't talk him out of the championship.

"All I know is that a national championship has started in the dream world and I'm representing the County of Dallas and I'm doing this with Anvil," said Ron.

"Ron, I think you need to speak to someone, maybe a psychologist," said Mariah.

"Look Mariah, Anvil promised to help me win the national championship in my dream life since she couldn't help me achieve it in my real life," said Ron. Mariah is now being taken over by frustration because she just doesn't know how to help her husband snap out of this fairy-tale, and all Mariah could do is to scream at her husband insisting this foolishness has to stop.

Ron smiled and stood up from the bed as they continued this conversation, he then turned to Mariah and subtly told her this dreams won't stop, it can't stop now until after the championship.

Anvil will come and practice with him on Wednesday and they'll compete on Thursday at the state level.

"You mean you'll train with Anvil on Wednesday in your dream and by Thursday, you'll represent this county at the state level?" asked Mariah.

"It might look strange to you but it was real," said Ron. Mariah couldn't take this any longer, and she quickly got up from bed and hurriedly walked out of the room in a brisk and brash manner as the conversation gets weird and weirder. Sadly, the words coming out from Ron's mouth aren't just the words from the lips of a pathological liar, rather they are his experience, and he isn't ready to shirk them off.

With this new twist, Mariah felt it's best to get her daughter involved, she then called Monica to express her concern over their dad's recent behaviour.

"Monica, can you hear me?" asked Mariah.

Monica told her mum the network is bad, and ended the phone call, then dialled her mum again.

"Hello Monica, how're you?" asked Mariah.

"I'm fine, mum, how're you and dad doing?" asked Monica.

Mariah didn't hesitate to hit the nail on the head, as she quickly steered the conversation into Ron's new passion because he's losing it. "I told you the other time, your dad was fake-smiling," said Mariah.

"What, what's wrong with dad?" asked Monica.

Mariah tried to scare the pants off her daughter, stressing her dad keeps dreaming about him and Anvil in horse racing competition. Sadly, she's isn't able to pass the seriousness of her concerns to her daughter. It's glaringly obvious that this isn't merely serendipity of some sort, but a challenge that's quite close to a real life stuff.

"Oh, I thought it was something serious," said Monica.

Mariah had to bring Monica up to speed, as she said it is, and that this isn't just a dream, because his interpretation of the dream looked like real life stuff. Yet, despite her mum's exasperation, Monica did a good job to calm her mum, and urged her to give her dad some time, and if the situation persists she'll have a word with him.

"How's your sister?" asked Monica.

"Bianca is fine, we were together this morning, and how's Fanny" asked Monica.

"Fanny is fine and that's the only one thing your dad never forgets, despite his poor state of mind," said Mariah.

By Wednesday the following week Anvil and Ron practiced for the horse racing contest at the state level in his dream. While their practice section continues Ron couldn't help but exclaimed about the rigorousness of this practice.

"Training here takes more of our energy," said Ron.

"It's good to help us keep fit, if we must win," said Anvil.

"Then I'll need to help you improve further on your ambling gait," said Ron.

"Just do whatever you think is necessary to help us win this race," said Anvil.

While still in his dream and practicing with Anvil, Ron asked Anvil why they aren't training in their usual Lone Star Park in Grand Prairie in the Dallas County. This is the dream world, after all, Ron is just a guest, and Anvil is a citizen of the after-life, and so, who's best placed to show Ron the best training ground, if not Anvil. Anvil made it clear to Ron that this is the state championship, and they've to prepare differently, even at that Ron hinted that he doesn't think he has come across most of these horses before.

"This isn't just a County competition; you'll see horses from various Counties in the state of Texas," said Anvil.

Ron insists he knew most of the best performing horses in the entire state of Texas, but most of the horses he's seeing on the racecourse training alongside them are new faces.

"All the horses you see here have passed into after life," said Anvil.

"You mean they're no more living in the physical world?" asked Ron.

Even as they practise Anvil took time to show Ron around as well as give him a little history about the participants in the after-life.

"Yes, you see that horse practising over there?" said Anvil.

"Yes, what about him?" asked Ron.

"He's called the 'Red Thunder,' he's the strongest, but not the fastest horse here," said Anvil.

"Is the horse that powerful?" asked Ron.

Anvil gave Ron a brief profile of "Red Thunder," and said the horse belonged to one of the ancient "Native American kings" it was a special breed, and the secret about his breeding has been kept away. There's this strength and tenacity that's particular to Red Thunder because that horse was bred for war.

"Is he the rider?" asked Ron.

"Yes, when a sport horse passes on at death, the rider continues with her when he or she dies," said Anvil.

Anvil and Ron continued as they visited another racecourse, Anvil then showed Ron another horse. "That black horse, the one on the extreme right is President Roosevelt's racing horse," said Anvil. Ron was quite delighted and asked to see if he could meet the former President of the United States, even if it's just for a handshake. "If that's his horse, then where is President Roosevelt, and I suppose he should be around somewhere?" said Ron.

Ron is a guest in the dream world, and Anvil has a championship to win, so he made Ron forget about his familiarity tour and rather, urged him to focus on his trainings.

Ron now understands that the relationship between a horse and a rider extends into the after-life, yet he's keen to know if riders in the physical world visit and ride with their horse that has passed into the after-life. Anvil had to make it clear that horses only ride together with their owner when they both have passed on, but she's only doing this because Ron couldn't move on.

"But I hear of Jockeys riding on their dead horse in their dream," said Ron.

"Yes it happens on few occasion then it stops, but you're different," said Anvil.

"Ok, Anvil, give me speed," after five minutes of riding, Ron changed the command "change your gait common...," said Ron.

After spending the entire night practising with Anvil in the dream, Ron woke up the next morning being Thursday, he then turned over on the bed and facing Mariah.

"Mariah, are you awake?" asked Ron.

"What's it, Ron? Don't be sloppy. At least you can see my eyes opened," Mariah retorted.

Ron didn't grasp the fact that this fairy tale about him and Anvil is getting Mariah upset, yet he went on and on, mouthing off to Mariah that Anvil was looking so fit for their state championship tonight, and describing how well they trained last night. For all it's worth, Mariah knows for certain that Ron wasn't suicidal but was rather despondent, and this dream doesn't explain anything.

"You're at it again; Anvil is dead, why don't you just let Anvil be?" Mariah chuckled.

"Remember I told you Anvil will come on Wednesday for practice against Thursday's race at the state level," said Ron.

"And how do you know Anvil is fit for your race?" Mariah queried.

"Because we trained together, and she even took me to places," said Ron.

Mariah now finds her husband insufferable, and her displeasure quickly morphed from irritation to frustration and then agitation as she tried wriggling herself from her husband's fairytale, yet he didn't stop but proceeded to give Mariah a full chronicle of the horse racing championship in the after-life. She felt Ron is now prodding her with his menacing newly found friendship with Anvil.

"Enough of this, Ron, I'm tired of hearing all these," Mariah retorted. She then turned and faced the other side of the bed.

"But tonight is the racing contest at the state level, and I thought you'll be excited about that," said Ron.

"I'm not, because I'm not interested in this foolishness," said Mariah.

"Ok sorry, if you feel disturbed," said Ron. He came down from bed and went to the living room. By Friday morning Ron woke up from sleep after the state championship race in his dream and turned to Mariah as before.

"Mariah, we won the racing contest at state level last night," said Ron.

"I can't go on like this, never!" Mariah exclaimed.

"Look Mariah, I just want to let you know Anvil did well, and the Governor of the state of Texas was there," Ron insists.

"The other time it was Mayor Brown, this time it's the Governor of Texas?" she asked angrily.

"The other time it was at the County level but this time, it's at the state level," said Ron.

Mariah angrily got up from bed, she was quite infuriated by this turn of events, and nothing upsets her the most than the feeling of being entrapped by the unfolding twists precipitated by Anvil's demise.

"I must do something about this before it gets out of hand," said Mariah.

This time she has decided to go a step further in addressing this murky situation, not just by her quiet displeasure.

"Mariah, why should I make such a thing up, I'm just telling you the truth," said Ron.

Mariah needs help and who's best to lean on in times such as this if not Kenny Walter, she didn't hesitate as she quickly took her shower and hurriedly rushed to the park to meet Walter to help her speak to Ron. Mariah met Walter in the bar inside the park garden cooling off with a jug of beer.

"Mariah, how're you?" asked Walter.

"I'm good, and you're having a good time, I suppose," said Mariah.

"How's Ron?" asked Walter.

Mariah's warm disposition suddenly melts away, the moment the conversation was steered into Ron's welfare. "Walter, I'll need your help with Ron," replied Mariah.

"What's it about Ron, is he coming back to the race?" asked Walter.

Tears rolled down her cheeks, as she reiterated that her husband is losing it, and she hadn't the slightest clue about what's wrong with her husband.

Walter seem to think he understands the workings of Ron's mind, as he was quite upfront and said he knew Ron isn't interested in racing without Anvil, but he hasn't any idea he's having problems. Mariah quickly put the conversation back into perspective, and she opened up to Walter that Ron has problems, and she wants him to have a word with Ron. "About what, Mariah?" asked Walter.

"He talks about continuing his race with Anvil in his dreams," replied Mariah.

"What you're talking about isn't new, and most jockeys find themselves riding their dead horse in their dreams," said Walter.

While Mariah thinks of her husband's problem to be something more clinical, Walter decided to tell her the story of Old Jack. Walter on the other hand think that Ron's troubles could be nothing compared to the crazy story of Old Jack who refused the courtesy of a horse ride and decided to hit the road in the middle of a hot summer year, walking from Alaska to Texas on foot, having just a pair of old boots to shod his foot, an old cowboy hat to protect him from the heat of a scorching daylight sun and a bottle of whiskey in his hand for the road. It was common knowledge that Old Jack ended with his foot in his mouth, as he obviously ran out of courage but funnily didn't run out of luck as the hospitality of an Injun who felt the need to save the life of this perceived enemy became his rabbit feet.

Mariah wasn't here on a social call, as she insisted that her husband's situation is worse compared to what Old jack suffered. She then said she understands that Old Jack ran out of courage, but this is different, that her husband talks about being enrolled in a championship, in his dreams.

Walter was lost as to what the problem really was, yet was willing to speak to Ron if that would help.

"Thank you, Walter, please help me do this," said Mariah.

"Mariah, do you care for a drink or anything?" asked Walter.

"Thank you, I'll be just fine," Mariah said, then left moments later.

Two days later, Kenny Walter visited Ron to find out what the problem could be but met him sleeping in the stable. Mariah tapped her husband on the leg to wake him up.

"Ron wake up, Walter is here to see you," said Mariah, while still giving him a tap on the leg.

"Oh, Mariah, why're you doing this to me?" Ron muttered, as he woke up and sat on the floor of the stable.

"What did I do? Walter is here to see you," said Mariah, even as Walter was standing right there with them. Ron protested, he groused, and continued muttering that Mariah didn't even allow him to finish feeding Anvil before waking him up. Downing one's sorrows in a bottle of whisky some days doesn't come easy but this isn't the case. Arguably, efforts to help Ron come around has been nothing other than grasping at straws, and funnily, this one will use a bit of luck to come out good.

"Stop this, Ron," said Mariah.

"No, Mariah, Anvil was eating and then you woke me," said Ron.

Mariah looked helpless, as she turned to Walter who is standing by and witnessing the drama first hand. "Here you go," said Mariah.

Walter saw for himself what he's about to deal with, he then asked Mariah to leave him alone with Ron, and minutes later Mariah left. Walter sat on the floor next to Ron who's already sitting on the floor of the stable.

"The floor of the stable isn't the most idyllic spot to sit but funnily you seem to find this spot somewhat comforting," said Walter.

"Because I find solace sitting here," said Ron.

"Ron, what's happening?" asked Walter.

"Nothing, as you can see I was sleeping then Marian woke me up," said Ron.

Walter then asked him what it is about this dream with Anvil, and he then proceeded to ask what it's all about.

"Ok, Anvil came to me in my dream and promised to help me win the national championship," said Ron.

"But Anvil is dead, Ron, how can you win national championship with Anvil?" asked Walter.

"At the moment Anvil and I have won the county qualification, moved on to the state, won the state championship. So, we'll be representing the state of Texas for the national championship on 19th of July," said Ron.

Walter was rattled by the preciseness of these dreams and more so, the fact that the dream take the form of a real life events. "This dream is a one-off thing, isn't it?" asked Walter.

"No, it's not, next three Thursdays from now which will be the 19th of July Anvil will come for me, and we'll represent the state of Texas at the national level," said Ron.

Walter just couldn't get his head around this, and without further hesitation he asked Ron why he's competing in a dream instead of competing in real life. Ron had to hit the nail on the head and said, actually, Anvil came back because he refused to compete with another horse in real life.

"How can Anvil come back?" asked Walter.

"She said she has been watching me from the heavens, and noticed I've refused to ride another horse," said Ron.

"Then why're you refusing to compete with another horse?" asked Walter.

"I can't, Walter, Anvil and I are soul tied and we've a special bond," said Ron.

Walter wasn't quite prepared for this, he thought he was just coming to offer a few words of encouragement to a friend but this is out of the blue, and more than a handful for him, yet he just wouldn't tuck his tail and run off. "What sort of fatuous and unexplained bond is this that has kept you bound to a dead horse?" Walter asked.

"It's all a mystery, Walter," said Ron.

Walter told him it's possible to bond with another horse aside Anvil, saying all he needed is some time, he then asked about Fanny, before making it clear that he can easily bond with Fanny. "It's not as easy as you think, Walter," replied Ron.

"Do you know you've completely withdrawn from your loved ones?" asked Walter.

Ron looked at Walter and tried making light of the situation by disproving Walter's claim of him being completely withdrawn, he smiled as he looked into Walter's eye as if there isn't any monster shut away inside him in the person of Anvil. He insists he's at home and surrounded by those who love him, and he isn't withdrawn.

Walter quickly dismissed Ron's excuse and told him he's only physically present at home but not emotionally attached to his family, and his inclinations hasn't helped either because it's as if there's something pressing his button. Despite knowing that this is something out of the ordinary, Walter still hadn't the faintest idea of what to do to break his friend from this vortex.

"I don't think my condition is as bad as you've just painted," said Ron.

"Yeah, it is, except you don't want to see it," said Ron.

"Ok, I'll try taking things slowly, but…," said Ron.

Walter interjected, as he's keen to help Ron snap out of this mystery that has held him bound. "But what?" asked Walter.

"I sometimes hear Anvil beckoning," said Ron.

"From yonder, I suppose?" asked Walter.

"Of course, yes!" said Ron.

"Anvil is dead and shouldn't have any reason beckoning," said Walter.

"Hmm, I get you, Walter," Ron said in a soft spoken voice.

"Ron, we'll need to talk more about this, but for now, I suggest you see a psychologist," said Walter.

Walter had a hell of ride with Ron, and after an intense period of talking Walter seemed to have failed to help Ron snap out of his despair, he then got up from the floor and left Ron after bidding each other goodbye. Moments after Walter left Ron inside the stable, Mariah walked up to him, to inquire the outcome of their conversation.

"Walter, how did it go?" asked Mariah.

Walter confessed to Mariah, he now understands her troubles, and the situation isn't quite a twinkle, it's rather a complicated one.

"Now you understand what I'm going through, what do we do about this?" asked Mariah.

Walter had an opportunity to take a peek into what goes on in Ron's mind, yet he seemed to have done a bad of it, and all he could tell Mariah was that the bond between Ron and Anvil is hard to decipher. Mariah equally seems not to get it as she insists Anvil is dead and that bond no longer exists. Sadly, the race in the dream world is real and Ron has actually been enrolled in the national championship, but as far as the physical world is concerned this is all a mere blab.

"This isn't just about the century old bond between the riders and their horses, there's more between Ron and Anvil," said Walter.

"I'm his wife, and I don't see anything more special," said Mariah.

Walter brainstormed with Mariah and suggested that Ron should see a psychologist. Funnily, Mariah sees Walter's suggestions as a tall order, and said she doesn't think Ron will listen to her.

"Yeah, but you need to try, just look for a way to convince him," said Walter.

"Ok, I'll do whatever I can to help my husband," said Mariah.

Walter urged Mariah to just keep him posted, and if she wants him to come over, he will. Walter then took some steps towards his car as he attempts to leave, but walks back to Mariah. "Hmm, hold on, I'll get somebody to speak with him," said Walter.

Mariah is worried sick and wants things sorted as soon as possible, and she interjected immediately and asked Walter when he intends to do that because she doesn't think she can continue like this much longer.

"That will be tomorrow, let's be hopeful," Walter said then leaves.

The next day Kenny Walter came with a Priest to speak with Ron, and Mariah was on hand to meet them the moment they alighted from the car. She opened the door to let them into the house.

"Hello Mariah," said Walter.

"Hey Walter, you're welcome," said Mariah.

The Priest walked up to Mariah and stood by her side. "Hello madam, sorry for your loss,"

"Thank you, and good morning, reverend," replied Mariah.

"Ron, how's he?" asked Walter.

"Same same, Walter, do you expect to hear something otherwise?" asked Mariah.

"Where's he?" asked Walter.

Mariah replied in quite a soft tone, and points to the stable, as she informed him that her husband is in the stable as usual. Walter then turns to the Priest. "He's in the stable, please come with me," he said.

Interestingly, just as Walter and the Priest took some steps towards the stable, Mariah felt the need to get her concerns off her chest. "Excuse me, Walter, just a minute," said Mariah.

Walter then turned to the Priest. "A minute reverend, I'll be back," he said and walks back to Mariah.

"The priest, what about him?" asked Mariah.

"Hmm, I brought him to speak to Ron, maybe it'll help," said Walter.

"How certain are you, do you think he'll make a difference?" asked Mariah.

Walter replied Mariah saying he doesn't know if this move will make a difference but he just needed all the help he can get to help Ron back on his feet. Mariah remains nervy about getting a priest involved, yet remained open-minded. She then told Walter that he's sounding as if there's something mystical between Ron and Anvil.

"Mariah, I don't know, let's just explore all options," said Walter.

"Ok, give it a try, thank you for everything, Walter," she said. Walter returned to the priest, and moments later Walter and the priest walked into the stable. "Hey Ron, how are you doing?" asked Walter.

"I'm fine, Walter, and you're welcome". Ron then turned to the priest. "Hello reverend," said Ron.

"Hello sir, you're Ron, I suppose?" asked the priest.

"Yes of course, you knew my name already," Ron said, and smiled.

Walter then formally introduced the Reverend to Ron. "This is my friend, Ron. I've told you a little, maybe you should hear from him," said Walter.

Interestingly, the moment the priest stepped into the stable, there was a flicker of recognition but Ron kept it to himself. The priest then asked Walter to excuse them and leave him and Ron alone.

Walter turned to leave but stopped suddenly, then turned to Ron. "Let him in, and let him help you," said Walter.

"Hello Ron, what's going on with you?" asked the priest.

"I'm fine, reverend, do you recognize me?" asked Ron.

"Not really, have we met before? You know I meet a lot of people," said the priest.

"Not a regular meeting, though, I usually come to you for confession," said Ron.

"Ok, lots of people come to me for confession, and I don't judge them or hold their sins against them, is your confession peculiar?" asked the priest.

"Yes of course, that's why I've the feeling you may know me, maybe not by face, but by my confession," said Ron.

The priest then asked Ron to tell him more about himself, and asked what his confession looks like, even though what was said during confession stays in the confession box, and typically, the Priest doesn't discuss people's confession with them once confession time is over, but now that Ron opened that door, the Priest decided to explore that line of conversation.

"I'm the jockey that comes for confession before he runs a race, now I suppose you know me," said Ron.

"Hmm, it's you, Jesus Christ!" the priest exclaimed, and then moved his seat closer to Ron.

This conversation has taken a new twist for this Priest, it's now glaringly obvious this two has a history together, and this opens up a door for a more open and honest conversation.

"Now you understand," said Ron.

"You didn't come for confession before this race, did you?" the priest queried further.

"No, I didn't," said Ron.

"Because I didn't remember taking your confession," said the priest.

"Of course, I didn't, and this is entirely my fault, I should've come for confession," said Ron.

"Why didn't you?" asked the priest.

Ron said he went to town with Mariah, and she wouldn't give him space to do that, and this is the first time he went for a race without going for a confession.

"Why didn't you come with her, and make her a part of what you do?" asked the priest.

"She isn't meant to be a part of it, it's meant to be between me and my horse," said Ron.

"Why the confession, you don't go to church and you aren't a practising Christian, are you?" asked the priest.

Ron confessed he of course doesn't go to church, but the confession is meant to keep him clean. The priest was lost as to what Ron meant by keeping himself clean because Ron sounds like a man who just arrive with a time machine and has lost track of time.

"How symbolic is this, and how does this affect your race?" asked the priest.

Ron was quite upfront in his conversation with the priest, he spoke quite freely as if they've known each other forever. Ron went further to explain that keeping himself clean helps his body and his soul to connect with his horse, and maybe some support from the Big Man in the sky.

"The Big Man in the sky, you mean, God?" asked the priest.

"Of course yes, I know he'll support me when I'm clean," said Ron.

The Priest steered the conversation away from the edgy mystery that has kept Ron bound, to the reality on ground, the Priest then fixed his gaze on Ron one more time and told him the autopsy revealed his horse was sick, and Anvil didn't die because he didn't come for confession. Sadly, the Priest's words wasn't well received because it didn't soothe Ron's pain, rather it exacerbated it.

"Reverend, don't justify Anvil's death, please don't do it," said Ron.

"But your horse is dead and you're slipping into depression," said the priest.

"Don't worry, reverend; I've a handle on this," said Ron.

The priest isn't one to be described as a person who isn't an ethical character, and he had no choice but to let Ron know that from what he has seen, Ron isn't ok, unless he promise he'll do something about himself.

"I'll be fine, reverend. I just need some time to grieve for Anvil," said Ron.

"It isn't out of place to grieve, but you don't have to remain in grief, you've to move on," said the priest.

"There will be no moving on, reverend, even after grieving, it would just be me being myself," said Ron.

The Priest turned and points to Fanny. "That horse over there, is it yours?" he asked.

"It's mine," replied Ron.

"Then carry on with her, and continue your racing," said the priest.

"No more racing for me, I can't race with any other horse other than Anvil," Ron insists.

"A lot of people feel the same way; let's get you out of this emotional state first before talking about racing," said the priest.

Ron steered the conversation into the very grey area his wife and friends are grappling with, as he told the priest his interest is in winning his championship in his dream world.

"What's it about your dreams?" asked the priest.

"It's just me and Anvil in my dream; she wants to help me win the national championship," said Ron.

The Priest realised this isn't just a man grasping on straws, this is more than mere mystery, the priest had to put things back into perspective. "Riding your horse in a dream isn't out of place, but the idea of your horse visiting you at specific dates and time, and wanting to help you win a championship she couldn't win for you in real life is quite strange," said the priest.

"This isn't strange, it's reality, just believe me," said Ron.

"You'll need to see a counsellor," said the priest.

"That's not necessary, and I'm in control of my situation," said Ron.

"Do you pray at all?" asked the priest.

"No I don't, except that I come for confession, which's a one off thing," said Ron.

The priest reached into his bag and brought out a bible and handed it to Ron. "Take this, study it and pray with it," he said.

"Ok, I'll try," said Ron.

The Priest gave one last try to see if he can awaken Ron's appetite for the need to reintegrate into the society. "Hmm, are you plagued by any thought of you and Anvil?" asked the priest.

"The Spring is here and I just can't get my mind off memories of me and Anvil walking under the Cherry Blossoms," said Ron.

"In life, there's a time and season for everything under the heaven, there's time to be born and there's time to die, time to mourn and time to merry," said the priest.

"These times and seasons you talked about shouldn't justify Anvil's death," said Ron. The priest reminded Ron there's much more than cherry blossoms, he told Ron there's a lot to hope for in spring, there's the rain drops, the butterflies, the blooming spring tulips. He assured Ron that no winter lasts forever, and no spring skips its turns, and that spring is here because winter yielded to spring, and this too shall pass.

"If you say so, reverend, but if given the choice, I love to remain drowned in that blissful dream of a Texas man," said Ron.

"Is this edginess or a man in a dark place?" the priest asked again.

"Let's say, a man feeling a little alienated," said Ron.

"Let me pray with you," The priest prayed with Ron. "I've to get going, and I'll continue to pray for you," said the priest.

The priest leaves the stable, and Mariah rushed to the reverend as he leaves the stable. "Reverend, how did it go?" asked Mariah.

"He's in a bad shape," said the priest.

Walter interjected and asked the priest what he advised they do next since efforts to get Ron back to himself seem to have largely failed, the priest then advised that Ron should see a counsellor. Seeing how the efforts of Kenny Walter, and even that of a priest failed to make Ron come around, Mariah quickly asked to know how to go about this, saying she doesn't think her husband will be willing to make such move.

"Just put a call and book an appointment on his behalf," said Walter.

"Ok, I'll give it a try, and I hope it works out," said Mariah.

"We've to get going, please keep me updated," said Walter.

The Priest then held Mariah by the hand, and prayed with her, then promised he'll be praying for her and for her husband.

Just as the Priest turned to leave, "just stay strong," said the priest.

"Thank you, reverend," said Mariah.

Bianca and Monica wanted to return home immediately after their exams, but they have a one month university trip to the Himalayas organised by a charity for which they have paid to be a part of even before Anvil's death. Mariah urged her daughters to go ahead with their planned trip as opposed to coming home to cheer their depressed dad up.

CHAPTER

SIX

The visit to the Psychologist

Mariah gave the priest suggestion of speaking to a counsellor a thought, and funnily, she has managed to summon the courage to give it a go. She then walked into the stable to inform Ron he needs a counsellor.

"Ron, I'm calling the Doctor," said Mariah.

"Why, are you alright?" asked Ron. He then stood up from the floor to show he cares.

"It's not me, Ron, it's you," she said.

"How do you mean it's me?" asked Ron.

Mariah just went straight to the point, telling her husband he's depressed and they can't continue like this, and he'll need to speak to a counsellor.

Ron on the other hand seems not to be getting a grip of how bad the situation has deteriorated, he quickly asked Mariah if it's about the dream when he protested she woke him up when he was feeding Anvil, he then went on to say he's sorry.

"Ron, we can't continue like this, you'll have to speak to someone about this," said Mariah.

Ron wasn't quite pleased with this new line of conversation as he reminded his wife he has been speaking with people. After all, he just finished speaking with the priest after talking with Walter.

Mariah reminded Ron that his conversation with Walter didn't yield any positive results, so it's best to take things further.

"What do you want me to do?" asked Ron.

"You don't eat, you're withdrawn from your family and this isn't fair on us," Mariah protested.

"But I'm always home with you, come on baby sit with me," said Ron. He then spread some straw on the floor of the stable, she sat on it and he sat beside her. "You know I love Anvil as well, why're you doing this to me? I need you," said Mariah.

Ron held Mariah by the hand and passed his other hand around her shoulder and pleaded with her to give him a little time to put himself together. Even though he meant no harm, Ron doesn't need to go about stamping his feet in disapproval to prove to his wife he doesn't like her latest suggestion.

"I'm trying to save my family, I'm trying to save us," said Mariah. Sadly, time isn't a luxury Mariah can afford at this point, particularly when her husband remained illusory, and she suddenly began to weep. Ron tried to pull her to himself but she stood up and walked into the house.

"Oh please, Mariah, I'm fine, you don't have to do that," said Mariah.

That evening Mariah decided to put a call for an appointment for a counsellor for Ron.

"Hello, this is Mariah Rogers speaking," said Mariah.

"Good evening, what can we do for you today?" hospital reception.

"I want to book an appointment for my husband," said Mariah.

The hospital receptionist requested for Ron's details, including his social security number. He then asked what the appointment is about.

"He is suffering bouts of situational depression," said Mariah.

The receptionist then asked if Ron is aware of the appointment and Mariah sounded positive as if Ron was in on it, and the appointment was booked.

Later that evening, Ron left the stable and came into the house, took his bath and went to the table to eat his dinner which was the only food he ate that day. Immediately after Ron settled in for the night, Mariah breaks the news that she has booked an appointment for tomorrow.

"Mariah, I told you not to do this, you know I can't leave the house now," said Ron.

"Your stay in the house has strained our family to its limit, where's the Ron I use to know?" asked Mariah.

"I'm trying to be there for you and the kids," said Ron.

Mariah have been able to cope with her husband being withdrawn, but she was quite upfront in letting her husband know what spooks her the most, as she said can't continue with this story of him and Anvil competing in the dream. Everything she could grasp with, but this story about competing in the dream makes her husband less predictable.

"Then what do you want me to do now?" asked Ron.

"Make up your mind to see the counsellor tomorrow, I'll be there to support you," said Mariah.

Ron looked on, and asked Mariah if his visit to a counsellor will make her happy. Interestingly, Mariah's response wasn't quite as straight as Ron would've wanted.

"I'll only be happy if I see a change," said Mariah.

"Ok, I'll be there tomorrow, I want to make an effort for my family's sake," said Ron.

The next morning Mariah accompanied Ron to visit a counsellor, it's time for Ron to go in, but Mariah asked if she should come with him but Ron told her not to worry that he'll be just fine.

"Ok just tell her everything," said Mariah.

"Ok, Mariah," Ron said, and walked in to see the doctor.

"Hello, good morning, I'm Doctor Cheryl Anderson, and you're?" asked the doctor.

"Ron Rogers," he replied.

"You're welcome," said Dr. Cheryl.

"Thank you," replied Ron.

Immediately after dispensing of all pleasantries, the doctor then went straight into the business of the day, as she asked Ron to tell her about his depression and then inquired further about how he's actually feeling now. Ron's response wasn't just illusory, he was still in denial as he told the doctor he actually don't know why his wife called it depression.

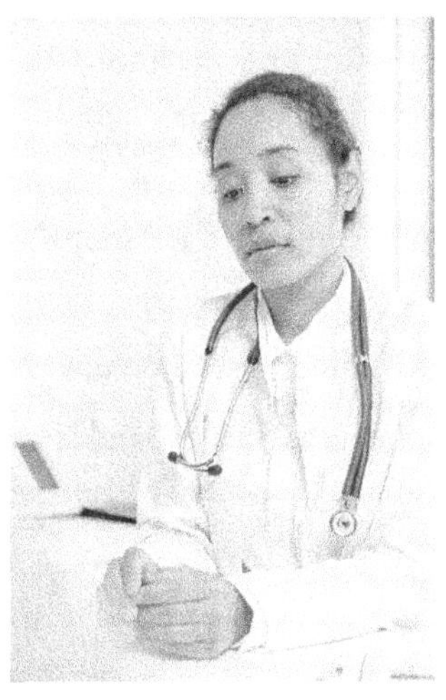

"Your wife booked the appointment, I suppose, and from her observation she concluded you were depressed?" asked Dr. Cheryl.

"Yes," said Ron.

"Ok, but is there a change in your usual lifestyle **and** routine?" asked Dr. Cheryl.

Ron hesitated then opened up, and said his horse died and he's mourning Anvil.

"Oh, sorry about your loss and who's Anvil?" Dr. Cheryl.

"Anvil is my best friend, my horse," said Ron.

"Ok, and how have you been mourning your Anvil, where do you stay to mourn Anvil?" asked Dr. Cheryl.

Ron told the doctor he stays in the stable and he doesn't go out, and the doctor then queried further by asking him much time he spends in the stable. Ron replied and said he stays in the stable from morning when he wakes up until maybe in the evening, then he'll come back into the house.

"But how has your family felt about this, are they happy with your present life style?" asked Dr. Cheryl.

The doctor seem to have a little peek into Ron's life and realised he's just finding it too hard to let go, and quitting old dreams is the toughest.

"I don't know actually, but they felt I shut them out of my life," said Ron.

"Does your wife and children love Anvil?" asked Dr. Cheryl.

Ron replied saying of course they do, and stressed that his family loved Anvil so much, just that they've been able to cope with the shock in their own way.

"Do you care about your family? Your wife and children do you love them," asked Dr. Cheryl.

"Yes, I love them to bits," replied Ron.

"If you love them this much, don't you think it'll be better you stop spending your entire day in the stable?" asked Dr. Cheryl.

"Yeah, you're right, just that Anvil and I have this special bond," said Ron.

"How much do you love Anvil?" asked Dr. Cheryl.

Ron smiled and said he love Anvil so much, and that's why he's finding it hard to let go.

"I'm not happy about Anvil's death, but do you prefer that it's either Mariah or any of your daughters that died?" asked Dr. Cheryl.

"Of course not!" exclaimed Ron.

"No? But that's what your action is saying; you've chosen Anvil over them," said Dr. Cheryl.

"But I don't see it that way," said Ron.

"As you said earlier, your wife and kids were equally touched by this loss, but your present action is about to tear your family apart," said Dr. Cheryl.

"If you say so, what do you expect me to do?" asked Ron.

The doctor then suggested to Ron that he can go into his stable, but he shouldn't spend more than an hour in the stable during the morning time, and same should apply in the evening. She advised that Ron should rather start spending more time in the house.

"Ok, I'll try to do as you've asked," said Ron.

"And make sure you eat at least twice a day, your next appointment will be next week Monday, If you make progress then you won't need medication," said Dr. Cheryl.

"Thank you, doctor," said Ron.

The doctor then urged Ron to take it easy on himself. They bid each other goodbye, and Ron left the doctor's office. Mariah got up from her seat and walked up to Ron as he came out of the doctor's office. "How did it go, Ron?" asked Mariah.

"It went well, and I'm sorry for all the pain I've caused you, now I get it," Ron said and gave Mariah a hug.

Mariah was stunned at Ron's confession and was happy his meeting with the counsellor was a step in the right direction. "Oh, I'm happy for you," she said.

"I'll try as much as I can to make this work, you've been wonderful," said Ron.

Mariah smiled she as told Ron she's relieved to hear this, and whatever happened to her husband in that meeting with the doctor makes a lot of sense and she wants more of it. They held hands as they walked in locked steps to the car and left.

The next Monday Mariah was quick on her feet to get Ron ready for his next appointment with the counsellor.

"How're you, Ron?" asked Dr. Cheryl.

"I'm fine, good morning," said Ron.

The doctor went into the business of the day as she asked Ron to tell her about his new routine, since after their last session.

"I no longer spend the whole day in the stable, except when I'm with Fanny," said Ron. The doctor then asked who Fanny was.

"Fanny is my daughter's horse," said Ron.

"Do you take Fanny for a ride sometimes?" asked Dr. Cheryl.

"Yes, I do," said Ron.

"Good to hear you now spend time in the house with your wife, do you sleep well?" asked Dr. Cheryl.

"Yeah, I sleep well and always dream about Anvil and I in a race," said Ron.

"This dream with Anvil, is it regular, and how often do you dream about Anvil?" asked Dr. Cheryl.

Ron's response was that it depends on whether there's a horse racing contest in the dream world, Ron's mention of racing contest now opens up a new line of questioning that the doctor seemingly seek to pursue. The doctor then quarried further and asked him if he sees himself riding Anvil in a racing contest in his dream.

"At the moment, we have a national competition and we just won at the state level," said Ron.

"This championship you talked about, how does it work?" asked Dr. Cheryl.

"We won at the county level and represented this county at the state level, and won," said Ron.

"What's it about this national horse racing competition, how'll you go about that?" asked Dr. Cheryl.

Ron was quite upfront in his bid to tell the interesting tale of his conquest in the dream world, and this is about his partnership with his riding partner. He didn't hesitate to tell the doctor that the national horse racing championship will take place on the 19th of July which is two Thursdays from that day. He hinted that Anvil will come to him in his dream a day before for them to practise and the next day they'll compete.

"Do you drink plenty of alcohol?" asked Dr. Cheryl.

"I used to, but since Anvil died I take only a little alcohol," said Ron.

This dream is now a new twist that would require additional attention, and the doctor concluded that from what she has just heard she'll have to place Ron on medication, she then wrote some prescription for him.

"Thank you," said Ron.

Doctor Cheryl proceeded to ask Ron if there's a place where jockeys go to relax and spend time with each other. Of course there is, as he quickly pointed out that they usually meet at the Lone Star Park, and it's the place they relax to have fun. The doctor then urged Ron to do more of outdoor activities, and urged him to spend about two hours daily in the park with friends for the next one week.

"Ok, thank you," said Ron.

"Make sure you take lots of fluid and eat well," said Dr. Cheryl.

They said their goodbyes and Ron left the counsellor.

Interestingly, a week later, Ron went to sleep on the 18th of July, and Anvil visited him for them to practise for the national horse racing contest that will be happening the next day 19th July.

"Ron, how're you coping?" asked Anvil.

"I'm coping well, and at least my fitness is perfect," said Ron.

"I'm talking about your mind set, because it plays an important role when racing in the dream world," said Anvil.

"I need to win this championship coming up tomorrow," said Ron.

"I hope you understand that racing in the dream world isn't the same as the physical world," said Anvil.

"Why isn't it the same?" asked Ron.

Anvil reminded Ron that the dream world is a world of unlimited possibilities, so he must win this race in his mind, before he can win it on the track, but in the physical world he must be good on the track first before his mindset can come in to assist him.

"But when we practiced for the championship at state level the other night, we did a lot of fitness exercise," said Ron.

"Is it the night I told you about the Red Thunder?" asked Anvil.

"Yes," said Ron.

"You called it fitness, but I was preparing you mentally," said Anvil.

"How does this mental preparation work?" asked Ron.

"It involves a problem solving strategy, called design thinking, this strategy is employed to challenge your automatic thinking, to see how things really are," said Anvil.

Ron seems to realise he's training alone and there wasn't any other horse around, he then asked Anvil to know why she didn't take him to where other horses are practicing.

Anvil reminded Ron, that this is the national horse racing championship finale, he'll see the best horses in the United States perform tomorrow, and he doesn't want him to train alongside them, so he doesn't get intimidated. Anvil understands that Ron could get nervy by acts of some of the horses competing at the national level, and this could be quite intimidating and could leave quite an impression on him. Not to mention the feelings of butterflies in his stomach that could precipitate into a knee jerk performance.

"Do they have special skills?" asked Anvil.

"Some of them run at the speed of light, but it's all a mindset thing, and you can beat them with the right mind set," said Anvil.

"Is that the reason why you're talking more about mindset?" asked Ron.

"Now focus your mind as we practice our ambling gait, your mindset plays a big role here," said Anvil.

While Ron was still dreaming in his sleep, Mariah woke up as a result of the noise of a neighbour's dog barking, she looked through the window and felt she saw someone walking in the dark within the neighbourhood. Mariah panicked and tapped Ron, asking him to wake up.

"Ron wake up, wake up, can't you hear that dog barking?" asked Mariah.

Back in the dream, Ron serendipitously had a feeling Mariah wants him, he quickly told Anvil he has to return to the physical world.

"Why? We still have training to do," asked Anvil.

"Mariah wants me and I've to return," said Ron.

"Ok, you can go, but make sure you sleep well tomorrow night because if you don't then you've missed out of the championship," said Anvil.

Ron woke up from his sleep. "Ooh Mariah, what's that! Why can't I just have a peaceful night sleep?" Ron retorted.

"What's it with you? There's someone lurking in the dark in our neighbourhood," Mariah retorted. The sleep in Ron's eyes disappeared immediately, as he quickly jerked up from bed, and asked to know where she spotted the marauding trespasser, he then pulled the curtain slightly apart and peeped through the window.

"I saw somebody walking in the dark," she said.

"Are you sure? Remain inside the house," said Ron. He then quietly went into his draw, brought out his pistol, opened the door slowly and went outside. Just as Ron made his way outside the house, Mariah whispered to Ron to please be careful.

He walked around for about ten minutes, scanning the surrounding of his house and even went into the stable, he then came back into the house. "There's no one there," said Ron.

"I thought I saw someone," said Mariah.

"Ok let's go back to sleep, you just cut short my practice," Ron retorted.

"What practice are you talking about?" asked Mariah.

Ron quickly told Mariah not to worry about it, so as to avoid opening the door to a new line of debate. The next night which is the 19th of July, and the night of the national championship, Ron took sleeping pill to enable him sleep as long as necessary. Ron needed to avoid a repeat of the drama of the previous night where Mariah thought she saw something that look like a boogeyman lurking in the shadows of the night.

"Mariah, I don't want you to disturb my sleep," said Ron.

"Why, so you can run around with Anvil in your dream isn't it?" asked Mariah.

"No, I'm taking sleeping pills," said Ron.

"Why are you taking sleeping pills? You've been sleeping well," said Mariah.

Ron hinted that she woke him up last night and he couldn't go back to sleep again. Talking about this matter in a dimly lit bedroom in this cold breezy summer night won't change the course of events particularly now that Ron is in a much better spirit to compete than he had expected. Yet his wife urged him to stop being tiresome because he's beginning to punish her ears with his tale about racing with Anvil. With Ron playing the victim's card, Mariah then slowed down to avoid goading him.

Mariah on the other hand made light of Ron's concerns, as she unblinkingly told Ron she knew what he's up to, she then reminded him tonight is Thursday 19th isn't it.

"What about it? I said I need an opportunity to sleep, is it too much to ask?" Ron protested.

"Tonight is the night of the national championship you talked about," said Mariah.

"What about it? I said I need opportunity to sleep, is it too much to ask?" Ron protested again.

Mariah realised Ron's insistence means he doesn't want her taking a peek into his cloak and dagger any further, and Mariah realised further conversation might spook Ron.

"Don't worry, I won't wake you up, and even if I see someone walking in the neighbourhood I'll allow you wake up by yourself," said Mariah.

The stage is now set for Ron and Anvil to compete in the United States national horse racing championship. Anvil was a horse with a pedigree in the land of the living, and new to competing in the dream world. Yet, she's keen to put up a show, in which even the labyrinths hiding away in plain sight will still find it an arduous task crossing that finish line before Anvil, in a classic case of more than meets the eyes.

Commentary: Ladies and gentlemen, I'm Jonathan Green, and I'll be running your commentary in today's national horse racing championship finale in the dream world, this race is organised only for the departed in the entire United States.

I must confess that we've a new contestant representing the State of Texas, who passed on recently, but surprisingly she was able to outrun all other horses that came her way to get to the finale. However, her riding partner, Ron Rogers, is still among the living but decided to partake in this championship that's meant for those that have passed on because of his love for Anvil. Though, Anvil as they said was a highly respected horse in the land of the living because of her pedigree.

The temperature is perfect, the weather is perfect and emotions are running high. The President of the United States Horse Racing Association is here, and the President of the United States is also present to make this horse racing contest a memorable one. President Franklin Roosevelt will be representing the Committee of Past Presidents of the United States in this championship, and the winner of this contest will get a handshake from Mr. President.

Commentary: Ladies and gentlemen the race has started, as you can see, the Kariaste, the horse with the speed of lightening is leading the race, right behind him is the Floempror, the horse that runs at the speed of light, but the spectators are anxious as

Anvil, the horse without a description just moved from the sixth place to the third place.

Ladies and gentlemen we are into the last one hundred metres of this race, Anvils is making a show with a surprise move against floempror and she's now in the second place in this race, and we're into the last twenty meters of this contest. Interestingly, Anvil and his riding partner from the land of the living is making an impression and also making the emotions of the spectators to run riots because she's springing surprises. As you can see, Anvil has just speed past Kariaste, the horse with the speed of lightening, and she has just crossed the finish line. Ladies and gentle men we now have a new national champion in Anvil and Ron Rogers.

Ooh, what a surprise, the horse without a description, the new entrant into the land of the departed has won today's horse racing championship contest. Immediately after the race, Ron couldn't help himself but asked Anvil how come they won this race.

"I told you it's a mindset thing," said Anvil.

"The speed of some of these horses is unimaginable," said Ron.

"What do you expect from the best horse in each state in the United States?" asked Anvil.

"So, this mindset thing was the reason behind our winning?" asked Ron.

"Yes, the dream world is a world of unlimited possibilities, so your mindset determines your pace," said Anvil.

Anvil hinted him that the President of the Unites States horse racing association is here, even the President of the United States is here. She then suggested they go to the podium to collect their trophy and get their hand shake from Mr. President. Ron and Anvil went to the podium to collect their trophy after which Ron shook hands with the President of the United States horse racing association, and then Mr. President, the President of the United States. They took photographs, and the occasion was filled with pomp and pageantry, with flares and fireworks lightening up the sky.

Ron was filled with joy as he couldn't help but thanked Anvil for giving him an opportunity to share in this experience. "Ron, nothing gives me joy than seeing you celebrated at the national stage," said Anvil.

Ron enjoyed all the fun particularly the photo ops, he then asked Anvil if she will involve him in future horse racing championships in the dream world. Sadly, Anvil made Ron understand that this place is for the departed, and she just came to help him fulfil an ambition she was unable to achieve in the real world, following her early demise.

"What about the trophy?" asked Ron.

"I'll keep the trophy and our photographs here until you pass on and join me, but try to live a good life and get old before you pass on, I'll be waiting for you even till the next two hundred years," said Anvil.

"Can you wait that long?" asked Ron.

"Some of the horses you saw here have been here for over a thousand years after uniting with their riders," said Anvil.

"Does it mean I'll not see you again?" asked Ron.

Ron wasn't quite impressed when Anvil told him their exploits in the dream world is over, as the national horse racing championship curtain closes. For all it's worth, this experience will leave a lasting impression on Ron. Though, Anvil isn't quite as heartless as the boogeyman lurking in the shadows in dark alleys, she told Ron they might be having a one-off leisure ride in his dreams but that's just it.

"Will you stay until I join you?" asked Ron.

"I'll be a chariot, when you pass on I'll come as a chariot to pick you, and after our reunion I'll go back to a racing horse," said Anvil.

"But you're a horse, must you be a chariot?" asked Ron.

Anvil took time to explain to Ron that she'll be a chariot during her time of waiting for Ron, because she would've no racing partner, but when they're reunited she'll go back to being a racing horse.

"Ok thank you, Anvil, you've been a good friend and partner," said Ron.

"Ron, be good, be cheerful, ride with Fanny, live a happy life, till we meet again," said Anvil.

They bid each other goodbye and he woke up from his sleep.

Immediately Ron woke up from his sleep, he turned to Mariah who's on her side of the bed.

"Mariah, we won," he said.

"What, your race with Anvil?" she asked. At least Ron already told her of his national championship contest happening on the 19th. He then smiled and said he's currently the new United State horse racing champion.

"Then where's the trophy?" asked Mariah..

"It's with Anvil," said Ron.

Mariah was quite rattled as she protested being gutted because this whole racing in the dream thing has turned into some kind of madness. This news seemed to touch a nerve, and she isn't appreciative of his candour. Ron didn't stop talking about his conquest, he just didn't stop as he insists Anvil will keep the trophy for him until they reunite maybe fifty years from now, that's if he lives above a hundred years.

"Enough of this," Mariah protested as she walked out on her husband, to the sitting room and continued her sleep on the couch.

Days later, Ron visited the counsellor for the fifth session, and funnily, he isn't looking forward to any race in the dream world this time. Consequently, the counsellor is spared further surprises.

"Good morning, Doctor Cheryl," said Ron.

"How're you doing, Ron?" asked Dr. Cheryl.

"I'm fine. At least, I'll say I'm good," said Ron.

"How is your social life?" asked Dr. Cheryl.

"You mean my social life? It's fine," said Ron.

"Yeah, I know from our last sessions, you're beginning to go out, what about leisure rides?" asked Dr. Cheryl.

"Yeah, I do that, I go out for leisure," said Ron.

Doctor Cheryl asked Ron about his horse riding, she wants to know if Ron has returned to horse racing. Ron didn't hesitate as he unblinkingly reminded the doctor of his earlier position on this matter, as he insists he's no longer getting involved in a horse racing contest.

"Why?" Dr. Cheryl surprisingly asked.

"As I told you earlier, I'll not race with any horse other than Anvil," Ron insists.

"I'm not talking of racing, what about Fanny? Do you ride her around for leisure, horse riding is something you enjoy doing isn't?" asked Dr. Cheryl.

Ron accepted that he rides Fanny around to keep the horse fit because his daughter isn't home, she's in school. "Each time you visit the park, try to go to the park with your horse, at least for leisure," said Dr. Cheryl.

"But I do that already," said Ron.

The doctor tried changing approach as to precipitating an appetite for horse racing, but in doing this she had to re-orientate Ron's mindset from a person fulfilling an obligation of merely keeping the horse fit to a person in the company of friends, and riding a horse.

"Do it for leisure this time, as a person doing what he likes but not as a person trying to help the horse stay fit," said Dr. Cheryl.

"I'll do that," said Ron.

"With this, your phobia about horse racing will go away. What about sleep, do you sleep well?" she asked further.

"Of course yes, I sleep well," said Ron.

"Ok that's good, what about your alcohol intake, how's it presently?" asked Dr. Cheryl.

Ron insists he has told her earlier, that he's a light drinker and he drink a maximum of two jugs of beer a day.

"What about the dreams you talked about, I meant the racing competition in your dream life?" said Dr. Cheryl.

"I told you Anvil would come a day before the national competition," said Ron.

"Yes, you told me," said Dr. Cheryl.

Ron was all smiles as he narrates how Anvil came the day before the national championship and they practiced at length, and the next day 19th July, Anvil came to him again on the day of the national horse racing championship and they competed.

"This is quite strange, and what happened during the contest?" asked Dr. Cheryl.

"Yeah, we won the national horse racing championship," said Ron.

"You mean all these happened last week Thursday, what about the trophy, where's it?" asked Dr. Cheryl.

"Yeah, last week Thursday was the horse racing contest at the national level, Anvil and I represented the state of Texas," said Ron.

"I mean the trophy, where's it?" Dr. Cheryl.

"I left it with Anvil," said Ron.

"You mean Anvil is with the trophy, in the dream world?" asked Dr. Cheryl.

This is quite a thorny and strange subject for the doctor, and one she'd to grapple with. The doctor remain open mouthed, as she listened to Ron's escapades with this Anvil, and she can't help but reach for tapes of Ron and his former riding partner doing great exploits on the racecourse. Yet there's more than meets the eyes with Ron's dreams.

"Yeah, though I can't bring the trophy to the physical world, but we actually won the race," Ron insists.

She then proceeded to ask Ron that now that the championship is over, does he still dream of racing with Anvil. Ron's response gave her some relief, as he said the dream has stopped. After all, Anvil only wanted to help him win the national championship since they couldn't win it in real life and he has done that.

"Good to hear the dream has stopped, but if the dream continues I'll want you to let me know immediately," said the doctor.

The doctor then urged Ron to continue with his medication, and always go for leisure rides. Ron thanked her then left the counsellor's office as the session came to a close.

After several visits to the psychologist Ron was able to pull through the depression he suffered as a result of Anvil's death. His conversations, his countenance and behaviour were restored; he became the lively Ron he used to be, just that he has maintained his position of not racing in any competition.

Now that he has signed back to life, it's time for Ron to bring closure to Anvil. Ron and Mariah had to pay Walter a visit, particularly now that he's is ready to see what the post mortem result said concerning Anvil's death.

"Hello Ron, how are you?" asked Walter. He then turned to Mariah and welcomed her.

"Ooh, thank you Walter," said Mariah.

After they finished exchanging pleasantries, Ron told Walter he has come collect Anvil's post mortem result.

"Why now?" asked Walter.

"Because I'm bringing a closure to Anvil's death," said Ron.

"What do you mean by closure? I don't seem to follow," replied Walter.

Mariah quickly interjected and reminded Walter that Ron wants to move on, and he shouldn't take him back to his dreams. She then urged Walter to please give them the post mortem result so Ron will know what caused Anvil's death.

"What about the racing contest in his dream?" asked Walter.

"We've finished the championship and we won," said Ron.

"When was this championship concluded?" asked Walter.

"Two Thursdays ago," said Ron.

Mariah interjected and reminded Walter that Ron wants to move on, and urged him not take him back to his dreams. She then requested Walter to give them the post mortem result so Ron will know what caused Anvil's death. Revisiting this conversation could mean pulling the rug from under her husband's feet, and patronizing him won't do the trick either. Walter opened the draw and brought out the post mortem result, then handed it to Ron. "The cause of death is cardiac failure," said Walter.

Ron opened the envelope and suddenly became emotional again, but Mariah isn't ready to allow her husband fall off the wagon again. "Cardiac failure, that's strange!" Ron exclaimed.

"Despite giving Anvil all the required medical attention, she shouldn't have died of cardiac failure," Mariah retorted.

Walter understands in no uncertain terms that Mariah doesn't want her husband slipping back into a state of emotional despair, he then reminded Ron he has mourned Anvil already, and there isn't any need going into deep thought.

"You're right, I've come to seek closure and that's what I've to do," said Ron.

"At least, we know the death of Anvil isn't your fault," said Walter.

Ron wasn't particularly pleased with Walter's effort to put him in the right, and his reply was unblinkingly stern as he asked Walter why he thinks he can justify Anvil's death.

"Ron, we now know the cause of Anvil's death, give me the envelope let me keep it," said Mariah.

Ron immediately stretched forth his hand and handed her the envelope because holding onto this envelope implies holding onto the past. Funnily, the past isn't the most idyllic place for Ron to be at this point.

"Ron, I'm happy for you, I've been seeing you around with Fanny, and sometimes in the bar, that's a very big improvement," said Walter.

"The visit to the counsellor worked, she helped him learn to go out again," said Mariah.

Walter was happy as he confessed he's happy to see Ron back on his feet, and hopefully he'll soon be on the tracks again.

"That'll never happen," Ron protested.

"Walter thanked Mariah for taking a good care of Ron, but Mariah in turn thanked Walter for being of immense assistance to her family during those bleak moments.

"Ron isn't just a jockey, he's my friend," said Walter.

"Thank you for taking charge of all these, Walter. I think we've to get going," said Mariah.

"Wait a minute. I've got something for you," said Walter.

"Something, tell me about your surprise," said Ron.

Walter pulled open the drawer again and this time he brought out travel holidays tickets and hands them to Ron. "Take them, a fully booked holiday for you and Mariah," said Walter.

Without opening the envelope and reading the contents on the tickets, Mariah quickly interjected as she asked Walter where the holiday will be. Walter then spoke softly as someone letting out a secret, and said. "Havana, don't you want a visit to Cuba? I guess dancing Salsa shouldn't be a bad idea," said Walter.

Mariah exclaimed "fully booked, you said!" Mariah is known to frown at surprises, but this time she seemed to like this surprise. She then turned to Ron with a smile before collecting the envelope containing the ticket from Walter. "Let me have a look, I've longed to visit that Communist nation," she said.

"Hmm," Ron mumbled as he gave Mariah a nudge and reminded her she never expressed interest in travelling to Havana. Walter stood up as he reminded Ron his holiday is booked, and urged him to take his wife to Havana and have some fun. After all, it's been long since he actually spent time with Mariah outside Texas because Anvil's premature demise put their lives on hiatus.

Walter stood up as he reminded Ron his holiday is booked, and urged him to take his wife to Havana and enjoy some fun. After all, it's been long since he actually spent time with Mariah outside Texas.

Mariah on the other hand was nudging Ron to grab this gesture of goodwill, and suddenly Ron brightens up and thanked Walter. "You've made Maria's dream of dancing salsa with me come alive and I equally like the idea, I suppose," said Ron.

"Ron, we've fifteen days to be in Havana!" exclaimed Mariah.

From the moment Mariah stepped out of Kenny Walter's office she bizarrely began preparing for her trip to Havana Cuba. Two weeks later, Mariah and Ron arrived the Jose Marti International Airport in Havana.

Mariah pointed at a cab driver carrying a cardboard with their names on display. "Hey Ron, look at that, that's our names on a cardboard," said Mariah.

Ron laughed as he wore a cheeky grin on his face. "Ahhh! the cab man, he's here for us, I think I like this," said Ron. They then walked up to the cab man.

"That's our name you put on display," said Mariah.

"Ron Rogers and Mariah Rogers, is that you?" asked Jagger.

"Yes of course, my name is Ron, and my wife Maria, you seem to be our driver," he said. Ron then stretched his hand for a hand shake with Jagger.

"My name is Jagger, and I'm going to be your driver, welcome to Havana," he replied.

Jagger helped Mariah and Ron with their bags and quickly loaded their stuff into the boot of his car and asked them to jump into the cab, so he could take them to their destination. "Where are you taking us, do you've an idea of the hotel we are meant to lodge in?" asked Mariah.

"Yeah, the Blue Ostrich Hotel is your destination isn't it, room twelve, double bed?" said Jagger.

"Oh, spot on," he chuckled, and wait a minute, are we to pay you for this service?" asked Ron.

"Of course not, this is part of your package, you booked an all inclusive holiday, didn't you?" asked Jagger.

Ron and Mariah eyed each other. "Yeah, yeah, we did," said Ron.

"We are spending a week in Havana, are you driving us all through or some other driver will take over at some point?" asked Mariah.

Jagger is known for his smiles and warm disposition, and creating a friendly ambience is one of his key strength. "I'm at your service for the next one week, and I'm meant to give you good service. Please I'll appreciate it if I'm highly recommended," said Jagger.

"Who does the recommendation?" asked Mariah.

"You of course, the hotel won't engage me any longer if a customer recommends me poorly," said Jagger. Ron was upfront in their conversation, and he jocularly asked Jagger if he has been poorly recommended at anytime.

"Fortunately not, my customers like me, and maybe I'm lucky perhaps," said Jagger.

"No, maybe you're a good guy, I guess," said Ron.

It didn't take long before Jagger took the last turn through the bend that led to the hotel.

Moments later, they approached the hotel reception, with Jagger by their side showing them the way.

"Hello, good evening, welcome to the Blue Ostrich Hotel," said the Receptionist.

"Good evening," said Ron. He then hands the receptionist their booking invoice, she collected it and spent some time on the system dealing with their bookings. Minutes later, she hands back their booking tickets. "Room twelve, all inclusive holiday package," said receptionist.

"Excuse me, and what are we entitled to?" asked Mariah.

"Hmm, your double bed room, breakfast, lunch and dinner, transportation around town," said the receptionist.

"Does it include dance, like, I mean dance during a night out," said Mariah.

Ron interjected and told Mariah he doesn't think night-out dancing is covered in the deal, yet felt since this is Cuba where every visitor would want to dance salsa perhaps it should be a part of the deal.

"I'm sorry; I don't get you," said the receptionist.

Ron was quick to speak up for Mariah, telling the receptionist Mariah wants to know if the cab driver will take them to places where they can have some fun dancing salsa.

"Oh my God, every American coming to Cuba wants to dance salsa!" the receptionist exclaimed.

Sadly, the receptionist expressed her prejudice and funnily played into Mariah's hand, and Mariah's expression of exception to issues is one that's in constant motion. "Hey don't be dismissive, and I don't think it'll be out of place sharing in that experience," said Mariah.

"Sorry about that, just that whatever activity you intend to engage in isn't a part of the package, because that's optional and preferences differ," said the receptionist.

"Hmm, I get it, meaning all you offer is the basic, what everybody would want?" Mariah said.

"Yes, sorry we don't offer some of the services you expected," said the receptionist. She then turned to Jagger, and asked him to please take their bags upstairs.

As they made their way upstairs, Mariah then asked Jagger to please wait behind because he'll be taking them to the boulevard, because she and husband needs to dance salsa tonight.

"Madam, I'm not taking you to the boulevard for salsa, I'm taking you somewhere else," he replied.

"Where, if I may ask?" asked Mariah.

"Err.., salsa? I'll take you down town, to Central Habana, a place for a good drink and a good dance," replied Jagger.

Mariah was glad, it's like providence brought this driver her way, and she sees this trip as a head start to a new beginning after Anvil's demise and the pain precipitated by her loss. "Thank goodness, you know what I wanted, you're taking us there?" asked Mariah.

Ron felt the need to take things slowly, he quickly interjected and said he thinks resting for a while before setting off for the downtown shouldn't be a bad idea. Mariah on the other hand seems to have things all planned out, as she interjected and reminded Ron that she asked Jagger to stay behind because they aren't leaving immediately.

The idea of asking a business man to sit down idly and wait for nothing seemed antiquated. Ron understands the mindset of a businessman like Jagger, and suggested to Mariah that keeping Jagger here idly would mean a waste of his time, time is money, and their contract with him doesn't include a waste of his money.

"Then what do you suggest?" asked Mariah.

"Jagger, its 6.pm, pick us up by half seven, you've got about an hour thirty minutes, use it to make some cash for yourself," said Ron.

"Ok, good idea, I'll be here by half seven, see you then," Jagger said, then leaves the hotel room.

Two hours later, Ron and Mariah arrived Central Havana, and they walked straight into a salsa dance hall. After spending about an hour in the bar, Mariah felt the need to turn the outing into a pulsating night out. "How long will you hold onto your glass of bourbon?" asked Mariah.

She looked on as her husband held onto the glass of bourbon forever, her patience grew thin and she couldn't help but express her exasperation to her dawdling husband.

"Aren't you dancing with me? I came here to dance salsa and not to share in your drinks galore," Mariah retorted.

Ron smiled, then gulps the Bourbon in the glass and stood up, "let's do this," he said, as he took to the dance floor after two shots of Bourbon, he then pulled Mariah to himself, urging her to show him her moves on the dance floor.

"I don't know how to do the dance steps," she said, then turns to Jagger.

"Teach me how to do this," said Mariah.

Jagger stood up and left his drink on the table as he attends to Mariah's request. "Ok, there are four beats per measure, move your feet to the beat of the music, like this," said Jagger.

Mariah watched and began mirroring Jagger's dance moves as she perfects her steps. "Ok, this is becoming interesting," she said.

"You should do this by moving your hips and upper body in coordination with the basic foot work," said Jagger.

Ron watched and also learnt a few tricks as Jagger gave Mariah a head start. "Ok Mariah, let us give this a try," said Ron. Jagger watched as Ron and Mariah was at it, and coached them all along. "Your foot work must go with the beat, and your movement must be influenced by the cha-cha mambo and the African styles," said Jagger.

"Ahhh, Mariah, you seem to be getting it," said Ron.

"Have you forgotten the fact that I'm a good dancer," said Mariah with a smile.

"Of course, I haven't, but you're displaying so much energy, and I can see you adding your own flair to this," said Ron.

Mariah burst into laughter "How?" she asked.

"Hips don't lie, Mariah. You're swinging your hips to accentuate your movement and I like that," said Ron. "That's what hips are meant for, they're meant to be swung," said Mariah.

"You two seem to be doing just perfect, and I think I should leave you to it," said Jagger.

"Ok Jagger, thank you, I guess I should have some good time with my wife," said Ron as he continued enjoying his salsa dance moves with his wife until they returned to the hotel hours later.

The next Morning, after a pulsating outing the previous night, "honey, its 11.am, we can't be in bed all day?" said Mariah.

Ron turned over with a smile, saying they came in late last night, and he's still reminiscing the fun of the previous night.

Mariah didn't hesitate to remind her husband that the fun he was reminiscing was for yesterday, and she then urged him to get ready for the day's outing, because Jagger his on his way. Ron seems to think Mariah is pushing her luck, and said they shouldn't expect Jagger to take them for salsa during the day because people only go to dance at night.

"I know, and we aren't going for dance, he's taking us somewhere else, I won't remain cooped up indoors with you when I'm supposed to be having fun outdoors," Mariah protested.

"Where should that be, if I may ask?" asked Ron.

"He called it Fusterlandia, he said we would love it," said Mariah.

Ron got up from bed, and walked across the room as he prepares to take a shower. "I hope we do," he said. He then stopped suddenly and focused on Mariah.

"What's it, and why're you staring into my eyes with this intensity?" asked Mariah. Ron turned around. "No, nothing," he said.

Mariah quickly followed him from behind. "There must be something, that look is beyond nothing, what's it, Ron?" asked Mariah.

"It's you," said Ron.

"Me! What is it about me?" asked Mariah.

Ron quickly put on a smile, but his cheeky grin speaks more than a thousand words, meaning there's more in his heart than he's letting out. Mariah's insistence forced Ron into confessing he never knew his wife is still this active. "You displayed some energy yesterday, I began asking myself if this is truly my wife on the dancing floor," said Ron.

"Don't insult me, you cheeky man. Do you think I'm old, because I'm not," Mariah protested jocularly.

Ron apologised to Mariah saying he's sorry, just that he was taken aback to see his wife enjoying the grove of the dance floor as he reminisce his youthful moments with his wife. Ron then decided it's best to seize the moment and make the best of it with his wife.

"Yeah, because you made our lives tenuous over the death of Anvil, when was our last holiday, or when last did we even have a good laugh?" said Mariah.

Ron confessed he just realised how much he has made Mariah suffer, because Mariah didn't hesitate to accept this offer from Walter the moment he pulled the tickets out of his drawer.

"I've been indoors with you, pained over a long period of time mourning Anvil, though, I'm glad Walter made this offer," said Mariah.

Thirty minutes later, Jagger arrived and picked Ron and Mariah up, and they then made their way to Fusterlandia. Interestingly, while in the cab, Mariah pointed to a beautiful art work. "Hey, Ron, can you see that?" she asked.

"Yes, it's beautiful, what a beautiful piece of art!" exclaimed Ron.

Mariah turned to Jagger, and suggested he should've stopped, so they can have a look at that, and then continue to their destination. Jagger felt good with himself as he funnily replied her, saying that's their destination and he knew she would like it.

"Oh, thank you, you've a good taste for art," said Mariah. The car slowed down and parked.

Jagger got down from the car, Ron and Mariah followed suit. Jagger then took them through the street in stroll. "This is a three-dimensional neighbourhood art work," said Jagger.

"Oh my God, what a bombastry of colour and creativity!" exclaimed Mariah.

Ron seem to be on the move even as Mariah dawdled a bit, as she enjoyed the eye catching artwork littered all over this street, and funnily each single piece of art is a masterpiece on its own. Mariah is now lagging behind, and felt Ron's pace isn't allowing her catch her fun, she couldn't help but protest. "Hey, why're you in a hurry? Allow me to take a good look at this, I'm here to feed my eyes and have some fun," protested Mariah.

"How come there is art work everywhere in this neighbourhood?" asked Ron.

"That's what makes it interesting, and that's why we called this place a street of art work," said Jagger.

Mariah needed to memorialise this outing she then brought out her camera, and urged others to wait, because she needed to take some photographs. Ron and Jagger stood by and watched as Mariah takes photograph, and suddenly, Ron got sucked in by Mariah's interest in pictures, he suddenly join Mariah and asked Jagger to please take some good shots of them if he doesn't mind.

"No, not at all, take a pose, let me take a snap of you," said Jagger. Ron and Mariah held onto each other as if they were held bound by teenage crush, while Jagger snapped them as much as they wanted and they also took a few snap shots with Jagger.

"We need a place to rest and drink something?" said Ron.

"If you need somewhere to relax, that spot over there is best, good drinks and the environment is refreshing," said Jagger.

Moments later, they walked into one of the nearest bar that was suggested by Jagger, and Ron exclaimed, because he couldn't just believe that there seems to be more art work inside the buildings than what they've seen in the street. More so, the live band was quite scintillating.

"That makes this street an interesting place to be," said Mariah.

Interestingly, Mariah is already anticipating her evening outing for her salsa dance class with her husband. At least she has had some fun, and wants to save the rest for evening, and not long after they took their seat she reminded them they would need to return to the hotel in an hour's time.

"Why? We would've to stay a little longer than that, let's have fun," he then turned to Jagger. "Get the waiter to get us something to drink," said Ron. After a refreshing time-out, they then returned to their hotel room to rest a bit before their evening outing. By evening of same day, they returned to Central Habana where they had fun dancing salsa the previous night, and it also proved to be a pulsating night out as the fun wasn't disappointing.

The next day, Ron and Mariah were waiting for Jagger and were discussing about the fun they've had so far, and while their conversation persists Jagger drove into the hotel premises as the couple engage themselves in his appraisal. "Hmm, here comes the devil," said Mariah.

Minutes later Ron and Mariah joined Jagger in the cab, in playing the conventional woman's role, she's keen to know where the days' tourism will happen, and asked Jagger where he's taking them.

"Hmm, Playas del Este," he said.

"Playas del what? Say that again, please," she asked.

"Playas del Este," he said again.

Ron interjected and asked what sort of attraction it is, and funnily, they've given Jagger a clean bill of health thus far, and there isn't any need questioning the fun lined up for the day.

"It's not too far from Havana's city centre, and it's a beach, just like your Miami Beach," said Jagger.

"You mean, it's a beach?" asked Ron.

"Yes it is, it's a lovely place to be, it's a stretch of palm-fringed beach," said Jagger.

"That's lovely, I love to have a feel of what your beach looks like," said Ron.

Jagger smiled and promised they'll love the beach, moments later they arrived Playas del Este. Ron was open-mouthed at the breath taking view of the beach. "Oh my God, Jagger, this place is lovely, and it reminds me of Miami Beach," said Ron.

"No, this place is different; it's more serene than the Miami Beach I know," Mariah.

Jagger was all smiles the moment Mariah said she likes the beach because her approval determines if the day's outing will be fun or not, he then said he's glad they like this place. Jagger became jocular as he mentioned to them that he do bring his family here on important family days. It's obvious to this couple that Jagger is a dark horse who has a lot to offer this couple as they seek out the best tourist attractions in Havana.

After spending about an hour walking barefooted in the beach, Mariah approached a couple passing by and holding bowling balls of coconuts with straws inserted in them. "Hey, where did you get that, I think I like it?" asked Mariah.

The couple pointed towards a Kiosk. "Over there," they said.

"I think I would like to have one of those," said Mariah.

Interestingly, Ron wasn't consulted after the conversation between Mariah and the couple, but he suddenly noticed Mariah walking towards the Kiosk. "Wait for me, Mariah, I need one as well," said Ron.

Mariah stopped and waited for Ron to join her, she then muttered, and said Ron doesn't seem to be interested, but Ron held her hand after catching up with her, they then walked down together. Ron then called out to Jagger, who's some distance away.

"Why don't you come with us Jagger? You equally deserve one of these," said Ron.

Jagger immediately hurtled closer before taking smaller steps to catch up with them.

"Ok, thank you," Jagger replied and followed Ron from behind.

Moments later while they were walking around the beach sipping from their bowling balls of coconuts Mariah realised Ron's attention is focused on some horses in the beach. "I supposed it isn't what I'm thinking?" asked Mariah.

Ron smiled with his cheeky grin on full glare, he then turned to Mariah. "What are you thinking, Mariah?" he asked.

"Your attention has been focused on those horses, this is a holiday and we're meant to do things differently," said Mariah.

While Mariah was trying to avoid what she regarded as the 'Pennsylvanian circus,' in which Ron and Bianca left her to herself and spent a major chunk of their holidays hovering around horses and stables. Ron didn't hesitate to remind Mariah that holidays are meant to be fun, yet they continued walking barefooted on the beach, sipping from their coconut balls. After about five minutes without reference to those horses, Mariah responded to Ron's earlier comment about holiday being fun. "Just the two of us, is fun enough," said Mariah.

"Yes, it is, and I'm not complaining, but those horses are meant to add to the fun, that's why they're here," said Ron.

"Ok, what do you want? Don't make it look like I'm standing in your way," said Mariah.

"I want to ride on one of those for a few minutes maybe," said Ron.

Mariah suddenly realised this is a good thing, after all, her husband who isn't willing to ride any other horse aside Anvil, is now willing to ride a horse he knew nothing about, she then exhaled. "Ok, let's do this," said Mariah.

They walked to where the horses are leashed, Ron then pointed to one of the horses. "I like to ride on this," said Ron.

"This white one, and is it because it reminds you of Anvil?" asked Mariah.

"Yes, actually, but no horse can take Anvil's place," replied Ron.

"Whatever," Mariah retorted.

Jagger had this disquieting thought that suddenly overwhelmed him and became apprehensive as Ron attempts to climb on the horse, he became fearful for Ron as so many thoughts ran through his heart. He then urged Ron be careful so he doesn't fall off from the back of the horse, but it's obvious that you can't teach the wolf how to live in the forest.

Mariah looked at Jagger and burst into laughter. "Jagger, don't worry, he won't fall," she said.

"Has he done this before?" asked Jagger.

"Of course yes, he's used to this," said Mariah.

"Climb on Mariah, let's do this together," said Ron.

"No Ron, carry on, while I watch you race," she said.

Ron climbed on the horse, rode for about thirty minutes demonstrating various horse racing skills and later returned to Mariah and Jagger.

"Jagger, do you want to try?" asked Ron.

"No, no, I'm ok," replied Jagger.

"Why, give it a try?" Ron insists.

"I'm fine, I've a phobia for horses," he said.

Mariah interjected to stop Ron from pestering Jagger any further. "Let him be, and you don't have to force him," she insists.

"Ok, I guess I'm done riding, but this is fun," said Ron.

Mariah laughed before spilling the beans on her reason for supporting the move, she didn't hesitate to acknowledge she's glad he's able to build the courage to ride since the death of Anvil. "Let me return the horse, I'll join you in a moment," said Ron.

Minutes later, Ron returned to Mariah who's eager to dip herself in the waves. "I need a dip, this is a beach, people don't go to the beach and leave without diving into the waves," said Mariah. They then returned to the kiosk and bought some swimming trunks, and changed into them before walking in locked steps for a dip. Ron held Mariah by the hand and suggests they dive in together. The experience was quite exhilarating and refreshing as well. They'd so much fun and enjoyed all that the beach had to offer before returning to their hotel.

After spending time enjoying all that the length and breadth of Havana has to offer, the last night of the holiday in Havana is here, and Mariah wants to make it count.

"Jagger is here, and I guess it's time to go,"

"Two more minutes, I'll be with you," said Mariah.

"Meet me downstairs, I'll be in the cab with Jagger"," said Ron. Moments later Mariah joined Ron and Jagger.

"This is the last night of our holiday in Havana and I must confess this holiday has been fulfilling and refreshing, but guess what? I want something different," said Mariah.

"Something different, like what?" asked Jagger.

"Visit somewhere new for tonight's salsa dance," she said.

Jagger thought to himself, and decided to offer them something new. "I guess you're right, and you should have a feel of salsa dance somewhere different from central Havana," he said.

As usual Mariah was upfront in asking Jagger where he intends to take them tonight, Jagger knows the terrain and knows the right dance hall where tourist treats themselves to a good salsa dance. He quickly suggested that a salsa dance in the grand boulevard Paseo del Prado, would be just perfect.

"Paseo del Prado, where's that?" asked Ron.

"That's the most beautiful street in Havana, bordering the old Havana," said Jagger.

Mariah wants to know what makes Paseo del Prado beautiful, she then asked. "Is it because it's the most beautiful street in Havana, or it's just a nice place for a good dance?" she asked.

"Because it's both, tonight you'll be dancing salsa in style, and you'll definitely like it," replied Jagger.

"Ok, I guess we are good to go, let's pay Paseo del Pradeo a visit," Ron said.

Mariah is organically a cautious person, but this time she's willing to take the plunge because she's quite up for it. It didn't take long before they arrived Paseo del Prado, and funnily, Mariah didn't wait to be convinced before exclaiming she likes this place.

"I'm certain you don't need me hanging around, and I guess I too need a partner to dance salsa as well," said Jagger.

Mariah was quick to get on with it on the dance floor, and thanked Jagger saying they won't need to be instructed tonight.

"Yeah, you're right, your dance moves explains it all. You don't need instructing anymore," said Jagger.

Mariah then smiles, and said she's now the one who should be instructing others. "I can see, you've perfected your dance moves," said Ron.

Ron then urged Jagger to go have his fun, and said he will signal him when it's time to go home. After dissipating so much energy on the dance floor, they returned to their hotel for the night. By morning, Jagger had to take them to the airport so they could board their flight back home, they said their goodbyes and exchanged contacts. Jagger watched as they boarded their flight and they waved each other one last time.

The holiday to Cuba will remain memorable, and by afternoon, Ron and Mariah return to Dallas, and Bianca was in the stable with Fanny when she realised a cab stopped in the front of their home. "Hey, dad is back, hold on Fanny, I'll be back, and be good, ok," said Bianca.

Immediately Ron stepped out of the car, "good to be home. It was actually fun spending quality time with you, Mariah," said Ron.

"Tell me all about it, maybe we would have to do this again, I can't wait for a repeat of this trip," said Mariah.

Bianca rushed towards her parents as they stepped out of the cab. "Mum, dad, welcome, and good to see you," said Bianca.

Ron gave Bianca a hug, saying he missed her, and kissed her forehead.

Mariah followed suit and asked Bianca how she's doing.

"Mum, I'm good, though I missed you and dad, how's Havana, how're the people, are they friendly, did you dance salsa?" asked Bianca.

Mariah couldn't wait to enter the house and rest her feet, but Bianca's too many questions seem to hold her hostage, and that needs to wait for later, or she needs to ask them in piece meal. "You ask too many questions, why don't you give me space to answer your questions one after another?" said Mariah.

"Ok, I get you, did you dance salsa?" asked Bianca.

"Yes I did, and it was fun, I feel like going back," replied Mariah.

"Is the place beautiful, and how're the people?" Bianca asked again.

"The people are friendly, warm and hospitable," said Mariah.

As they walked into the house, Mariah's eyes glanced around to see how tidy the house is, even as Bianca called out to Monica, saying mum and dad are here. Monica rushed out from her room and met her parents in the balcony. "Dad, mum, welcome, how was your trip, I suppose you'd lots of fun?" asked Monica.

"We had fun, lots of it, I must confess," said Mariah.

Monica got a bit cheeky with her dad, she was saying the truth actually, and she wasn't just being cheeky, cheeky, as she told him he looks a little different, and he now looks wrinkle free.

"That was the exact thing I told him, he doesn't seem to believe me," said Mariah.

"The trip was meant for dad, for the two of you actually, to help you return to your normal life," said Monica.

Ron smiled as they tell of his looks, he seems to be sucked in by this appraisal of his looks, and Bianca interjected and asked her dad what he got for her. Mariah didn't allow Ron to respond before telling Bianca to be patient because she got lots of stuff, girly, girly stuff for them and said she's certain her girls would love them.

"I can't wait to see what you've got for me," said Bianca.

Monica was quick in her bid to get the table set as she informed her parents' there's food in the kitchen, and that she made something, because she's certain they must be famished by the time they get home. Funnily, Ron needed to start with a chilled glass of water, and then asked Bianca to please squeeze some lemon in it.

Days later, while Bianca was in the park with her horse Fanny, an unlikely friend in the person of Albert came calling, with something in mind.

"Have you come to train with your horse?" asked Albert.

"Of course yes, I need to keep her fit," she replied.

Albert expressed a view held by many other regular visitors to the park as he reminded Bianca that the way and manner she trains with her horse makes him feel she could end up a Jockey one day. Bianca didn't hesitate to relegate this concern to the bin as she insists she didn't have any intention of being a Jockey, and she's just having fun with her horse.

"What's her name?" asked Albert.

"Oh, her name is Fanny, I named her after my best friend," said Bianca.

"Your best friend in school, I suppose?" asked Albert.

Albert soon got all chatty, chatty, but Bianca don't seem to be in the mood for a long chat, yet she kind of gave Albert some audience. "Yes of course, but why all these questions and I hope I've made my stance clear to you," Bianca insists.

Bianca's fiery remark didn't deter Albert who insists Bianca's response the other time isn't good enough. Sadly, engaging in drudgery in his attempt to drive his point home will rather make thing croak than win him Bianca's heart.

"Which of it did you not understand, I said I'm not interested, why don't you leave me alone?" she reiterated. Funnily, Bianca is placid, but that doesn't count as predictable when presented with a Kool-aid she isn't willing to drink.

Albert seem to be a very methodical in his questioning, funnily, the more he presses on, the more Bianca's interest in this conversation seemed to recede. Yet, he continued pressing as he urged her to give him a chance to prove his love for her, Bianca remained undoubtedly upfront as she insist she doesn't need him proving anything, because she isn't ready for a relationship now.

Albert wouldn't want to be the loser in his quest for Bianca's heart, he then urged her not to tell him to stop trying to win her heart, saying she's just too beautiful to be ignored and he can't just let go of her.

"Albert, please stop bothering me, I'm not ready for a relationship," Bianca retorted.

"Ok, I get it, but will you consider me when you're ready?" asked Albert.

"Ok, I'll give it a thought, you seem to be a nice guy," replied Bianca.

Interestingly, while the conversation between the pair persisted, Bianca looked and saw her sister coming from afar, and needed to discharge Albert before her sister catches up with her.

"Thank you for giving me hope," said Albert.

"But I haven't promised you anything, please you've to leave," said Bianca.

Albert wasn't quite impressed as Bianca suddenly became feisty, and chasing him away, he didn't hesitate to protest the manner he's been chased away, and asked if he has said anything wrong.

"No, you haven't said anything wrong but that's my sister coming, and you've to leave now," said Bianca.

Albert turned around and saw Monica coming from afar, he then quietly tucked his tail between his legs and crawled away at Bianca's request, and a minute later Monica walked up to Bianca.

"Where have you been?" asked Bianca.

"I went for some shopping, and who's that guy?" asked Monica.

"An acquaintance from the past," replied Bianca.

Monica laughed as she introduced some jokes into her sister's response which she considers smoke and mirrors at best, after all, she knew it was her sister who asked this acquaintance to leave because she saw her coming. "An old acquaintance with a mission I suppose?" asked Monica.

"What else do you think he's doing, if not asking me out?" she asked.

"Err.., do you like him?" asked Monica.

"Why're you asking? You never showed me your new boyfriend," Bianca protested.

Monica was quite open with her sister. "You know I'd a boyfriend in school but I ditched him because he isn't the kind of man I want for my future and for now there isn't any new boyfriend," she insisted.

"Though, I know you will find somebody else very soon," said Bianca.

Monica insists she isn't in a hurry and queried why her sister is keeping things from her, but Bianca on her part also insisted she wasn't keeping any secret from her big sister, stressing she already told Albert she isn't ready for a relationship for now.

Though, Monica didn't hold back in her brief assessment of Albert and said the guy seems like a nice guy, and asked what his name is.

"Does it matter?" Bianca protested.

"If you like him you can give him a try," said Monica.

"Though, that'll be when I'm ready to date, but why did you trace me to the park?" asked Bianca.

Monica needed a ride, and said she knew her sister will be in the park and she wants Bianca to give her a ride home. This is an unlikely request that Bianca isn't keen to accept as she insists Monica shouldn't complain over her armature riding skills.

"I know about that already, I just want to enjoy a ride with my little sister," said Monica.

"Climb on, let's go home," Bianca said, and they rode their horse home.

Weeks later, it was Sunday morning, Ron Rogers woke from his sleep and was held bound by the urge to visit and say a thank you to the priest for coming to his aid during his dark moment. He suddenly rose from the bed and stood on his feet, but had to win Mariah over first if this thought will last the next minute.

"Honey, today is Sunday," he said.

"Everyone knows what day it is, what about it?" asked Mariah.

"Honey, get dressed, we are going to church today," he said.

Mariah isn't one that tolerates surprises, particularly one that relates to visiting church.

"What church, and where's this thought coming from?" she asked.

Ron needed a good alibi to strengthen his move, he needed some convincing to do for Mariah to come on board. He then intimated Mariah saying he spoke with Kenny Walter a day before, and he reminded him of the need to say thank you to the priest.

"Then call him on phone and say thank you," said Mariah.

"That would be rude, don't you think so?" said Ron.

Mariah thinks the idea of her entire family attending church service just to say a thank you to the priest lacks tack and void of common sense, as she insist they don't have to attend church to thank the priest.

"What about the priest that left everything behind to pay me a visit, even when he doesn't know me?" said Ron.

"He's doing his job," said Mariah.

Sometimes there's no logic to this, and things don't always line up straight as they should but this time it's quite a different kettle of fish. Even though Mariah hadn't the faintest idea of what her husband is getting at, she wouldn't want to pull the rug off his feet.

"What about me, what's my job, is it to sit down and be cared for?" asked Ron.

"Ok, if you insist, then the church should be ready to have us as guests," said Mariah.

"I longed to be in a church service, maybe this is the opportunity," said Ron.

Mariah is keen to understand Ron's intention, because she didn't want this visit to be a decoy to lure her into becoming a habitual church woman. "This is a one off thing, isn't it?" Mariah retorted. Instead of giving a straight answer, Ron jocularly said it depends on how attached his soul is to today's service.

"Don't bet on it," said Mariah.

Ron finished with Mariah then proceeded to knocks the door to Monica's room "Monica, we are going to church, get ready," he said.

"What, church!" exclaimed Monica.

"Yes of course, we're going to church," insists Ron.

Monica was taken aback with her dad's sudden appetite for church, and didn't hesitate to ask him where all this is coming from as she registers her protest, and insisting she isn't up for this. Ron pressed on in his organic fashion, and even though he's used to having his way with his girls, they seem to be resisting this time.

"The priest was there for me, during those difficult times and it isn't out of place to attend service to say thank you," said Ron.

"But why today?" asked Monica.

"Why not today? Today is the best of days," Ron insists.

Sadly, this hypothesis didn't fit the premise upon which this family has lived their lives all along, and this sudden premise needed being questioned, particularly when it's going to distort their lifestyle. After all, her dad was doubly lucky to be visited by a priest whose church they hardly attend, she then realised it wouldn't be out of place to go with her dad to say a befitting thank you to the priest. "I don't like this idea, but I'll go with you," said Monica.

Ron then left Monica and walks to Bianca's door and knocked, "Bianca, get ready, we're going to church," he said.

"Seriously, is this a joke or what?" asked Bianca.

"No, it isn't," said Ron.

Bianca was spooked by the idea of going to church, her initial reaction was like that of a person who's suffering from the impact of the feelings of butterflies in her stomach, as she questioned her dad's motives "What business do we've going to church?" asked Bianca.

"I need to say thank you to the priest that was there for me, when I was down," said Ron.

"Ooh, not a bad idea," she replied.

Interestingly, Ron cleared the air and that caused a sudden change of disposition in Bianca and she became quite upfront and have no qualms joining her dad to church. Two hours later, Ron and his family left for church and they arrived the church premises not long after they left home. Sadly, it was embarrassingly obvious as the anxious feelings of having butterflies in their stomach seem to leave them all nervous, and cagey. Ron had to urge them to get down from the car.

"Ahhh! This is odd, and I can see mum looking so cringy," said Monica.

"Don't use me to cover your unease about this," said Mariah.

"You're all acting as if you're going to the electric chair, Mariah, this is our fault, we didn't introduce our girls to church that's why they find this to be odd," said Ron.

After dealing with their fears, they all got out of the car and join the church service.

After the mass, Ron waited to see the reverend and then asked his family to come with him, as he walked towards the priest's office.

"Where are we going, dad?" asked Bianca.

"To see the priest, he's waiting for us," said Ron.

"Honey, we need to be fast about this," said Mariah.

"Hello, reverend," said Ron.

"Good to see you, Ron, and how're you doing?" he asked.

"I'm fine reverend, I just come to say thank you," said Ron.

The priest then turned to Mariah, and welcomed her to church, they then exchanged pleasantries. "God has done it for you, are these your daughters?" the priest asked further.

"Oh pardon my manners; this is my daughter Monica, and my daughter Bianca," said Ron. The priest stretched forth his hand for a handshakes with Monica and Bianca "Hello, welcome to church," said the priest.

"Thank you, reverend," said Monica.

"I've been praying for you, Ron, and I'm glad you're back on your feet," said the priest. It wasn't a bad experience for Mariah and her daughters after all, the priest then prayed for them and they left and returned home.

Days later, Ron Rogers and his family were in the living room watching the television. Monica had a slice of Pizza in her hand. "Hmm, why is this pizza so spicy? We'll need to make a complaint," she said.

"You can't make a complaint, Monica. It's meant to be spicy because it's a new menu," said Bianca.

"Then why did we go for it?" asked Monica.

"Dad wants to have a taste of it," replied Bianca.

Ron walked into the living room and soon made himself comfortable before asking Bianca to get him a can of coke, so he could eat his pizza with it. Mariah interjected and jokingly told her daughters their dad has made them earn the sobriquet of a pizza eating family.

"I'll need to make something else, I can't eat that," said Monica.

"I'll eat the pizza with dad," said Bianca.

Mariah gave Bianca the kind of look that speaks volume, as if she's saying here you go again. Bianca got the message communicated by her mum's look, but cared less, and after all, her dad is there to take her side.

"Your choices aren't those of a lady, you're always with your dad in all things," said Mariah.

"Mum, I'll make something just for you and me," said Monica.

While Monica was in the kitchen trying to make something, it's like the noise of spoon and pot reminded Mariah that Monica hasn't brought back stuff from school since she graduated, and it's glaringly obvious that rules of the jungle doesn't apply here, and Monica had to answer to her mum.

"Monica, you graduated three months ago and your things are still in school, why aren't you bringing your stuff home?" said Mariah.

Monica protested, as she insisted that she passed them on to Bianca, and her little sister can't be in school and in need of her things, and she's still expected to bring them back home. "Mum, don't mind her, I only took a few of her things and asked her to bring the rest of her things home but she refused," said Bianca.

Mariah knew her daughters could be everything but skulduggery, yet she didn't like the fact that are daughters are giving her the run around, and so she seem to want to roughen them up a bit. "Monica I want all those things returned to this house as soon as possible," Mariah insists.

"Bianca has denied I left my things to help her, she now makes it look like I forced them on her; remember one good turn deserves another," said Monica.

"Monica, don't worry I'll help you bring all of it back, the next time I return home," said Bianca.

"Yes, that's my little sister," replied Monica.

"I'm not inviting you for my next birthday party unless you stop calling me little sister," Bianca said jocularly.

While the conversation was still going on, a phone call came in and Monica stepped aside to attend to the phone call.

Mariah gets put off when her daughter walks out on her, particularly when she's still speaking, she then turned to Monica and yells at her asking where it is she's going because she isn't finished with her. Monica hinted her mum she had to pick a phone call, she then excused herself and walked to the balcony to attend to the phone call.

"Hello, this is Monica on the line, and who am I speaking with?" asked Monica.

"This is Nicky Howard calling from the Bright Stone Power International, good to hear you're Monica," she said.

"Yes, I'm Monica, thank you," replied Monica.

"You applied for the position of an accounts officer in our company," said Nicky.

"Yes, and I've been interviewed," said Monica.

"Congratulations your application for employment has been successful," said Nicky.

"Ooh, oh my gosh!" exclaimed Monica. She held the phone to her ears in excitement. "I can't believe this, thank you, thank you very much," she said.

"When do you intend to start? You've two weeks to do that," said Nicky.

Monica couldn't wait to start as she quickly accepted the offer and agreed to start in less than two weeks, at least to start documentations. Lucky for her, she has her best in New York, and accommodation might not be a problem.

"Ok, that'll be good, congratulations once again," said Nicky.

Monica thanked Nicky and then walked straight into the living room to join her sister and her parents. She then exclaimed, "I've gotten a job, people!"

"Ooh, thank goodness, Monica, are you serious about this?" asked Mariah.

"Of course yes, I'm dead serious, mum. Oh my gosh, I'm so happy!" exclaimed Monica.

The news took Bianca by surprise, not just because it's too good to be true, but this means separation from her sister. She looked lost and her first reaction was to confirm her fears, and she was quick to ask Monica where the job is located.

"New York, and I'm so happy," said Monica.

Bianca's fears were exacerbated with the mention of New York, after all, it's now obvious that there's going to be some distance between these sisters. "What about me, Monica, you're leaving me behind?" asked Bianca.

"No, little sister, I'm not leaving you behind, I'm only preparing a way for us," said Monica.

"Can I come to New York?" asked Bianca.

"Of course yes, I'll have to get a place quickly for your sake, so you can feel at home whenever you come visiting," said Monica.

Mariah felt touched by Bianca's cold response to this good news, and not to put too fine a point on it, she then rebuked Bianca asking what makes her think Monica will forget about her. Ron was looking so excited as he walked up to Monica and gave her a big bear hug, he then turned to Bianca and assured her Monica wouldn't do a thing like that.

"Oh, thank you, dad, we must celebrate this," said Monica.

"You're right, drinks on me, everybody get ready, tonight we'll be celebrating in style," said Mariah.

"Where are you taking us, dad?" asked Bianca.

"We'll be spending time at the park resort," said Ron.

"Oh, that'll be nice," said Bianca.

Moments after the excitements over her appointment dies down, Monica immediately began putting things in place for a new life in New York City, but this can't happen without Megan, her best friend. Monica stopped for a moment, and decided to give Megan a phone call, but Megan was on phone with Karen, her fiancée. "Karen, where are you?" asked Megan.

"Babe, I'm on my way to your place, is anything the matter?" he asked.

Megan had a long day because she'd to improvise to work after being denied the privilege of driving her car to work. She quickly dispensed of all the flattery, and then asked Karen to come and pick her up because she's waiting for him in the front of her office.

"What about your car, what happened to it?" asked Karen.

"I left my car at home, a car broke down at the entrance of my estate and I couldn't wait for it to be towed away," she said.

"I'm close to your office, meet me outside the gate," said Karen.

Megan came out of her office and joined Karen "hey babe, how was your day?" she asked. Karen didn't allow Megan to settle in before passing is hand around Megan's neck even as he's keen to acknowledge he'd a great day at work. It didn't take long before the pair arrived Megan's place.

While their conversation persists, Monica's phone call came in. She reached for the phone, picked the call and then muttered that she had it in mind to call Monica. "Hello Monica, congratulations," said Megan.

"Megan, you knew about the offer?" asked Monica.

"Yes, of course! It's my place of work." Megan apologised, and said she was to call her immediately she left her office but her fiancée has been all over her like a dog in heat since they stepped into the house.

Monica smiled and asked Megan if it's the same Karen, her fiancée that works in the bank, that's being characterised as a dog in heat.

Megan was only bantering, and making jokes, nothing more, she accepted it's Karen she's describing as a dog in heat, but it's all a mere banter.

Monica couldn't help herself as she held the phone to her ear and listen in while these two messed about, she then joined in the banter, and urged Megan to attend to Karen so the heat can go away. At least it's just for the two of them.

"Sorry to disappoint you Monica, the heat never goes away, this guy is from a place they call Blackheath, have you heard of that before?" asked Megan.

"Yeah but that's in England or somewhere, I don't know, really," said Monica. They all burst into laughter, and the laughter quickly turned hysterical, Megan then continued with her line of banter, and said she has no idea of which of the black heaths, but she knew for sure that Karen is always running after her.

Monica continued laughing. "Oh my gosh! You've got jokes Megan, since you're in love with him and the two of you want to get married then you've to make the best of it," said Monica.

"Yeah you're right, he's my man, I'm keeping him and will go the extra mile to make him happy, or maybe it's just me that's overreacting," said Megan.

"You know you've got jokes and the short time I spent with Karen when I came to New York last month for interview, I realise he has jokes as well," said Monica.

"You're right Monica; we are two people with lots of humour," said Megan.

Monica had to chip in her request for help with where to stay when she eventually moves to New York as she reminded Megan she'll be staying with her until she gets a place.

Megan has no qualms having Monica around for a while, after all, they have been friends since school, and their friendship has been going on forever. Megan was quite upfront as she reminded Monica, now that she's moving from one state to another, where else will she stay if not with a friend.

Monica was glad to know that Megan had her in mind, and promised Megan not to worry because she won't take up much of her space so she can have time with Karen.

Interestingly, with Karen, Monica wouldn't be in a hurry to look for another place, because Karen is a nice and understanding guy with a good heart, at least Monica once had a taste of his humour.

"Megan you made this job possible, thank you very much," said Monica.

For all it's worth, Megan was quite passive with accepting a thank you from her friend because she considered such to be a corrupt flattery. She urged Monica she doesn't need a thank you from her, after all they're friends. "Our friendship has been going on forever, right?" said Megan.

"Yes, of course, we'll talk tomorrow, give Karen some attention, I can hear him at the background," said Monica.

"Don't mind him, he has been tickling me all these while. Ok then, let's talk tomorrow," said Megan.

After the phone call with Monica was over, Karen became cheeky with Megan, as he asked her why she's quivering even when he has his hands around her.

"You're tickling me and sending tremors down my spine yet you're asking, why I'm quivering," Megan protested.

"That aside, is it me you described as being on heat?" asked Karen.

"How best can I describe your action?" asked Megan.

"Ok, let's say the bank official is on heat," Karen said, and they both burst into laughter, then continued frolicking around while Megan made dinner for two.

Later that evening, Ron was looking his best as he offered to give his family a treat in celebration of Monica's job offer, something he did in quite a long time. He walked out of the house and headed for the car, flanked by his wife Mariah, and his daughter, Bianca. While Monica followed them from behind as they leave the house.

"Ahhh! I like this atmosphere," Ron said as he walked into the Lone Star Park bar flanked by his wife and daughters. They stopped in the middle of the bar to decide on were to sit. "Where do we sit?" asked Bianca.

Mariah then pointed to a vacant table among others. "Let's go over there," she said.

They soon made themselves comfortable after choosing a table for themselves in the bar. It has been long we enjoyed a family outing like this," said Mariah.

"Dad hasn't been himself since the death of Anvil," said Monica.

Mariah was upfront with her daughters, as she said their dad was a wreck after the incident with Anvil, but their dad is beginning to return to his real self.

Bianca turned to Monica and nudged her with her elbow then exclaimed, saying their dad really loves Monica because the first family outing since the death of Anvil is to celebrate her sister.

"I'm his first child. So, permit me to enjoy some priority, and I hope you are aware dad loves you more?" asked Monica.

"I know, and you don't need to remind me of that," said Bianca.

"What about me, his wife, if the two of you're fighting over his love, do you know he's mine?" asked Mariah.

While his wife and daughter got chatty, Ron raised his hand to get the attention of the Barman, and it didn't take long, the barman is on hand to take their orders.

"Hello Ron," said James.

"How are you, James?" asked Ron.

"I'm fine; and I can see you're having a good time with your girls," said James.

Ron smiled as he reminded James the fun couldn't be any better with his girls by his side. James proceeded to take their orders after the brief exchange of pleasantries.

"What do you care?" asked James.

"Ask them what they care to drink, just get me two shots of Bourbon," said Ron.

Mariah turned to Ron and smiled. "Your dad likes his Bourbon," she said.

James then turned to Mariah and her daughters, and asked them what they care to have. Mariah requested for a glass of white wine, but suddenly seem to realise herself after placing her own order. "Ooh, the same for the three of us," said Mariah.

Monica protested immediately, as she accused her mum of over-reach for not allowing them to make their own choices, after all, they aren't kids anymore. Mariah on the other hand stuck to her guns, insisting there isn't any other choice other than wine, and she forbids her girls from drinking whiskey or brandy.

"Mum, but the wine you just ordered still has alcoholic content," said Monica.

Mariah went softly, softly, not to spoil the evening and the fun after the strong opposition from Monica. "I'm not stopping you girls from drinking alcohol, I'm only limiting your alcoholic intake," said Mariah.

"But dad just ordered two shots of Bourbon," said Bianca.

"Your dad has the right to live his life the way he likes, you girls can do as you please when your time comes but for now, we play by my rules," said Mariah.

Monica insists on her mum not making a choice for her, she then turned to James and ordered a glass of Chardonnay. Mariah smiled as she gave Monica a long side-glance. "The lady in you'll always show forth," said Mariah.

"Yes mum, I've got class, I've got taste, and that makes me a lady," said Monica.

Bianca seems to toe her sister's line, as she asked James if they have something sweet and tangy. "Yeah, I'll make something up for you," said James.

"Ok, but make it nice," said Bianca.

James finished taking their orders and left, and minutes later brought the drinks. As Ron held onto his glass of bourbon, he asked Mariah and the girls if they would like to eat something.

"I'll take chicken with my wine," said Monica.

Bianca wants something different, suggesting she want to have real food, while her mum and dad wanted chicken just as Monica. Mariah then asked James to give the three of them chicken and Bianca real food.

James turned to Bianca "what food do you care for?" he asked.

"Give me steak and potatoes, and I want onion gravy with it," she replied.

Moments later, as they enjoy their meal, Monica used this friendly ambience to encourage her dad to return to horse racing. "I can't, Anvil's departure marks the end of horse racing for me," Ron retorted.

Monica pressed on as she tried to patronise her dad into going back to the sport he love dearly, as she insists she doesn't see anything wrong for him to try being happy again, urging him to race with Fanny.

Ron shook his head in disapproval and spoke in no uncertain terms that he isn't going back to horse racing, but if he chose to take on any sport, then he'll have to go back to being a Rodeo once again.

Bianca turned to her dad and reminded him of how he's fond of talking about his days as s Rodeo cowboy, but she has never seen him engage in it.

Ron smiled, and told Bianca he was the best Rodeo cowboy in Pittsburgh Pennsylvania when was growing up. "Why did you stop?" asked Bianca.

"I found love, I found your mum and realised she's a fan of horse racing, that was when I switched from Rodeo to being a Jockey," said Ron.

Monica turned to her mum. "Mum, can you hear that, and why aren't you saying anything?" asked Monica.

"What do you want me to say? What your dad said is the truth," said Mariah.

Bianca quickly interjected as she took aim at her mum who always nags her to death for her interest in horse racing, she then turned to her mum and reminded her she doesn't seem to support horse racing in any form.

Mariah is now on the defensive, as she decided to address Bianca's punchy remark about her not being in support of horse racing. "How come your dad was able to go this far if I don't support horse racing? When you've a family you try to balance things to keep them safe," said Mariah.

While the conversation persists, the music "I was Born to be a Cowboy" by Red Steagall began to play, the song is Ron's favourite, and it did provoke a response in him. He then stood up, and whispered in quite a soft tone to his wife. "Ahhh, this is my music, let's dance, Mariah," said Ron.

Mariah wasn't forth coming, and she passively dismissed Ron's offer, and then muttered. "I'm not here to dance to the amusement of your fellow Jockeys," she said.

"Hmm, mum, why don't you show off some of your salsa dance moves? Dad said you're good at it," said Monica.

Mariah looked away as she insists, this isn't a salsa dance hall.

Monica then interjected and steered the conversation to her dad's choice of music and said she really don't know why her dad loves this song so much.

Ron stood up and turned to Bianca. "Come and dance with daddy," he said. Bianca gave her hand to her dad as she stood up and they walked in locked step to the dance floor.

Minutes later, while the dancing was going on Bianca rested her head on her dad's chest as they danced. Mariah looked on as Bianca and her dad graced the dance floor, and didn't know when jealousy took over, she then thought aloud. "Bianca, why're you resting your head on your dad's chest, is he your boyfriend?" asked Mariah. Interestingly, Monica overheard the words her mum just muttered, and was surprise at what her mum was driving at. "Oh my gosh! Mum, are you jealous? She's your daughter," exclaimed Monica.

"I know, I'm just talking," replied Mariah.

"But I saw it in your eyes as they became as wide as saucers," said Monica.

While on the dance floor, Bianca then asked her dad a question she has always asked him, she asked him again, why he love this song so much.

"Because I'm a Cowboy," he said.

Bianca then reminded her dad that he no longer race, so he can't continue the claim of being a Cowboy.

"Yeah, but I stopped racing as a champion," said Ron.

Monica laughed as she asked her mum not to worry, and said when Bianca finishes dancing, she'll return her man to her, and she then asked her mum if she should get her more wine to help her calm down.

"Why do I need to calm down, am I up or something?" Mariah retorted. They both laughed, and steered the conversation away from her mum's jealousy.

Ron and Bianca danced for about thirty minutes then returned to their table, but moment after the dancing, Kenny Walter walked past and saw Ron and his family, he then walked up to Ron. They exchanged pleasantries, and he then told Ron he was watching as he danced on the floor with his daughter. "The Salsa dance in Havana is still fresh in my memory, thanks to you," said Ron.

"Good to know the holiday wasn't in vain," said Walter.

"I never knew you were in, when did you come in?" asked Ron.

"I've been around, and I must say I'm happy to see you return to your usual happy self," said Walter.

"Hello Walter," said Mariah.

Walter then focused on Mariah, and appreciated her for doing a good job on her husband, at least her efforts on her husband have paid off, but Mariah on the other hand returned the appreciation to Walter. "Thank you, my family owe you some gratitude, and thanks you for the trip to Havana," said Mariah.

Walter then begged to take his leave, as he urged Ron and his family to enjoy the night while he retires for the day.

It was quite an interesting night out with his family, Ron and his family returned home after spending about three hours in the park. Later that night, as they returned from the night out and returned to their various bedrooms, Bianca walked into Monica's room.

"I thought you were already asleep, Bianca?" asked Monica.

"No I'm not, I can't sleep," she said.

"Why aren't you able to sleep, and why's your face like that?" asked Monica.

Bianca didn't hesitate to let her sister know she's missing her already.

"Seriously?" asked Monica.

"Yes, of course, I want to sleep in your room, so I can spend more time gazing at your face?" said Bianca.

"Oh, you're welcome, come to bed if this is where you've chosen to pass the night," said Monica, as she moved to create space for Bianca in the bed.

Bianca climbed into Monica's bed, and then protested that she has always said it, that Monica's bed is better than hers.

"Yes of course, it should, and why not?" asked Monica.

"That's cheating, and I know mum loves giving you the best of everything," said Bianca.

"What about dad giving you the best of everything? And if I must remind you, the bed is now yours," said Monica.

Bianca interestingly has something else in mind, the bed isn't what she wanted because she made her concerns glaringly obvious, and being able to visit New York whenever she feels like it is her obvious interest.

"If that's all you wished for then your wish is granted, for your sake I won't stay too long with Megan before getting a place for myself," said Monica.

"Yes, now you're talking. I'll come over whenever I like, wear the best of your dresses and hit the town," said Bianca.

Monica understands quite well that with Bianca things are always easier than said, particularly when she has a horse to attend to. She then cheekily asked Bianca if she's sure she could leave her lovely Fanny behind to have the fun you just described.

"I'll miss you, Monica. You know it's sometimes difficult being alone with mum in the house," said Bianca. Monica entreated Bianca to stopped stressing about her being in the house alone with their mum, rather she should be focusing her energy on being in New York with her.

"I'm happy for you Monica, and this is a sign of better things to come," said Bianca. The pair didn't go to bed immediately as they chatted all night reminiscing their lives together, but Bianca seem to be missing her sister already, and the feeling of being left is quite new, and something Bianca has to get used to.

Monica empathised with her sister but turned the whole thing into banter, as she asked Bianca to stop sounding as if she can't stay without her, after all, they've been apart for the past three months when she was in school.

"I get you, though, this is our new normal," said Bianca.

Two weeks later, Ricky arrived the Lone Star Park, and walked straight to the receptionist then asked of Walter's whereabouts. James replied Ricky, saying Kenny Walter is in the office, yet asked Ricky if Walter is expecting him, and he hopes there isn't any problem.

Ricky got pissed, and accused James of asking too many questions at the same time, yet said he's willing to answer the first question. "Which is?" asked James.

"Yes, Kenny Walter is expecting me, and please tell him I'm here," said Ricky.

James looked on and speechless because he finds Ricky insufferable, he then told Ricky to his face that he's a strange fellow and urged him to take his seat while he inform Walter of his presence.

"Ok, thank you," said Ricky.

James walked into the office and informed Walter that Ricky Trump is here to see him. "Ooh, I've been expecting him, where's he?" asked Walter.

"He's in the reception, should I ask him to come into the office?" asked James.

"No, I'll meet him right away," he replied. Walter stood up immediately and left the office to meet with Ricky.

"Hello Ricky, thank you for coming, is she here with you?" asked Walter.

"Of course yes, she's outside, come and take a look at her," said Ricky.

They both went outside, Ricky led the way, and Walter followed. As they approached the horse that's still some distance away, Walter then asked if she's a thoroughbred.

"Yes, of course, and why did you insist on a sparkling white horse?" asked Ricky.

Walter made his intentions known to Ricky as he told him he's giving the horse as a gift to a friend who lost his horse to cardiac arrest.

"Is the horse a sparkling white horse?" Ricky queried further.

Funnily, Ricky knew Anvil but had no knowledge that Walter is referring to Ron Rogers and his horse, Anvil. Walter then told Ricky he's getting the horse for a friend who signed out of life after the death of his horse, and he just realised his friend is beginning to return to his usual self.

"Ok, this isn't a bad idea," said Ricky.

"Give me a minute," said Walter. He then brought out his phone and dialled Ron's phone.

"Walter, how're you doing?" asked Ron.

"I'm fine, Ron. Please I want you to come over to the park," said Walter.

"When, are you expecting me now?" asked Ron.

Walter couldn't wait, he wants Ron to come to the park immediately.

"Err.., Walter, why the urgency?" asked Ron.

Walter didn't want to divulge too much to avoid getting Ron spooked, he urged Ron to come over immediately so he could take look at something, and he'll be waiting. "Ok, I'll be with you within the hour," said Ron. As Ron attempts to leave the house, Mariah called him back and asked him where it's he's headed, and why the hurry.

"I'll be back soon, Walter wants to see me," said Ron.

"But your lunch will soon be ready," said Mariah.

Ron was already at the door as he speaks with Mariah, and all he could say to Mariah was that he will soon be back, and she should get the table ready.

In less than an hour, Ron was already in the park, while Walter was waiting for Ron in his office. "Thank you for coming, Ron. Please come with me," said Walter.

Ron then followed Walter "Ahh, Walter, why the urgency?" asked Ron.

Walter and Ron walked to where the horse was and Walter then asked Ron to take a look at the horse. "Ooh, what a beautiful horse! She looks wonderful, who's riding her and what's her name?" asked Ron.

Walter fixed his gaze on Ron, and said the horse is waiting for him to name her. Ron was lost as to what Walter was getting at, he then queried Walter asking why it should be him to name the horse and not her rider.

"Ok, let me make this easy for you, this is a gift from me to you," said Walter.

Ron chuckled, and said this feels good, then thanked Walter, yet said he doesn't want the horse. Walter was taken aback by Ron's refusal to accept his gift.

Walter has been upfront with gifts, the tickets to Havana worked perfectly well, but this gift seemed awkward and didn't go down well with Ron. "What's it, Ron?" Walter asked, and accused Ron of making him look like a man holding the hat and clowning around.

Ron tried not to put too fine a point on his comment, but subtly reminded Walter that he doesn't intend to be discourteous then proceeded to ask why he's doing this. "Ron, I saw you dancing on the dance floor of the bar the other night and that made me realise you've signed back to life," said Walter.

Ron finds Walter's explanation not to hold enough water, as he accused Walter of trying to take away the memory of Anvil by giving him a white sparkling horse that has a resemblance with Anvil, and he doesn't think that's a good move. Walter is now left hanging, he's now looking more like a man baking a pie in the sky, or chasing a rainbow rather, yet had to press on and can't back down at this point.

"With her, I believe you'll be encouraged to race again," said Walter.

"I've told you that I've signed out of horse race and that's it. The trip to Havana doesn't mean Anvil's memory has been relegated to the bin," said Ron. The unbridled look in Ron's face speaks volume and clearly explains he's quite uncomfortable with this conversation. Things almost got awkward when Walter reminded Ron that this fantasy with Anvil has to stop, emphasising that they were mere dreams and no matter how interesting his dreams might be it lacks the touch of reality. He then fixed his gaze at him once again and said sweet dreams are still made of dreams after all, and nothing more, he couldn't help but conclude that

Ron has been caught up in the vortex of a fairy-tale life. Ron on the other hand, interjected and insists he's caught up in nothing, just that he isn't interested in riding again. Walter remained open-mouthed as Ron blatantly threw his act of goodwill back at his face, he then points to the horse, and asked Ron what he expects he do with the horse now that he has placed the order.

"Give her to somebody else or you can return her to her owner," said Ron.

Walter wasn't quite impressed with Ron's ineptitude, he took a deep breath, followed by a sigh, before asking Ron why he's making this whole thing quite difficult for all who cares about him. "Give me time, Walter. I must confess you're a good friend, and you've showed me so much love, but this isn't the time," said Ron.

Walter agreed to give Ron some more time as he just requested, yet reminded Ron that getting a horse as white as this that has a perfect resemblance with Anvil isn't always easy. "Don't misjudge my disposition, I'm not being apathetic," said Ron.

Walter isn't buying any of Ron's excuses as he has proved to remain aloof of the obvious around him when it comes to horse racing, otherwise how come he remained unfazed despite efforts to get him out of the woods and return him to the tracks. Gestures such as this are meant to help Ron take those little steps that will eventually restore him back to his glory days, but he has made things bizarrely awkward for this friend of his who just wants to help. It's obvious that big doors swing on small hinges, and Ron has chosen not to take those little steps and have rather decided that gestures that will make him relegate Anvil's memory to the past aren't worth it.

"Walter, I know the efforts you're putting to help me get back on my feet," said Ron.

After the back and forth, Walter felt it's better to return the friendly ambience between them, he then urged Ron to wait, at least, for drinks and possibly something to eat before he leaves.

"Ah, Walter, my tummy is already reserved for Mariah's food, she's making me lunch," said Ron.

Walter turned to Ricky and advised Ricky to go with the horse, Walter then apologised to Ricky for his troubles. "Walter, I've to return home, Mariah is expecting me to return to her," he said. Ron then left Walter and Ricky behind to sort themselves out. "Give me something to take care of our transport," said Ricky.

Walter dipped his hand into his pocket and brought out some money, and handed it to Ricky. "I think this will do?" said Walter.

"Yeah, thank you," said Ricky.

An hour later, Ron arrived home, and Mariah was already waiting as he walked into the house. "Yes, I'm back; it's just a short conversation between Walter and I," said Ron.

Mariah interjected and reminded Ron the table is set, and urged him to go straight to the table because he wouldn't like eating a cold food. Ron then thanked Mariah for knowing what he liked and how he likes his food.

"Why did Walter want you so urgently, is there a problem?" asked Mariah.

"There isn't any problem, he just gave me a gift of a white horse that looks like Anvil," said Ron.

Walter's love for Ron meant he was willing to go the extra mile to get Ron back on his feet, funnily, the very ones you think will never hurt you always seems to be the ones that does and that's what they say about love.

"Oh, that's thoughtful of him, where's the horse?" asked Mariah.

"I turned it down, no horse can replace Anvil," said Ron.

Mariah went ballistic over Ron's refusal to accept Walter's gift, as she asked him what he meant, he turned it down. Mariah got pissed with the fact that a man went through a great deal of trouble to buy her husband a horse in a show of love and he turned it down. Ron insists he has made his point about racing with another horse, and doesn't want to debate this any further.

"Ok, suit yourself, but I think it's rude turning down such a gift," said Mariah. She reminded her husband that Walter has been overly nice to him since Anvil's demise and throwing his gift back at his face isn't the humane response to such act of kindness.

CHAPTER

SEVEN

Bianca and Fanny joined the race

Bianca was in her last year in school and was home because the university was on break, and decided to take part in the County horse racing championship contest, but for this to happen, she needs to get her dad onboard.

After spending time with Fanny in the stable, she walked into the living room. "Dad, we need to talk," said Bianca.

Mariah thinks Bianca's conversation can wait for later, and asked her to join her in the kitchen. After all, she has been with Fanny since she woke up.

"She will join you but she needs a little more time with Fanny, and she's talking to me," said Ron.

Mariah insists the talk can wait, Bianca is on holiday and this is the only time she can give her some help, Bianca had no choice but to get her concerns in the open immediately. "Dad, Fanny and I want to take part in the next horse racing championship," said Bianca.

"No, no, I don't think it's a good idea because you're in school," said Ron.

It was as if Mariah was hit by a ton bricks the moment Bianca opened her mouth to speak about taking part in the County's horse racing contest. She quickly reminded her husband of her initial disapproval of buying Bianca a horse. "Ron, when you bought her a horse, I knew it would lead to this," Mariah yelled.

"How did you know, Mariah?" asked Ron.

"You knew her obsession with horses, yet you bought her a horse," said Mariah.

Bianca interjected, and urged her mum to let her be because the decision with what she does with her life lies solely with her. Mariah isn't prepared to put up with what she considers a lame excuse, and said she isn't prepared to go through another heart ache.

For all it's worth, her dad is yet to recover from Anvil's loss and it's affecting the family greatly.

Bianca isn't having her mum smash her dream of becoming a jockey, she quickly reminded her dad that it's been eighteen months since Anvil's death and he hasn't raced since then. She paced up and down for a while as her mum threw a spanner in her dream of becoming a jockey, and instead of bending over she decided to give the situation a kicking as she walked back to her dad, and then looked into his eyes and reminded him this family can't hide away from what it's known for.

"Enough of this madness, Bianca, you're in school," insists Mariah.

Bianca continued to drive her point home, as she insists, school will resume in a month's time and the racing contest will take place in three weeks time. Funnily, of all Bianca has said, the only comment that got to her dad, was that 'a horse racing family is now shying away from what they're known for.'

"You're right, Bianca. We can't shy away from what we're known for," said Ron. Sadly, Ron's assent got Mariah going ballistic, and she's about to roughen things up. "Ron, are you going along with this madness, Fanny may not have the desired racing strength and skills," Mariah insists.

"I'll train her and Fanny," said Ron.

Bianca erupted with laughter, and jumped her dad with a big hug. "Thank you dad," she said. "Instead of putting Bianca up for this, why don't you train Fanny and race with her yourself?" asked Mariah.

Ron stood on his earlier position as he insists he'll never race again, and that he can only ride horses for leisure, but not in any contest. Mariah remained mortified by Ron's decision to put Bianca up for this, and she isn't going to sit on her hands and let it fly. Sadly, her ability to muscle Bianca to do as she's told might be a bit limited now that her husband has just given his blessing to Bianca.

The rarity of these accidents makes them the more shocking that makes Mariah to look like someone merely crying wolf, Ron wonders when his wife became a fatalist. He then turned to Mariah and asked to know why she owes the pleasure of pouring cold water on her daughters' credibility.

"Mum, I'll be fine," said Bianca.

"Bianca, I'm only trying to get my head around your mental switch from a Veterinary Doctor to a jockey," said Mariah. Funnily, this ship has sailed, and Mariah's sulking can't turn the tide this time. The next day after expressing her interest in the racing contest, Ron took Bianca to the park to meet with Kenny Walter, and to inform him of his daughter's interest in the upcoming horse racing championship.

When they arrive the park, Ron asked Bianca to wait while he go and get Walter, and moments later, Ron joined Bianca at the table where she's seated, and told her Walter isn't in the office.

"Do we go back home then?" asked Bianca.

"Let's wait for him, he'll be here shortly," said Ron.

"Ok then, let's wait," said Bianca.

To keep a warm and friendly ambience and also shorten their waiting time, Ron thought it best to order something to drink while they wait for Kenny Walter. Ron then asked Bianca what she cared to drink, and went a step further to ask if a glass of Brandy will do.

"No, mum will kill me, just give me a glass of red wine," said Bianca.

Ron tried to make light of Bianca's modest living to make her loosen up a bit, he then reminded her she'll be twenty three by next month and about to become a jockey. At least, a little alcohol won't do any harm. "I know, just that mum has her ways and I'm not up for her nagging," said Bianca.

"Aah, Mariah! exclaimed Ron.

"Why're you laughing, dad?" asked Bianca.

Ron had to explain to Bianca that her mum is a good woman, attached to her standards, and red lines that aren't meant to be crossed. Interestingly, while the conversation persists Kenny Walter walked through the bar attempting to go to his office. "Hey, Walter," said Ron.

Walter stopped to say hello to Ron, and then turned to Bianca and asked if she has come to spend some time with her dad at the park.

"Yes, but I've actually come to see you," said Ron.

Walter pulled out one of the seats by the table to seat with Ron and Bianca but quickly got up and asked Ron to give him a minute so he could handover his bunch of keys to them at the office.

Bianca seems concerned that Walter might torpedo this move even before it's put on the table. Immediately Walter turned and left for the office, she turned to her dad and asked if he's sure about Walter giving his blessing to her intention to race at the championship level.

"Walter is my friend, he wouldn't deny you that opportunity," said Ron.

Minutes later Kenny Walter returned and joined them, and immediately he took his seat among them, he asked if he should order drinks.

"No, we're fine. It's my daughter Bianca," said Ron.

"What about her?" asked Walter.

Ron didn't hesitate to tell Walter his daughter wants to take part in the next racing championship coming up next month.

This is a big ask from Ron, and Walter thinks this isn't a good idea. Ron quickly adjusted his seat so he could look Walter eyeball to eyeball, and insists is daughter can do it, as he queried Walter's reasons.

Walter has seen too many racing accidents, and contesting at championship level isn't just a free for all. "These horses are racing at between sixty eight and seventy kilometres per hour, and Anvil ran much more than that, it's not for amateurs," said Walter.

"She will be twenty-three by next month," said Ron.

Walter tried dismissing Ron reason for putting his daughter forward, and said it isn't about her age, it's about the risks associated with top class speed.

"Don't worry about this, Walter. I'll prepare her mentally," said Ron.

Walter has been boxed into a corner, and he's now likened to a man presented with a Kool-Aid that would result in nothing but a ghastly outcome. If this goes wrong, he would have to answer to the horse racing fans, not to talk of another visit by the renowned Florina Banks. Walter then turned to Bianca, and asked if she's sure she can do this, Bianca nodded in the affirmative and was quite upfront in her response as she insists she sure can.

"Is she racing with Fanny?" asked Walter.

"Yes, she is," said Ron.

"Can Fanny withstand the stress, does she have the stamina? You know already that there's a difference between a sport horse and that designed for leisure," said Walter.

Ron reminded Walter that Fanny is a racing horse, and all she needs is to teach her special skills. Walter seem to be moving the goal post with every response Ron puts forward, he then moves the goal post further again. "What about Bianca, does she have the special skills to help Fanny win a race?" asked Walter.

"I'll pass my skills to her; let's just get her into the line up," Ron insists.

Walter couldn't help as he turned to Ron and told him he's sounding convincing, he then stood up and went into the office to get the forms.

Bianca couldn't hide her joy and immediately Walter left to pick up the forms, she turned to her dad and thanked him, saying she'll love to do this.

Moments later, Walter returned and handed the form to Ron. They thanked Walter for giving them the opportunity to do this and promised not to disappoint him.

Sadly, this isn't the kind of conversation Walter wants to be having with Ron. He's particularly keen to see Ron on the tracks doing the things he's known for. "When are you coming back to the race, Ron?" asked Walter.

Serendipitously, this isn't the kind of conversation Ron likes having, he looked away as he told Walter he isn't coming back to horse racing again because his racing partner is gone.

"What about Fanny, can't you race with her?" asked Walter.

Ron points to Bianca, and said Fanny belongs to Bianca, and Fanny isn't Anvil.

"No problem, coming back to the race is a step in the right direction," said Walter.

Ron thanked Walter, as they said their goodbyes. "Ok, Ron, I hope to see you around later," said Walter.

As she stood up and prepares to leave with her dad, Bianca turned to Walter and thanked him. While still holding her dad by the hand, she looked at Walter again and told him not to worry, as she promised she won't disappoint him. They then walked out of the bar and entered their car before leaving the park.

Now that her application has been accepted, it now behoves on Ron to pass his horse racing skills to Bianca as promised. Ron had to take Bianca to the Lone Star Park to train, and as they leave the house, Mariah looked on through the window in awe, saddened by this hollow feeling of helplessness as she watched them leave the house.

While the training commenced at the park, Bianca asked her dad to explain whatever training he's giving to Fanny.

Ron spent about an hour with Fanny to help improve Fanny's skill, and after some demonstrations Ron began explaining each demonstration to Bianca. "Ok, this is called the smooth-riding four-beat footfall pattern," said Ron.

"Ok, let me try," She then spent some time as she tried the smooth-riding four-beat footfall. "Dad, I can do it," said Bianca.

"Though, Fanny can do this naturally, but she needs some special skills," said Ron.

Bianca is a fast learner, and horse racing is already her thing, just that this time she has to train to win. Bianca then asked her dad what special skill he's talking about, Ron had to take Bianca's heart away from seeing horse riding as leisure but a relationship between her and Fanny.

"We call that the ambling gait," said Ron. He then climbed Fanny, and spent about an hour trying to make Fanny respond to his special racing commands. Bianca didn't hesitate to ask her dad if the commands he just displayed with Fanny is necessary.

"Yes it is, if you want to make a difference in the tracks, it's about a bond between you and Fanny," said Ron.

"Ok, if it's this necessary, then let me try," said Bianca.

"Yeah, go ahead, try to connect with Fanny, let her understand what you're thinking," said Ron.

Bianca tried the ambling gait for about an hour. "Dad this aspect looks more emotional," she said. "Yeah, it's about bonding, and with this, Fanny can get some special skills you desire," said Ron.

After a long day of practice, Bianca seem to be disappointed because her idea of racing wasn't discussed, she then told her dad he hasn't taught her about improving her riding speed.

Ron laughed, and tried assuaging Bianca of her concerns, as he told her speed is the last thing she'll learn, but they've done enough for the day. Bianca thanked her dad, and confessed she's beginning to see horse racing differently. They left the park after about three hours of intense practice.

Mariah is now feeling so suffocated, and there's no one to turn to, particularly now that Ron have taken side with Bianca. The next day Mariah had to call Monica to inform her of Bianca's decision to become a jockey, and she had to make her position clear on the matter.

"Hello mum, how're you doing?" asked Monica.

"I'm fine, how's New York City?" asked Mariah.

"New York is fine, life after school is sweet, how's dad and Bianca?" asked Mariah.

"Oh, that's why I'm calling," said Mariah.

"What's it, mum are they ok?" asked Monica.

"Yes, they're, but your sister wants to take part in the Dallas County horse racing championship," said Mariah.

Monica was taken aback by this news yet she told her mum Bianca is in her final year and she's supposed to be in school. Mariah couldn't help but let Monica know that her fears has come true as she insists that the moment her dad bought her sister a horse, she knew it would come to this. Monica's confusion is more about Bianca's ability to combine her education and horse racing.

Mariah considers Monica's concerns to be misplaced, and had to put the conversation in the right perspectives as she insists she isn't talking about Bianca's ability to combine horse racing and school. Mariah stressed that there are lots of horse racing related injuries and deaths, and all she's doing is to protect her family.

"I'll have a word with her on this, but I know it might be difficult talking her out of this," said Monica. "You've to do that quickly, because the other time I asked you to talk to your dad you stalled and I was the one who suffered when his situation deteriorated," said Mariah.

"I've heard you mum," said Monica.

Mariah insists she's doing this because if anything happens to Bianca, she'll be the one nursing her. With the heat fully turned on, Monica agreed to give Bianca a call and then promised to get back to her mum. It didn't take long after her phone conversation with her mum, Monica gave Bianca a call.

"Hello, little sister," said Monica.

"Hey Monica, how're you?" asked Bianca.

Bianca carefully avoided any mention of her horse racing interest because she feared that Monica will pour cold water on her horse racing interest.

"I'm fine, how's your holiday?" asked Monica.

Bianca didn't hesitate to say her holiday is fine, and she'd wanted to visit Monica in New York. Monica interjected. "Then why didn't you come? I would've loved it," she queried.

Bianca became cheeky, and said she would've loved to come to New York, take some of Monica's dresses for herself, Monica played along. "I'm certain, dad gave you money to do some shopping for yourself," said Monica.

"Picking the right clothes is one thing I don't know how to do. I like your choice of clothes, that's why I'm always interested in your clothes," said Bianca.

"I can send some to you through post," said Monica.

"You'll do that for me? I'll love it," said Bianca.

"You're welcome, and what's it about you entering a racing championship?" asked Monica.

Bianca didn't allow Monica finish her statement before interjecting, as she said she's sure their mum must have told her about her racing contest.

Monica had to play the long game to avoid making this a shouting match that will precipitate into ending the conversation prematurely. "Why didn't you tell me about this, at least we talked the day before yesterday and you never mentioned it?" asked Monica.

Bianca coiled in immediately, and said she knew if she'd told Monica about it, she wouldn't have approved of it. Monica had to appeal to Bianca's emotion to see if she could influence her decision, she then reminded Bianca she's the only sister she has got. "You know my life will be shattered if anything happens to you," said Monica.

Bianca urged Monica not to sound as if she's going to the slaughter house.

"I'm not trying to scare you by sounding as if you're going to the electric chair," said Monica. Funnily, each time Monica opens her mouth Bianca hears her mum speaking through her, all she hears is their expression of fear but no words of encouragement and support. "But that's how you're sounding," said Bianca.

Monica had no choice but to put it to Bianca that a lot of people have become disabled or died as a result of horse related injuries.

"I know mum put you up to this," said Bianca.

Monica had to come clean, as she said their mum is only worried because if things go south it will be her mum nursing Bianca.

Bianca had to change tact because picking a fight with Monica would mean fighting on all front, and that will leave her on the back foot. For all it's worth, Bianca had to keep things civil between her and her sister, she then begged Monica, saying she shouldn't hate her for this but the family should just let her do this. After all, nothing will happen to her she insists. "What about your school?" asked Monica.

Bianca assured Monica her school isn't affected by this because the racing championship is coming up in three weeks, while school resumes in a month.

"Helping you manage your obsession with horses is my biggest challenge," said Monica. Bianca continued her earlier line as she pleads with Monica and urged her not to worry about her because their dad is her trainer, and she will be fine.

"I don't know how mum will take this, but I'll see what I can do," said Monica.

Monica is now racing against time particularly now that the situation is down to the wire. She immediately put a phone call across to her dad, to discuss Bianca's horse racing interest with him.

"My angel, how're you?" asked Ron.

Monica was quick to dispense of all pleasantries, she went straight on to discuss Bianca's horse racing interest with her dad. She told him, Bianca just informed her he's her trainer.

"Yes I am, is there anything wrong with that?" asked Ron.

Monica knew for sure that her dad is quite an assuming man and getting through to him when his mind is set will require some moral suasion. She started by reminding her dad of the troubles her mum has been through since death of Anvil.

"Yes I know, but that has nothing to do with Bianca," said Ron.

Monica continued pressing her dad as she insists Bianca is supposed to be in school and not in the park riding horses. Interestingly, her dad who sees nothing wrong with Bianca's interest in a racing contest insists she's on holiday and the competition will be over before she resumes school.

"Dad, she's a lady and any horse related injury will not be good for her," said Monica.

Ron thinks Bianca's daring act of bravery to preserve the family's name is a good thing, and continued pestering from Monica and her mum to make Bianca cower out of the race, is petulant. "You're sounding like your mum, don't worry she'll be fine," said Ron.

"I'm actually sounding like this because the family doesn't need any more awkward moments," said Monica.

Realising that her further push against this racing contest will set her on a collision course against her dad, Monica had to retreat carefully to avoid an implosion within the family.

Days later, Ron and Bianca left the house for their fourth training session in the park.

"Today you're learning the dressage rules," said Ron.

"Dad, what skill is that?" she asked.

"These are rules you're meant to observe during racing contest," replied Ron.

"Bianca then asked her dad to teach her about these rules because she would love to know how to apply these rules. Ron started by explaining to Bianca that in every race a jockey must perform a combination of five of the leaping gaits he thought her, and all the forms of trot she has learnt. He then reminded Bianca, she can do halt and rein back but she mustn't gallop.

"Let me apply this rules in my race and see how my performance will be," said Bianca. She then climbed the horse and raced some distance, applying all the rules and did well at it.

"Ahh, you did well, make sure you apply these rules, even as you race at a very high speed," said Ron.

Bianca then asked her dad if this is all she should learn for the day, but he preferred she perfects the dressage rules because of its importance, yet he scheduled the next training session to be about helping Bianca race at a top speed.

"When will that be?" asked Bianca.

"Practice all you've learnt in the next five days, then we'll now combine all we've learnt in a race," said Ron.

"That'll be interesting," said Bianca.

Ron is now at the height of equipping Bianca with the skills she would need to be her best during the racing contest. The next training session would involve racing at top speed, using the ambling gait skills and applying the dressage rules in a competition, this is a culmination of all she need to know.

Mariah has been sulking over her inability to put the brakes that would stop this racing contest going ahead. Monica called her mum to feed her back on the outcome of her conversation with her sister and her dad.

"Hello mum, how're you doing?" asked Monica.

Mariah wasn't keen for pleasantries she's rather interested in answers, and she didn't hesitate to remind Monica of her conversation concerning her sister. Monica understands that in situation of this nature only cool heads will prevail.

"Mum, this matter should be approached with care, and didn't Bianca tell you I called her?" asked Monica.

"She did talk about your conversation with her," said Mariah.

"At least, I haven't been silent about it," said Monica.

Mariah expected that the conversation between Monica and Bianca will provoke a response that will result in her withdrawal from the racing contest. Sadly, Monica's last ditch effort seems not to have made any difference, and Mariah is quick to remind her Bianca is going ahead with the competition.

"I'm aware of this, which was why I'd to call dad," said Monica.

"What did your dad say?" asked Mariah.

Monica decided to choose her words carefully to avoid setting her dad and mum against each other, yet she made it clear and in no uncertain terms that her dad doesn't see anything wrong with Bianca taking part in this competition.

"Ok," Mariah muttered.

Monica understands what her mum's frustration could precipitate into, she quickly urged her to please handle this with care, so her relationship with Bianca isn't strained.

"You mean I should just let it go?" asked Mariah.

"Yes, you've to, and it's good for everybody in the family," said Monica.

The horse racing contest for the County of Dallas is at hand, and Bianca needs a Vet to certify Fanny fit for the race. She walked to her dad and urged him to arrange a medical check up for Fanny.

"You mean the usual routine check up before a race?" asked Ron.

"Of course yes," she said.

"That'll be done," said Ron.

Despite Ron's assurances Bianca seem to have concerns she needed to get off her chest, as she insists she wants the medical check done properly, and not the poor medical check-up that was done on Anvil. Ron quickly interjected to correct Bianca's erroneous view about Anvil's medical check-up, and Bianca's comment did actually spooked him. Ron looked away from Bianca as he insisted that Anvil had a proper medical check-up, and what happened to Anvil wasn't because of poor medical care.

Bianca noticed her dad has suddenly became emotional, she then apologised to her dad for talking about Anvil's care in that manner. Ron softens up his stance to keep the conversation up, he then told Bianca not to worry, that he also wouldn't want Fanny to suffer the same fate as Anvil.

"When will the medical check-up be done?" asked Bianca.

"That'll be a day before the race, and then you'll submit the fitness certificate on the day of the race," said Ron.

Mariah continued her opposition to Bianca's interest, and interestingly the day to the horse racing championship is now by the corner, and Monica think it's important for her to play the adult in the room. Mariah's position has arguably been dispiriting for everyone in the family, and Monica had to come home to support Bianca in her racing contest, at least to spur her mum's interest.

Bianca was with her dad in the stable, and surprisingly saw Monica stepping out of the cab. "Hey dad, see," Bianca said as she points to Monica from inside the stable.

"What's it?" asked Ron.

"See, that's Monica," she replied, and rushed out of the stable to welcome her sister.

"Hey, little sister, how're you?" asked Monica, as they walked towards the stable where their dad was. "You've come with your little sister thing," Bianca protested.

"Don't worry, when I've a fiancée I'll stop the little sister thing," Monica said jocularly.

"Ooh you'd better, because I've had it up to my neck," replied Bianca.

"Allow me to enjoy the privilege of being the big sister," she walked into the stable, and then turned to her dad. "Hello dad," said Monica.

"My sweet angel, you're welcome. You never told us you were coming," said Ron.

Monica told her dad the trip was meant to be a surprise, and that she has come to support her little sister, Ron was amazed to here of this unlikely support, despite earlier oppositions. "You travelled all the way from New York to Dallas just to support your sister?" asked Ron.

Monica smiled and asked if she had a choice, after being boxed to the corner, and after all, there's no need cutting off her nose just to spite her face. They all got chatty, chatty, and moments later, they all left the stable and walked to the house.

"You did that for me! I thought you hated me for doing this?" asked Bianca.

"It's your action I hate not you, I'll always love you and at least you know that," said Monica.

Mariah was surprise to see Monica, at least, if not for any other purpose, her daughter is home since she resumed her job in New York and that deserves some good moment. "You're here," said Mariah.

"Hello mum, I'm here," said Monica.

Mariah doesn't like surprises and this visit counts as a surprise, and Mariah isn't letting Monica off the hook without giving her the third degree. "But you never said you were coming?" asked Mariah.

"It was meant to be a surprise, and I came to support her in tomorrow's race," said Monica.

Funnily, Monica's response precipitated a sudden change in Mariah's deposition, and she didn't hesitate to ask Monica if she's also in support of this whole horse racing thing. Mariah is now feeling left out and it's now looking like it's her versus every other person. That's the thing about family, and strangely, the very ones you think will never hurt you always seem to be the ones who do. It's now expedient for Mariah not to only address the elephant in the room, but to accept this elephant as being a part of the room.

"Mum you remember what I told you on phone? Just give her the support," said Monica.

Monica tried to soften things as she urged her mum to go softly, softly on Bianca, she then passed her hand around her mum's neck and said she's only trying to ease the tension around here. Instead of dawdling further, Monica encouraged her mum to join the band wagon in support for Bianca, because it's glaringly obvious that this support won't cost her an arm and a leg.

"Ok, if you say so," said Mariah.

Monica stood up and as she said she's famished, and asked what food is there to eat in the house. She then walked to the fridge and opened it.

Bianca was quite happy to have her sister around, she then asked Monica not to worry and urged her to relax while she go into the kitchen and make something special.

"Tell me, how prepared are you?" asked Monica.

"Very prepared," said Bianca.

Monica seem keen to assess Bianca's horse racing skills, she then shifted the goal post further, as she asked Bianca if she's certain to make it to the top five.

"The interest of every contestant is to come first, but the first five? It's a yes!" said Bianca,

"Then you aren't just Bianca, you're now a professional jockey," said Monica.

Hours after Monica settles in, it's time for Bianca to take Fanny to the Veterinary doctor. Monica was in the balcony and asked Bianca where she's taking Fanny.

"For a medical check up," said Bianca.

"Is she sick? You know she's racing tomorrow," asked Monica.

"No, she isn't, this is a requirement before the horse can race, it's also good for Fanny's fitness," said Bianca.

"Which of the Vet doctors are you taking her to?" asked Monica.

"The one opposite the park, come with me please," said Bianca.

Monica retorted and reminded Bianca she just returned from New York, and she'll need to rest, but Bianca pestered her further saying if actually it's her Monica came for, then she should ride with her to the park.

Monica had to come down from the balcony and join Bianca "Then I'll do the riding," said Bianca.

"I'm your host and you're my guest, so let me ride you," said Bianca.

Bianca wanted to do the riding, yet Monica insisted Bianca is merely obsessed with horses but she can ride as well as Bianca does.

While the back and forth continued Bianca felt it's time to show off what she has under wraps to her sister. "Why don't you let me show you some of the skills I've learnt?" asked Bianca.

"Ok then, let's go," said Monica, as she climbed on and sat behind Bianca. They chatted and spent some time doing catch up as they ride along, and Bianca ceased the opportunity to remind her sister it hasn't been easy preparing for the racing contest. Monica seem to enjoy time alone with her sister, after all, they've been apart for a while. Funnily, while they ride along, Bianca suddenly put up a display of some of her recently acquired skills. These skills aren't new to Monica because she has always seen her dad do them, but she hasn't seen Bianca put up such a display before.

"What are you doing?" asked Monica.

"That's the ambling gait," said Bianca.

"Where did you learn that?" asked Monica.

"Dad thought me, and there are many other skills he passed on to me," said Bianca.

Monica was quite impressed by some of Bianca's impressive displays, she couldn't deny the fact as she accepted the fact that Bianca is now a better horse rider than she is.

It didn't take long before they got to the Veterinary Doctor. The Veterinary Doctor spent some time examining Fanny, and after a while of medical examination he told Bianca the horse is fit to race. Interestingly, Bianca memorialised the fact that it's the same Vet that checked Anvil before her last race.

"This is the very same type of medical check up Anvil did before her last race, isn't it?" asked Ron.

"Yes, and why're you asking?" asked the Vet.

Bianca then queried the Veterinary doctor further, and asked why Anvil died after he certified Anvil fit to race. The Veterinary Doctor picked offence as he asked her what it was she was insinuating, before asking if she thinks he didn't do his job properly.

Monica interjected and said Bianca isn't insinuating, rather she's saying Fanny shouldn't die like Anvil after he has certified her fit to race.

"The Veterinary doctor tried to assuage Bianca of her concerns, and told her not to worry, that nothing will happen to Fanny. He insists, Anvil ran at an exceptional speed, though she did it effortlessly that was why people didn't see the impact of her speed on her.

"Yet, she died," said Bianca.

"Be assured, Fanny will be fine, I promise," said Bianca.

Bianca seemed to strike some connection the moment she mentioned to the Veterinary Doctor she soon will be his professional colleague because she's a Veterinary Doctor to be, and in her final year.

"Oh that's good, maybe when you're through with study you'll work with us," said the Vet.

"That'll be a conversation for another day," said Bianca.

Two hours later, Monica and Bianca returned home from their visit to the Vet, and funnily their dad was already waiting because he has other things in mind planned for Bianca.

"Where have you girls been?" asked Ron.

"We went to the Vet to finalise Fanny's medical check up," said Monica.

"I know, but you stayed longer than expected," said Ron.

Ron wasn't impressed that they spent more time than necessary, Bianca had to explain to her dad that they went into the park on their way to the Vet's office because she wanted Monica to see some of the skills he has passed on to her.

"Dad, you've done a great job, Bianca is really good at it," said Monica.

Ron smiled and then turned to Bianca, before saying he's glad her sister considers her qualified for this contest. "Thank you dad," said Bianca.

Ron didn't hesitate as he quickly asked Bianca to get dressed because she's going out with him. For all it's worth, Monica has had a long day and quickly excused herself from any further activities. "I hope that doesn't include me because I need to get some rest?" asked Monica. "No, it doesn't," replied Ron.

Bianca equally protested going out with her dad, and insisted she's also tired. She practically begged him to move the appointment to another time because she's racing the next day and needed to rest.

Her dad was quite sympathetic with her plight, yet insisted that this can't wait, and that it has to be now. He then urged her to get dressed immediately. "Ok, give me a few minutes to wash up, and I'll be with you," said Bianca.

"Be quick about it," said Ron.

Minutes later Bianca joined her dad at the balcony. "I'm ok, dad, let's go," said Bianca.

Ron looked keenly at Bianca for a while, and shook his head in disapproval then asked her to change into something more decent. Bianca protested as she insists she's decent enough.

"Bianca, I never said it isn't decent. Something more decent, I said," said Ron.

Bianca exhales after unsuccessfully convincing her dad. "Ok, I'll be back," said Bianca. Ron then asked Bianca to please make it snappy.

Five minutes later Bianca returned and asked her dad how she looked, and her dad nodded in approval of her outfit.

"Yes good girl, let's go," said Ron.

They got in the car and drove off. Forty five minutes later, Ron drove into a Catholic Church premises and parked. "Dad, what's going on, and what are we doing here?" she asked.

"Tomorrow is your race, isn't it?" asked Ron.

"Yes, of course, but what has that got to do with our being here?" asked Bianca.

Ron's heart has been shattered into a thousand pieces, and mending it has so far proved impossible because some broken hearts can never mend. All Ron could do, is pass his skills and secret to his beloved daughter. "It has everything to do, and you're here to confess your sins," said Ron.

Bianca looked dumbfounded. "My sins!" She laughed sarcastically. "Dad, seriously, is this a joke or what?" asked Bianca.

Ron looked at Bianca and said this isn't a joke, and that he's just letting her into what he has done for the past thirty years. This is now getting weird for Bianca, and she's suddenly grappling with how to respond to this instruction from her dad.

"You mean you come here to confess your sins, and who do you confess to?" she asked.

It's glaringly obvious that this is new to Bianca and instead of providing an answer to Bianca's question, he told her the priest is right in there waiting for her to confess her sins. Bianca didn't hesitate to ask her dad what sin it was that he's talking about, and she quickly registered her protest because he's making her look like one filthy creature.

"You aren't filthy, when you go in there, you'll see lots of people confessing their sins. They aren't filthy, it's just making things right," said Ron.

"How long did you say you've been doing this?" asked Bianca.

"Since I started horse racing, thirty years ago," said Ron.

Bianca registered another protest and accused her dad of keeping too many secrets because they knew nothing of this. She then tightened the screws further as she suggested that even her mum and Monica knew nothing of this.

"No, it's a secret and I expect you to keep yours a secret," said Ron.

"Dad, this is funny, what makes you think I would want to do this, is it because we followed you to church the other day, once in our life time?" asked Bianca. She then laughed sarcastically and Ron joined her in the laughter. Funnily, Ron isn't keen to take this secret to his grave, particularly now that he has a protégé, someone to pass it on to, and that's the thing about love. "I'm showing you what I do, the choice is yours," said Ron.

"Ok, do other Jockeys do the same thing?" asked Bianca.

Ron looked away and said he doesn't think so because this style is personal to him, and he's passing it on to her. This secret isn't all for the taking, it's for Ron and his family alone. Bianca was worried sick about how this whole thing will work, yet with the feelings of butterflies in her stomach, her exasperation seems to suddenly get worst.

"You said the priest is waiting for me, did you arrange with him to bring me here?" asked Bianca.

"No, he's waiting for everyone, and not just you, you see that bell up there?" asked Ron.

Bianca looked up at the bell as it chimes and then said the bell is ringing but asked her dad what's it he wants to say about the bell. "Yes, that's a call for confession and you should go now," said Ron.

Suffix to say that Ron did a good job of assuaging Bianca of her fears, and he has just succeeded in taking away the kind of fear that makes a wolf look bigger. Bianca softens up as she suddenly assumes her dad's posture of a jockey.

"Ok, but I don't know what to say, and how does this work?" asked Bianca.

Ron then gave her further insight and said when she goes into the church she would see other people going before the priest and kneeling down, he urged her to just do the same.

Bianca insists she doesn't even know where the priest is, and asked her dad if she should just kneel down and keep quiet. Ron looked at Bianca and wanted to speak but Bianca interjected and asked what she should say when she kneels before the priest.

"You'll find the priest in there, after kneeling before him, say forgive me father for I've sinned," said Ron.

"Ok, forgive me father for I've sinned, that's all, and I'll start coming out," replied Bianca.

"The priest would ask you some questions," said Ron.

"Like what kind of questions?" asked Bianca.

Ron insists he doesn't know what questions the priest will ask, yet he encouraged her to just tell the priest everything and urged her to stop acting as if she's going to the electric chair.

"Ok, let me do this, I'm doing this for you, dad. If this would make you happy," said Bianca.

"Good girl." he kissed her forehead. "Go on, I'll be waiting for you," said Ron.

"Ok dad, I'll be back," replied Bianca.

This is a long shot and Bianca had to get on with it, head on, but she had to overcome the feeling of butterflies swarming down her stomach as she walked into the church and took her seat. Moments later, she walked and knelt before the priest and began her confession.

"Forgive me father for I've sinned," she said.

"When was your last confession?" asked the priest.

"Confession? Hmm, I've never done this before," said Bianca.

"What made you come for confession today?" asked the priest.

"I just need to keep my spirit and soul clean, and I feel it's something I've to do," said Bianca.

"Then how do you feel about being here today?" asked the priest.

"I'm glad I'm here, and it's cool," said Bianca.

"What are the sins you wish to confess?" asked the priest.

"My sins?" asked Bianca.

Bianca's edginess seem to disappear, this isn't as strange as she feared after all. She became more forthcoming with answers to the questions from the priest. Bianca's confession of wanting to keep her spirit and soul clean looks more like her dad's confession but the fact that she didn't mention horse racing meant the Priest wasn't able to connect Bianca to her dad.

"Yes, tell me about them and unburden yourself," said the priest.

"I used to get angry easily, I talk back at my parents, maybe a few lies, but I don't have a boy friend," said Bianca.

"Your sins are forgiven," said the priest.

"Thank you, father," said Bianca.

"When you get home pray, "our father," said the priest.

"Our father! Is it a kind of prayer?" asked Bianca.

"Yes, if you don't know how to say it, meet one of the sisters they'll teach you," said the priest.

Bianca interjected and told the priest not to worry, because her dad would teach her.

"Ok, you can go now," said the priest.

"Thank you, father," said Bianca.

Bianca stood up, and moments later, she joined her dad who's waiting for her in the car. "Ooh, you're back, and so soon I guess?" asked Ron.

"Hmm, it's a bit of fun, I've always heard my friends who are Catholics talking about confession," said Bianca.

"Now, you've experienced it, and the priest doesn't bite I guess?" asked Ron.

Bianca couldn't help but tell her dad of her experience, as she told her dad the Priest asked about her sins and how she has to mention them to him, yet concludes her sins all little sins.

"No sin is little, that's our perception, the big man in the sky takes every sin seriously, but I'm glad you've done this, make it a ritual," said Ron.

"You mean I must do this before any race?" asked Bianca.

"Yes, don't look down on what you've just done," said Ron.

"I don't know its significance, but ok, noted," said Bianca.

Ron reminded Bianca that what she just did, should be her secret, and urged her to keep it to herself. He then turned on the ignition of his car and they drove out of the church premises.

Bianca suddenly began pointing to the adjacent direction, and reminded her dad that's the way home, and asked where he's taking her. Ron smiled and said he knew for sure that her race is a day away and she must be nervous but he's taking her to the beach, so she can relax.

"Ooh, not a bad idea," Bianca said and smiled.

An hour later, they are already bare-footed and waking the beach with a cone of ice cream in their hands. Bianca couldn't help but told her dad that the thought of the racing contest is quite exhausting, and makes her nervous.

"I know, I felt the same before my first race," said Ron.

"Then this feeling isn't peculiar to me, it's a usual feeling," said Bianca.

"Yes, the feeling isn't peculiar to you, my trainer took me to the beach to ease off my nervousness, just as I'm doing to you now," said Ron.

Bianca then asked her dad which among his previous trainers he's referring to. "We call him the Bulwark, but his real name is John Longshield," said Ron.

"Oh, John Longshield, the one you've a picture of you and him on the wall?" asked Bianca.

"Yes, that's him, he's a gifted trainer who made me the champion I'm today," said Ron.

"What about Tommy Jones, is Longshield better than Tommy?" asked Bianca.

Ron doesn't pit his trainers against each other, rather he view them from the lenses of their individuality. He turned to Bianca and said, they're good in their own ways, Longshield started it and Tommy finished the job.

"Oh, I keep thinking about tomorrow," said Bianca.

Ron reminded Bianca that tomorrow will come and go, there's nothing to worry about, he urged her to go around and listen to the birds sing, and then jump into the waves. "Go, go, I'll be waiting," said Ron.

Bianca walks back to her dad. "Oh no, I don't have a swimming suit, jumping into the waves won't be possible," she said.

Ron smiled, and said he came prepared.

"How, dad, I don't get you?" asked Bianca.

Ron smiled, and asked her to check under his seat in the car that there's a swim suit right there, because he bought her one. Funnily, Bianca was amazed at the manner her dad choreographed this whole evening outing. "When did you buy it? You seem to have this trip planned out," said Bianca.

"Never mind, Bianca. Just make sure you've fun," said Ron.

Bianca gave her dad a big hug, and thanked him for his thoughtfulness. She then left, went to the car, picked up the swim suit, dressed up and rushed into the waves.

Bianca continued to splash through the waves, and at some point, she completely forgot she has a racing contest a day away.

An hour later, Bianca walked to her dad who was leafing through a cowboy magazine "Dad, it's time to go," said Bianca.

"How do you feel now?" asked Ron.

Bianca was quite upfront as she told her dad of her exhilarating feeling, and said she feels so good and at one point she forgot about the race completely.

"Oh, I remember that thought," said Ron.

"This experience is quite exhilarating, I feel so refreshed," said Bianca.

Nature has its own way of mesmerizing humans, but this time it's about hope, implying there's a possibility of having the last laugh.

"Are you sure you'd enough fun?" asked Ron.

"Yes of course, and thank you for bringing me here, the sea is something else, its therapeutic effect is second to none and it's fun," she said.

"Ok, time to go then," he said, and it didn't take long, they left the beach and returned home.

A day later, the Dallas County horse racing championship is here, and it's now time for Bianca to show forth what skills her dad has passed on to her.

TV Presenter: *Hello, I'm Chamberlin, your usual horse racing presenter. Today is another day in the history of horse racing in this County, just that there's a twist in today's story, and that has brought emotion into today's horse racing competition because we have a new jockey competing for the very first time. That person is Bianca Rogers and her horse Fanny, she's the daughter of our legendary jockey, Ron Rogers.*

Commentator: *Ladies and gentlemen I'm Martin Presley and I'll be running your commentary today. Grand Prairie is about to witness another emotional contest because the spectators are anxious about the outcome of today's race. At least, they knew Blue diamond has been the champion since the death of Anvil, but for Bianca and Fanny, they don't know what to expect.*

TV Presenter: *Martin, what do you think about Bianca and Fanny, can they pull surprises?*

Commentator: *Chamberlin, you just opened a Pandora's Box with your question. Bianca is still a young jockey and her horse Fanny is a Pennsylvania thoroughbred. Her father is a horse racing legend, he could pass his racing secret to his daughter, and therefore I don't want to underestimate her ability. I understand the spectators are suddenly having these funny feeling of butterflies in their stomach, but it's best to keep an open mind.*

TV presenter: *Ladies and gentlemen, viewers at home, the weather is cloudy and not encouraging, but the spectators are in high spirits.*

As we can see, the contestants are coming out to their tracks as the race is about to begin.

Commentator: *Oh, this is becoming emotional with the anxiety as to whether Fanny will beat Blue diamond to become the new horse racing champion.*

Commentator: *Ladies and gentlemen the race has started, Fanny is in Fifth place, with Blue diamond taking the lead as usual, this is becoming more interesting as Fanny moves to fourth place right in front of her is Beauty, the spectators are anxious as the tempo of this racing contest is now very tense. We're now in the last twenty meters of this race and ladies and gentlemen Blue diamond is still main- taining his lead and Fanny just moved to second place, and as you can see, emotions are running very high, ladies and gentlemen Blue diamond has won the race. Bianca Rogers and her racing partner, Fanny, came second, and however, Blue diamond remains the horse racing champion in the County of Dallas.*

TV Presenter: *Though, Blue diamond won the race, I see a rival in Fanny, Fanny's performance was spectacular, if her first race could be this fantastic, then Blue diamond has found a rival in her.*

TV presenter: *Martin, do you think Ron Rogers will be able to train Fanny to become the new Dallas county champion?*

Commentator: *Actually, Ron Rogers did a good job on Fanny and his daughter, but Blue diamond remains a force after the demise of Anvil. I see rivalry between Fanny and Blue diamond. Though, Chamberlin, I'm expecting to see Ron Rogers back on the tracks, Ron is a bundle of skills and a partnership between Ron and Fanny would've been perfect.*

TV Presenter: *Yes, the spectators are expecting to see Ron Rogers on the track once again, but ladies and gentlemen and viewers at home; it has been an interesting evening, thank you for watching.*

Monica and her mum couldn't hold back their joy as they rushed to Bianca's side.

"Little sister, your performance was marvellous," said Monica.

"But I came second," said Bianca.

Monica quickly corrected Bianca's impression of herself, and reminded her, it's just one jockey in the entire County that beat her, and told her she's going places with today's performance. Bianca's biggest surprise was, seeing her mum rushing to celebrate her.

"How are you? You did very well," said Mariah.

"Mum, are you sure?" asked Bianca.

"Yes of course, you performed beyond my expectations," said Mariah.

"But I thought you're mad at me?" asked Bianca.

Mariah quickly dismissed any animosity against Bianca, and asked her not to worry because that's in the past. "Let's enjoy your victory, this victory came about by dint of hard work, and your perseverance," said Mariah.

Monica began giving Fanny a rub. "Hey Fanny, you did well today," said Monica. "Where's your dad?" asked Mariah.

"He's on the other side," said Bianca.

"Don't worry, we're going to celebrate your victory," said Monica.

Mariah was all smiles, and she has suddenly set aside all the topsy-turvy that preceded this race. "I trust your dad, this victory won't go uncelebrated, and I know he must be proud of your performance," said Mariah.

A week later, Monica is already back to New York, and Bianca getting ready to return to school. Albert stood by the balcony and knocked at the door. "Hello, hello, anybody home?" he asked.

Mariah walked to the door, and opened to see who it was. "Hello, how may I help you?" she asked.

"Please, is Bianca at home?" asked Albert.

"Yes, she is, but who're you?" asked Mariah.

Albert quickly introduced himself as a friend, and told Mariah his name is Albert. Mariah quickly apologised to Albert for her probing questions, yet went ahead to ask Albert if his friendship with Bianca, is a friend, as in school mate or what. Albert decided it's best to introduce himself formally, he then told Mariah he lives in the County, and works with Oasis Veterinary, and Bianca is a friend.

"Are you a Veterinary doctor?" asked Mariah.

"Yeah, newly qualified, and I started working with Oasis Veterinary a few months back," said Albert.

Mariah's disposition changed and she suddenly became warm towards Albert, after all she was glad to know that her daughters' friend is a Veterinary Doctor and not a jockey as she has always feared. She then gave Albert a seat at the balcony. "Have a seat, she's having a shower, and she'll join you when she's through," she said.

"Ok, thank you," said Albert. Mariah then returns to the house, but immediately she walked into the living room, Ron asked who it was at the door.

"It's Bianca's friend, he said his name is Albert and he works as a Vet doctor," said Mariah.

Ron had a jockey's diary magazine in his hand when Mariah replied him about who it was at the door, he suddenly stopped surfing through the magazine and turned his attention to Mariah. "I know all the Vet doctors around here, but I don't know any Vet doctor with that name," said Ron.

"He said he joined Oasis a few months ago," said Mariah.

"Ok, I expect so," said Ron.

Mariah didn't hesitate to inform Bianca her friend is here immediately she leaves the bathroom. Bianca passively asked her mum which of her friends it was, and further asked where her guest was seated.

"I'm talking of Albert, the Vet doctor," said Mariah.

Bianca was lost as to who it was that's by the door, and funnily, the name Albert didn't ring a bell, and she quickly asked her mum which of the Albert she's talking about. She then insists the Albert she knew never said he's a Vet, and Bianca might find Albert insufferable because she isn't overly fond of people pussyfooting around her.

Mariah seems not to be letting her daughter off that easily, particularly now that her daughter seems to be evasive. She then urged Bianca to stop pretending she never knew Albert is coming to see her, yet informed her Albert is waiting for her at the balcony.

"Ok, I'll see whoever it's when I'm dressed," said Bianca.

Minutes later Bianca walked to the balcony to see who her guest was. "Hey Bianca," said Albert.

"Oh my God! It's you, how come you told my mum you're a Vet?" asked Bianca.

"Of course yes, that's what I am. Though, you never asked, and I know you're studying to be one as well," said Albert.

Bianca became curious and asked how he knew she's studying to become a Vet, and after all he didn't hear that from her. Albert leaked the source of the information to Bianca and told her it was mention during the horse racing contest's commentary.

"Were you there, I mean did you come to watch the race?" asked Bianca.

"Yes, of course, I came to watch you, and I watched every step and every move you made during and after the race. "Wow, that's strange, but what do I offer you, except alcohol? I've wine, red, or white?" asked Bianca.

"Never mind, I'm already on my way, and that will be for next time," said Albert. Interestingly, as Albert stood up to leave, Bianca then asked what the purpose of this visit was since he refused her offer, and was also leaving almost immediately she came to the door to know who her guest was.

"I don't want to be in the shadows anymore, and I've just achieved that," said Albert.

Bianca had to sound her note of caution again, as she reminded Albert she already told him she isn't ready for a relationship, and asked why he traced her home. Albert insists he isn't a bad guy and felt it's time he makes his interest in Bianca known to her parents.

"I was scared of you before, but now it just got worst," she muttered and then turned to leave.

"How, what have I done! And why do you like secrecy?" asked Albert.

"Secrecy about what, I'm not in a relationship with you, so why're you forcing it?" asked Bianca.

"The truth is, I love you, and I can't wait to show it," said Albert.

Bianca's disposition seem to be one of detachment, and Albert isn't making the best out of the moment either because his continued expression of love makes her blush and she's now interpreting it as Albert knowingly taking a mickey out of her. For all it's worth, Albert doesn't really intend to blindside her but she seem to be taking this whole thing the other way around.

"But if you want me to consider you, then you'll have to give me some time," said Bianca.

Albert looked into Bianca's eyes and said he's ready to wait until she's ready, yet he wants her to give him a time frame.

"Don't push your luck, and I've to start going back," said Bianca. She then burst into laughter, as she shook hands with Albert, but he isn't letting her off that easily, he then interjected and asked when he hopes to see her again.

Unsurprisingly, as Bianca turned to leave she jocularly reminded Albert not come to her house, and if need be, she will find him.

"Whatever, I'll find a way to see you," said Albert. He then brought out his card and handed it to Bianca. Funnily, she collected the card from him yet remained surprised as to its purpose, before asking him what the card was for.

"That's my contact, and you can call me whenever your mind is made up," said Albert.

"Ok, but don't bet on it, and I've to go now," she said and left.

Minutes later Bianca returns home, and funnily, she has some explaining to do to Mariah who seem to be convinced Bianca pretended not to know Albert, and she wants to know why. Bianca insists she never pretended, and she only said the Albert she knew never told her he's a veterinary doctor.

As far as Mariah is concerned, if it looks like a duck and quacks like a duck, then it must be a duck, and she hates creepy situations. It's either that Albert is creepy, or he's a good guy and her daughter is just making this whole thing look creepy. "Who's he to you, is he your boyfriend?" asked Mariah.

"He isn't my boyfriend, he's just a friend," said Bianca.

"Though, you've to be careful," said Mariah.

"Mum, what is it? I said he isn't my boyfriend," said Bianca.

Mariah suddenly became incensed and cautioned Bianca to stop quoting her wrongly, because she never said she shouldn't have a fiancée. "All I asked is for you not to rush into anything," said Mariah.

Ron intervened immediately and urged Mariah to leave the girl alone, he insisted that Bianca will be graduating from the University soon, and she's mature enough to decide what she wants for herself.

"Ooh, you've just joined her in quoting me wrongly, Albert seem like a nice guy, all I want is for her to take her time to know him better," said Mariah.

"Ok, I've heard you, mum. I'll take my time to know him better," said Bianca.

Days later Bianca returned to the University as her course draws near to its end.

In one of the weekdays, Bianca woke up and was getting ready to leave the room earlier than she usually does. "It's just 7.45am, where are you rushing off to Bianca?" asked Lisa.

"Aren't you girls going?" asked Bianca.

"Going where?" asked Kristin.

"We've a class with Professor Lax Carlson at 8.30am," replied Bianca.

"But we don't normally have his lectures on Tuesdays," said Lisa.

Bianca reminded them the day's lecture is a one-off thing, and that it was meant to compensate for the Professor's absence four weeks ago and was agreed upon in the last class. Kristin was taken aback because she has no knowledge of this impromptu lecture, after all she was in his last class.

Bianca then reminded the girls they left five minutes before the end of the class, and that's when this lecture was agreed upon.

"Are you waiting for Fanny?" asked Kristin.

"Yes, of course!" said Bianca.

Lisa then urged Kristin to hurry up and get dressed, saying who knows how valuable this class could be. It didn't take long before Fanny walked in.

"Hey girls, what's up?" she said.

"We're good, what's up, girl?" asked Kristin.

"Hey, Fanny, that's new isn't it?" said Lisa.

Fanny was lost as to what Lisa was about as her disposition was one of surprise. She quickly interjected and asked Kristin what it was she was talking about.

"The Pendant, it's beautiful, and it must have cost you a fortune," said Lisa.

"I don't know what it cost, it's a valentine's gift from Alex," said Fanny.

"Wow, Alex knows how to give good gifts, he's just like my boyfriend," said Kristin.

Lisa interjected and reminded Kristin she doesn't need to tell them about Andre, after all, everyone knows, he's good at taking care of a woman.

"Oh Fanny, it's truly beautiful, let me have a look at it, but you never told me about it?" said Bianca.

While Bianca touched the pendant to have a feel of the piece of jewellery, Fanny softly reminded Bianca she told her about the pendant, just that she doesn't seem to be listening.

Lisa quickly asked Fanny to please pardon Bianca, insisting that when it comes to matters of the heart, Bianca is always aloof.

Bianca finds Lisa's description of her quite distasteful, and she didn't hesitate to register her displeasure as she reminds Lisa that her insensitive comment was quite cruel and demeaning, and she doesn't like it.

"That's true, Bianca, you talk about nothing but horses," said Lisa.

"You don't have to blame her, she doesn't have a boyfriend yet, what contributions do you expect from her during such conversation?" asked Kristin.

Bianca realised she's suddenly became the centre of the conversation and her friends are taking turns in ridiculing her. Her choice of pet and social life is now being turned inside out, and made jest of. "What makes you girls think I don't have a boyfriend?" asked Bianca.

"Oh Bianca, that's bad, and why haven't you told me about him?" asked Fanny.

"That isn't true, when a woman is in love, you'll see the sparkles in her eyes, and there isn't any in Bianca's eyes," said Lisa.

"Lisa is right about a woman in love, and love has a way of showing itself through acts, looks and expressions," said Kristin.

These girls think that as it stand Bianca has nothing as her object of passion except horses. For all it's worth, she isn't some kind of sterile horse loving girl lacking of romantic emotion.

"You mean I'm lying or what? His name is Albert," said Bianca.

Fanny is Bianca's best friend, and insists Bianca doesn't tell lies with things of this nature, it means if Bianca says there's Albert, then, there's Albert.

Kristin didn't waste time trying to take a Mickey out of Bianca. "Are you sure she isn't referring to her horse as Albert," Kristin said and burst into laughter.

Bianca seem to have had enough, after all she's due in class, she then packed her books angrily, and walked to the door. "I'm off for class; you girls should think whatever you like," said Bianca.

"Wait for me Bianca, why're you mad at me?" asked Fanny.

Bianca continued without stopping, yet insists she isn't mad at Fanny but they have to hurry to class. It's now obvious she couldn't take any further banter from her sniggering friends. Fanny suddenly stopped at the door and rushed back for a quick pee, while Bianca waited for her outside the room. She walked a few steps further, and immediately reached for her phone, then dialled Albert's phone.

"Hello Bianca, are you ok?" asked Albert.

"Why the question? I'm ok," said Bianca.

"Seriously, I seem to be dreaming, I never expected you'll call me one day for whatever reason," said Albert.

Love have a way of finding its own, they say, and it's now obvious that pressure from these bantering friends seemed to send Bianca cowering and running into Alberts' open arms.

"I've just called, so you aren't dreaming," said Bianca.

"Are you at home or what?" asked Albert.

"Forget about where I am, I'm ready," said Bianca.

Albert was lost with the essence of this conversation, he then asked Bianca about what it is she's ready for because he doesn't seem to get her. Bianca was already pissed and incensed by her friends, and this phone call wasn't because she's ready for Albert, she had already mentioned Albert to save face, she's now following through with it. She then muttered, "why're you asking me as if you aren't the one chasing me around to be your girlfriend?" asked Bianca.

"It means you've accepted to be my girl?" asked Albert.

"Of course yes, you heard me clearly.

Albert was all smiles as he held the phone to his ear, it was as if he has just won a lottery, and didn't realise he has just asked Bianca if she's at home, and he would like to come down to see her.

"I'm in school, don't push your luck, and let's take things slowly," she said.

"Ok, however you want it, I don't mind," said Albert.

While the conversation persists, Bianca saw Fanny coming to join her, and quickly ended the conversation with Albert, so as to keep things under wrap.

CHAPTER

EIGHT

Walter has continually sought ways to help Ron return to the tracks. It's now over two years after the death of Anvil, Ron's position on this matter hasn't changed, yet Kenny Walter hasn't stopped trying to encourage him to race with Fanny. Presently, all Ron does is ride Fanny around for leisure, and in one of such occasion, Walter felt the need to have a word with him.

"Ron, you're here," said Walter.

"I'm just keeping Fanny company," replied Ron.

"I thought I saw you at the park yesterday, when did you leave?" asked Walter.

Ron replied Walter that he brought Fanny to the park for exercise, then said Bianca is in school and can't care for Fanny presently. Walter became jocular and reminded Ron that it's now over two years since Anvil's demise, and suggested to him that it's good he has Fanny, he then urged Ron to race with Fanny. Ron tuned to Walter and scolded him for not realising Fanny isn't Anvil, and can't be Anvil.

"Ron it's you that bought Fanny for your daughter, and I'm convinced you liked her that was why you bought her for Bianca," said Walter.

Ron wasn't having any of Walter's encouraging words because he finds him illusory, and quickly made it clear to him that Fanny is a brown horse and Anvil is a white horse, they aren't the same.

"But before the death of Anvil, you did ride fanny around," said Walter.

"That was for leisure, and I still do now," said Ron.

Walter looked on, and in his heart considers Ron to be quite as stubborn as a mull. At some point Walter had this feeling of indignation towards Ron, yet decided it's best being patient. "Remember you've a family, how do you take care of them, if you remain like this?" asked Walter.

Ron had to make Walter understand he isn't keen to make money from horse racing any longer. After all, Monica is through with her school and she's now in New York and Bianca is in her final year. It's now just him and his wife, and they'll cope.

"We'll talk some other time, Ron. " Walter said, and left Ron and Fanny to do their thing.

Two days later, Mariah got hint of the Dallas County horse racing Contest, and thinks the time is right for Ron to return to the tracks.

Mariah walked up to Ron while he's in the stable attending to Fanny, and asked if he picked the form for the upcoming Dallas county horse racing contest.

"Bianca will be taking her final exams then, so I don't think that will be necessary," said Ron. Mariah didn't hesitate to let Ron know she isn't referring to Bianca because she knew Bianca will be taking her exams then, so this shouldn't be about her.

"I'm not following you," said Ron.

Mariah had to hit the nail on the head and reminded Ron she's talking about him, and asked why he isn't picking up the form to take part in the racing contest. "I think I've made myself clear about the fact that I'm not racing again," said Ron.

"But you ride Fanny around more often, by now I believe your love for racing must have been reignited," said Mariah.

Ron accepted he rides Fanny around but that's only for pleasure, and not for a racing contest. "Maybe I'll have to go back to work," said Mariah.

Ron suddenly became apprehensive, he then stood up and went to Mariah and sat by her side. "I know I encouraged you to stop working, but you don't have to go back to work just because I refuse to go into the race," said Ron.

Mariah insists they needed money to run their lives and she just can't sit on her hands and do nothing. Actually, Anvil's death seems to have made the years vanish before their eyes, and Mariah is keen to make the best of what's left.

"Don't be in a haste to take a job, we can manage," said Ron.

Mariah insists she needed to take care of her family, and insists she isn't holding it against Ron if he can't race. She then pleaded with Ron to let her take care of herself, her husband, and her daughters.

"What if I get a job outside horse racing?" asked Ron.

"I thought we've brought closure to you and Anvil, why then are you still using Anvil as your excuse?" asked Mariah.

Ron felt Mariah is unnecessarily being tedious, and accepted he has brought closure to Anvil, but he doesn't want to race again. Mariah refused to be swayed by Ron's illusory excuses, as she made it clear that it's glaringly obvious that Anvil is still holding him back. Mariah stood up, and said she can't continue to hear this because she needed to dressed up and go to town, to make some moves in search for a job.

Ron looked on as Mariah had her shower, dressed up and walked through the door, to at least connect with old contacts, to make the job search easy. Ron rushed after Mariah, before she turned the ignition of the car. "Wait, wait, I'll look for something else to do," said Ron.

"Too little too late!" exclaimed Mariah, as she kicks the car and drove off.

In the ordinary sense this is succinctly an expression of love, but Ron understands that this isn't anything but leading him down the garden path, something he particularly will never acquiescence. Later that evening Ron went to the park with Fanny for a leisure ride, and Arnold seems to be in the park training. "Hey Ron, how're you doing?" asked Arnold.

"I'm fine, how's she?" asked Ron.

"Who?" asked Arnold.

"Blue diamond, of course!" exclaimed Ron.

"As you can see she is doing great, how is Bianca?" asked Arnold.

"She's in school," said Ron.

Ron had to keep up appearance, and he's obviously out of the woods but had to knit himself back to the horse racing association. His refusal to race with Fanny tells all around him that the feeling of hollowness hasn't fully gone away. As for Ron, this is nothing but an island in the stream and disavowing it will bring nothing but hurt.

"As I told you earlier, you did a good job in her, she will definitely be the horse racing champion one day," said Arnold.

"You're right, I'm off to the bar for a jug of beer," said Ron.

Arnold quickly told Ron he thought he has come to practice.

Ron stopped and reminded Arnold he's only here for a leisure ride, which explains why he's heading to the bar for a jug of beer immediately after he arrived the park. It's obvious that his friends have failed to realise that Ron and Anvil are one and the same.

That's how Ron sees it, one can't continue the sport without the other, because the abiding impression of Anvil is one of friendship and confidant, and Anvil obviously seems to have some auspicious presence over him.

"But last week you were with Fanny on the track practising, when I discussed my health with you, remember?" said Arnold.

Ron insists all that was just about leisure and has nothing to do with horse racing contest. Arnold quickly apologised for mistaking Ron's leisure ride for a practice for the next racing contest.

"Why?" asked Ron.

Arnold dipped his hand in his bag and brought out two forms, he then told Ron he picked two forms. "One for you, and the other for me," said Arnold.

Ron remained circumspect, and he finds conversation surrounding his returning to the tracks as an ill wind that won't do his friendship with close friends any good. This time, he was quick to urge Arnold to not just assume things that way. He looked at Arnold and asked if he's having a laugh or trying to be cheeky by this gesture. "I'm sure you don't want to climb that tree," said Ron.

"That's my bad, you can keep it in case you change your mind," said Arnold. He then passed the form to Ron, but these coincidences didn't go down well with Ron, as he quickly asked Arnold if Walter put him up to this.

"Kenny Walter didn't, I'm not his errand boy. Why would he put me up to this? I did this as a friend," said Arnold.

"No, I can't, you keep it," said Ron, as he withdrew from the form and left Arnold's hand hanging. Funnily, Arnold reminded Ron that Ron's name is already printed on the form, so the form shouldn't be with him. "Ok, bring it then since my name is already on the form, though thank you for having me in mind," said Ron.

Arnold smiled and said they were all happy to see him pull through the depression that resulted from Anvil's death. "Ok, I'm off to the bar," said Ron.

Arnold turned his horse around, but urged Ron to sleep on the form maybe he'll give it a second thought. Recently, every turn Ron makes, there's someone urging him to return to the tracks, serendipitously, his wife, Kenny Walter and now Arnold, seem to pressure him in one way or the other to race in the next racing contest.

That night Ron was at loss with the direction of his conversation with those closely associated with him, and even though he hasn't been overly fond of friends urging him to return to the tracks, this is now something that requires some attention. He didn't sleep that night as he thinks things through, and decided to give competing in horse racing another try.

Immediately he woke from sleep the next morning, he turned facing Mariah, and said he'll compete. Mariah was lost and quickly asked what it is he's competing in.

"The County horse racing championship," said Ron.

Mariah then asked to know what informed this change of mind because this is all coming out of the blue, since this conversation was laid to rest days ago.

"Arnold already bought a form for me, and he thought I would love to compete again," said Ron.

Mariah remained curious and insists she isn't comfortable with this sudden change of heart, and wants to know if a mere form precipitated this new decision. Ron is now boxed to the corner, he'd to hit the nail on the head.

"If everyone feels it's something I should do, then let me give it a try," said Ron.

"But, are you ok doing this? You know this requires the right state of mind," said Mariah.

"Yeah, I should be!" said Ron.

One week to the race, it's now obvious to all that the legend is back, and irrespective of whether his riding partner is Anvil or not, Ron Rogers is now where the attention lies. Kenny Walter and Bill Shannon met with Ron at the park.

"Hello Ron, how's your training going?" asked Walter.

"I'm fine, just that the idea of racing seems new," replied Ron.

Bill Shannon interjected. "Ron, it's been a while," he said.

"Of course Bill, it has actually been quite a while," said Ron.

Walter tried to avoid being perceived as vaguely illusive and immediately told Ron that Bill has something for him. After all, if you can't sing and certainly can't dance, you still must put up a show somehow by getting involved when it becomes necessary. "What is it?" asked Ron.

One interesting thing about Bill is his candour, and being upfront in getting his concerns off his chest is his primary character flaw because he has no time taking a panoramic view of a situation, he just grab his moment until it runs out of steam. He then hands Ron an envelope containing cash, and reminded him the fans seem to be interested in him.

Ron remained self-absorbing, and finds Bill quite commendable yet insists he doesn't need this. Walter had to step in as he attempted to manage this warm ambience that's suddenly gone sour. He had to set every erroneous thought aside, and told Ron he has been off the track for sometime so he needs all the cash he can get. Ron was taken aback by this sudden interest in him and Fanny, and funnily, questions what makes them think he'll win this race.

Bill thinks a lot more of Ron than he now does about himself, he reminded Ron that if he's able to make Bianca come second with Fanny, then nothing will stop Fanny from coming first if he take the driver's seat.

"So you trust my performance this much?" asked Ron. He then collected the envelope and puts it in his pocket.

Bill looked into Ron's eyes, and told him other betting houses are putting Arnold and Blue diamond forward, but their fans trust in Ron and Fanny.

"But these fans seem not to be there with me during my dark moments," said Ron.

Walter understands that Ron has gone into throwing tantrums, and assured him the fans were with him, at least they protested Anvil's death, and also supported Bianca in her race. Funnily, Walter took his time to let Ron know that sometimes our situations overwhelm us and we don't see clearly, and many will kill to enjoy the support of the fans as he does.

"Ron, you knew I was in your house a number of times, I gave you all that was due to you and I even added more," said Bill.

"Yeah, I'm aware," said Ron.

"Ok Ron, let's leave you to continue your practice," Walter said, and they both left.

The Dallas County horse racing Championship is here, and it's now time for the legend to show to the world he remains the man to beat.

TV Presenter: *Hello, I'm Chamberlin, your usual horse racing presenter. Today is another day in the history of horse racing in this County, just that today's horse racing is even made more interesting with the return of our legendary Jockey, Ron Rogers. Though, there's a twist in Ron Rogers return, that's this time he's not racing with Anvil* *but with Fanny. The anxiety of the spectators is whether Ron Rogers can win today's race with Fanny.*

Commentator: *Ladies and gentlemen I'm Martin Presley and I'll be running your commentary today. Grand Prairie is about to witness the return of a legend. Therefore, today's race is an emotional contest, because spectators are anxious about the outcome of today's race. At least, they know Blue diamond has been the champion since the death of Anvil, but can Ron Rogers do the impossible with Fanny? They don't know what to expect.*

TV Presenter: *Martin, what do you think, can Ron do with Fanny that which Bianca couldn't, can they pull surprises?*

Commentator: *Chamberlin, Ron Rogers isn't Bianca, if Bianca can come second, then what do you expect from Ron? I'm confident Ron will make Fanny a champion today.*

TV presenter: *ladies and gentlemen, viewers at home, the weather is bright and the mood is perfect and the spectators are in high spirit. As we can see the contestants are coming out to their tracks as the race is about to begin.*

Commentator: Ooh, *this is becoming emotional as spectators give Ron Rogers a standing ovation as he steps out with Fanny, at least in*

recognition of his legendary past. However, the anxiety as to whether Fanny will beat Blue diamond to become the new horse racing champion has just increased with Ron in charge.

The commentary: *ladies and gentlemen the race has begun, as you can see emotions are running high, Fanny, just moved from third place to second place, but the Blue diamond is still in first position, we are now in the last ten meters of the race, from my observation the tempo of this race has increased dramatically and Fanny seem to be contesting for the first position. Though, I can't believe my eyes, and from what I'm seeing, it seems Fanny has taken the lead, and . . . and, yes, Fanny just crossed the finish line. Fanny has won the race, Fanny is now the new Dallas County champion, and Ron Rogers have pulled it off.*

Sadly, Ron fell off his horse immediately he crossed the finish line, and the paramedics rushed to his side.

Mariah, who was already rushing towards her husband to celebrate his victory, increased her pace and ran faster to his side as he lay on the ground. "Come on, Ron, get up, please get up," said Mariah. The paramedics were also speaking to get a response from him, but sadly, Ron seemed not to be responding.

The CPR isn't working either, the Paramedic then turned to Mariah and asked if she's related to him. "Yes, he's my husband, and please do something," she said as she wept.

"I'm sorry, we did all we could," said the Paramedic.

The paramedics' comment came to Mariah as if she was hit by a ton of bricks, it actually deafens her. "What are you saying? Don't tell me you've done all you can," Mariah cried.

"I'm sorry; we've done the best we can," said the paramedic.

"What are you saying, is my husband dead?" asked Mariah.

"Yes madam, I'm sorry, he's dead," the paramedic replied.

"Ooh no, no," Mariah screamed and wept. "Ron, please come back, Ron, Ron, please don't do this to me," she cried.

This whole drama was unravelling so fast, Arnold jumped of his horse and rushed to the scene. "What, is it this serious?" asked Arnold.

"He fell badly, it was quite a fatal fall," said the paramedic.

Arnold grabbed Ron and sobbed. "Come on Ron, please Ron, you've got wife and kids, please don't leave us," Arnold cried. Arnold then turned to the paramedics and urged them to continue, and not stop CPR, but the paramedics insisted they've done all they could that they're just cracking his ribs, yet with the persistence of Arnold the paramedics continued with the CPR and rushed Ron to the hospital.

Kenny Walter rushed from the VIP stand to the scene and pulled Mariah who is still weeping away, consoling her. It took Walter some time to get to the scene because of the distance from VIP stand to the scene of the accident. Walter was quite terrified to see his friend helplessly on the ground, he tried grabbing his friend to jerk him back to consciousness but was prevented by the paramedics, he then focused on Mariah.

"Arnold, what's the problem with Ron?" asked Walter.

"I don't know but the paramedic said he didn't make it," said Arnold.

"Oh my God! Ron, please don't do this to us," Walter said and moved to Ron's side for the second time, then rushed back to Mariah who continued sobbing uncontrollably. "Ron, please, please don't leave me," cried Mariah.

"Come on, Mariah, it's ok, please calm down," said Walter.

Mariah was quite shaky as she turned to Walter who rushed into the scene in confusion as to what the problem with Ron was. After a moment with Ron, Walter left Ron with the paramedics, and walked to Mariah who's being consoled by Arnold. "Walter, we killed him, you know he never wanted to do this," said Ron.

"Don't talk like this, Mariah," said Ron.

Mariah continued sobbing while reminding Walter, Ron said he wasn't competing again, but they all talked him into competing with another horse. Sadly, Ron just bit the dust after testing the best of both worlds and the worst of both at the end.

"Please Mariah, think about your girls, you don't need to hurt yourself," said Walter.

Commentator: I don't know, but there seem to be a problem, Ron just fell off his Horse after crossing the finish line, the paramedics are already attending to him. But our new County champion seems not to be getting off the ground, and the spectators are worried.

The beautiful smile that changes the colour of the sky, enough to turn a dark cloud into a blue sky that Ron started the day with just fades away as the paramedics pronounced Ron dead on the scene. Ron's mystery seemed to take hold as the temperature suddenly began dropping like stone, and it's dropping fast. Yet, the Paramedics continued as they rushed Ron into their van, bound for the hospital.

TV Presenter: Martin I hope history won't repeat itself, this County can't afford to lose another champion jockey, (ten minutes later), ladies and gentlemen and our viewers at home, word reaching us is that Ron Rogers is dead, what a sad day? I'm short of words.

Commentator: Oh no, ha..., what a sad day for this County, a triumphant return has turned out to be a sad demise, and how can the Rogers Family overcome this grief?

TV Presenter: Ladies and gentlemen and our viewers at home we are ending this broadcast on a sad note, thank you.

Within the same hour of Ron's death, Lewis walked into the accounts department where Monica works. "Hello Megan," said Lewis.

"Lewis! It's been quite a while, where have you been?" said Megan.

Lewis is quite a fascinating character whose presence provokes banter because of the friendly ambience that precedes him. "Why're you sounding as if you missed my face?" asked Lewis.

"Stop sounding as if I secretly hated you with passion," said Megan.

Lewis and Megan seemed to be two peas in a pod, because of their humorous nature, and this makes it all fun as they enjoy each other's company. Lewis laughed as he described Megan as a mixture of humour and elegance which makes her charmingly wicked.

"You're kind of funny you know, that's why I always look forward to your dry humour," said Megan.

"You seem to be hooked on it, that's why you missed me this much," said Lewis.

"Hooked on what?" asked Megan.

"My humour, of course!" said Lewis.

"Your humour or your sarcasm, which one?" asked Megan.

Interestingly, Lewis isn't a man given to emotional outburst, and not without certain influence, anyway. He subtly reminded Megan he's surprised she cared enough to notice his absence, and then asked her about Karen?

"Karen is fine, but you just asked after him as if you've met him," said Megan.

"Any guy taking care of a pretty lady like you deserved to be asked after," said Lewis.

After their bantering exchange of pleasantries, Megan steered the conversation into a more matter of concern as she asked Lewis where he has been all these while. After all, she inquired of Lewis from Leo who has refused to tell of Lewis's whereabouts each time he comes to pay bills for their firm.

"I told Leo to keep it a secret," said Lewis.

"Secret, from whom?" asked Megan.

"You of course," Lewis then burst into laughter. "Actually, I went to France on an official assignment," said Lewis.

"That should be for about six months?" said Megan.

Lewis steered the conversation into something more personal as he suddenly looked a different direction and asked. "Who's she?" he asked. "Who is who? I don't understand what you're talking about," said Megan.

Megan was lost as to what Lewis was implying, but she then followed the direction of his eyes and realised Lewis attention was completely focused on Monica. "I mean, her, when did she join you guys?" he asked.

"Oh, you mean, Monica?" asked Megan.

"Is her name Monica?" asked Lewis.

"Yes of course, she's my best friend, and she'll be six months with us next week," said Megan.

A dramatic shift of his attention to Monica was quite a switch, and this could mean he needed time to process what his eyes have just seen, and possibly his heart has just been captured by Monica.

"You mean she has been here for six months while I've been wasting away in France, in the name of an official assignment?" Lewis said, and smiled.

Megan understood what that meant, and quickly chipped a note of caution, to curb Lewis's expression of exuberance. She whispered to Lewis and urged him to stop talking as if he owns Monica, and made it clear, Monica doesn't play around if he must know. "I don't care, I'm not a player either," said Lewis.

Megan tried to manage Lewis's expectation as she asked what makes him think Monica will be into him, the same way he has fancied her.

Lewis of course is aware that he could get turned down by Monica because this isn't a take all situation. He was quite struck by Monica's looks, even though he knew little about the personality behind the looks, yet he's convinced he has just met the woman of his dream. "I don't know and I don't have to lose faith, now that I've found her," said Lewis.

"Stop being naive, did you lose her or what, and why're you sounding as if she's an item?" asked Megan.

"Can't you see there's love in the air; she's also staring at me?" said Lewis.

Megan had to quickly correct Lewis's wrong impression of the sudden ambience created by the manner he's starring at Monica. "No, she isn't starring at you in love, she's starring at you in amusement," said Megan.

"Why? All I see in those blue eyes of hers is nothing but love," said Lewis.

Megan reminded Lewis, his childlike smile won't do the magic and that Monica's big blue eyes aren't just there for the taking, but they're rather reserved for the best man. She quickly reminded him that Monica is starring at him in surprise and wondered why he has focused his attention on her and that's very embarrassing.

"I hope I haven't blown my chances, what do I do now?" asked Lewis.

"Go to her and say whatever is in your mind, before she considers you a disturbed man," said Megan.

"Ok, I'll do that right away," said Lewis.

Just as Megan concludes with Lewis, she muttered under her breath and said Monica has been unusually quiet today and she just doesn't know why. A minute later, Lewis walked to Monica. "Hey Monica, I'm Lewis and I am pleased to meet you," he said.

"Why were you starring at me that way, your stare was embarrassingly obvious, and do you know how embarrassing that is?" asked Monica. "Before I say a word, please accept my apology for creating a wrong first impression," said Lewis.

Monica suddenly put up a cheeky smile that's quite puzzling as she told Lewis he just made the whole thing worst by coming over to her desk.

"I'm not the bad guy kind of man, you may have heard about me from your colleagues, my friendly disposition is what endears me to them," said Lewis.

"Why didn't you allow your disposition to endear you to me, before coming over?" replied Monica.

Funnily, the last thing Lewis would want is to be on the back foot, he didn't hesitate to tell Monica of his anxiety, as he asked Monica, what if he waits and somebody wins her heart before she comes to know his kind of person.

Monica burst into laughter. "Oh, is it a competition kind of thing?" she asked. Lewis then realised that a formal introduction is the best way to take away the creepiness in this conversation.

Lewis concurred to the fact that this is now a competition for Monica's heart, but he'd to introduce himself saying his name is Lewis, and he's a financial accountant, who has just been captured by her charm.

"I've heard a little about you and I know you're Leo's colleague," said Monica.

"Err.., well researched then, I went to France to restructure our Accounts department and I did that for the past six months," said Lewis.

"And you're going back, are you?" asked Monica.

Lewis was quite upfront with his feelings for Monica, and he didn't hesitate to let Monica know he won't be going back until he's able to get her attention. "What sort of attention do you need? You already have my attention," said Monica.

"I like you, Monica. You may not know me, but your friends will tell you more about me, and you'll find out the rest for yourself," said Lewis.

"Despite your poor first impression, I know you're a nice guy, but just as you said, I'll have to find out more for myself," said Monica.

"Oh thank you, but I'm particularly delighted to have met you," said Lewis.

Monica softens up, yet urged Lewis not to raise his hopes, and suggests they take things little by little until she's sure about saying yes or no.

Megan interjected and said Lewis is a sweet and innocuous young man, and it's just that he always makes a bad first impression. "Err.., tell me all about it!" exclaimed Monica.

"We'll talk about that later, let's go for lunch," said Megan.

Lewis laughed, and asked Megan if she's cunningly taking Monica away from him.

"Hmm ok, I'll join you in a minute," said Monica.

Megan then turned to Lewis and told him he has said enough, and reminded him he can't win Monica in one day, they then burst into laughter. Moments later, Monica joined Megan in the restaurant where they got chatty in their assessment of Lewis.

"Monica, Lewis seems to like you, and he's falling head over heels already," said Megan.

"I know, but I'm not giving in until I see some seriousness in him," said Monica.

"Don't worry; I know he'll show you he's serious," said Megan.

While the conversation was on-going, Monica asked a staff of the restaurant to switch the channel so she could watch her dad's race, not knowing the race happened thirty minutes earlier. Sadly, what she saw was nothing but grief from the news of her father's death.

"What! She dropped her fork on the table and screamed. No, that can be true," Monica cried. Megan didn't quickly see the news headlines and asked Monica why she's screaming.

"That's my dad on the news," said Monica.

"Oh my God!" said Megan.

Monica couldn't help herself with the shocking news that left her quite shaky, she then ran to the ladies, and stayed there to sob uncontrollably.

Megan stood up immediately and followed Monica, and comforted her all through. "It has happened, and there's nothing we can do about it," said Megan.

"My dad said he's no longer racing, they must have talked him in to doing it," said Monica.

"It's your mum, you should be worried about," said Megan.

Monica looked straight into Megan's eyes and said she hasn't been herself since she woke up today, and now she knows something bad was to come her way that day. "I also noticed you've been unusually quiet today, and I just couldn't place your mood, give your mum a call please," said Megan.

"Ok, let me give her a call," said Megan, she then dialled her mum's number.

"Hello mum," said Monica.

Sadly, it was Kenny Walter who picked the phone, Monica's mum is indisposed at the moment, as she's been comforted by Arnold and other friends of the family. "Hello Monica, how're you?" he asked. Monica told him she just saw the news concerning her dad, and asked if that's true, even as she continued to sob on the phone.

"Yes, it is, but I want you to be strong for your mum and your sister," said Walter.

"What about me? My world is shattered," replied Monica.

Funnily, Monica equally needs comforting, and Walter is treating her as if others were made of lace and she wasn't. "I know, and I'll be there for you, but for now please be strong for them," said Walter.

Monica then asked about her mum. "She's here with me, she can't talk for now, but I want you to come home tonight," said Walter.

Monica then asked if her sister is aware of this incident, Walter told Monica he doesn't think Bianca is aware but he'll give her a call right away, and let her know her dad is critically ill.

"Why tell her he's critically ill?" asked Monica.

Funnily, Monica thinks Bianca may have seen the news just as she did, and selling her a ruse about her dad being sick, will be sort of making a joke out of this sad tragedy that has befallen them.

"She might not be able to manage the news," said Walter.

Serendipitously, these two sisters knew their dad was going in to a race but had no idea the race is happening thirty minutes earlier than they thought. Funnily, Bianca has been tied down with an important school work, and hasn't seen the news of this incident.

"I'll be on my way right away, let me inform my office first," said Monica.

"Ok, but don't say a thing to your sister. I'll inform her myself," said Walter.

Immediately after his phone call with Monica, Kenny Walter had put a phone call across to Bianca who's just stepping out of lectures. Even as he dialled Bianca's number, he prayed silently in his heart for Bianca not to have heard the news, particularly now that he'd to lie to her.

"Hello Bianca, this is Kenny Walter," he said.

"Ooh Walter, how're you, I guess my dad won the race. I've been tied down by school work," said Bianca. "We're fine, and your dad won the race, but there has been an incident and we want you to come home tonight," said Walter.

"What incident! The trembling in her voice could be felt on the other side of the telephone. "Are my parents ok?" she asked.

Walter then told her it's about her dad. Bianca was now taken over by apprehension, as she stood statue-still and her ears keen to hear what it is about her dad.

"What about him?" asked Bianca.

Walter began speaking in a low calm voice, yet hid his emotional distress away from Bianca as he told her Ron was involved in a racing accident and he's critically ill. Sadly, Walter isn't just talking about Ron, the legendary jockey, he's talking about her dad.

"What, my dad? Oh my God, not again," she screamed.

"Yes Bianca," said Walter.

"Are you telling me the truth?" asked Bianca.

"That's the truth for now, Bianca," said Walter.

Bianca quickly asked if her sister is aware of this incident, even as tears rolled down her cheek. "Of course yes, I just told her about it, and she's already on her way to Dallas," said Walter.

Learning that her sister is already on her way to Dallas over this incident left Bianca with this gut wrenching feeling that got her overwhelmed. She didn't realise she has lost grip of her phone, and the phone fell on the ground as she continued to cry. "Ooh, no, why?" cried Bianca.

"Bianca, Bianca," said Walter. He couldn't continue the conversation, after all the phone is on the floor.

Lately, the Rogers family ordeal is likened to a life's buffet served, lined up without an end in sight and with ready host doing the dishing. Sadly, this is a kind of buffet they'd rather not taste. Thirty minutes later, Bianca called Monica to share her grief with her but the call didn't go through at first, and she was only able to reach her just as her flight was about to take off.

"Hey Monica," said Bianca.

"Little sister, how're you?" she asked.

"Where are you, and did they tell you about dad?" asked Bianca.

Monica replied her saying Walter told her about their dad, and she's on her way to see him and be there for their mum as well. Bianca continued crying, and all she kept saying was she doesn't want anything to happen to their dad. Even as she tried to keep her shattered emotions intact, tears rolled down Monica's cheeks as she spoke with her sister. "Don't worry, I hope you're coming?" asked Monica.

"Yes, I am," said Bianca.

"Ok, I'll be waiting," said Monica.

Sadly, Mrs Berkley who sat next to Monica in the plane knew she hasn't perfected her platitudes, even though she considers getting involved in people's private business an ethical minefield. She however got involved in Monica's as she turned to Monica "You're crying, are you okay?" asked Mrs Berkley.

"I'm okay. No, I'm not, I just lost my dad," said Monica.

"Oh shame, you've to be strong my dear," replied Mrs Berkley.

"Yeah, thank you," said Monica.

Mrs Berkley then asked Monica if she's on her way home now, but she could read Monica's disposition and understand she's grieve stricken, and decided not to push her any further.

"Yes of course, but please just give me some time to pull myself together," said Monica.

Bianca arrived later that even from school, only to meet Monica who's already home, and was comforting her mum. "Hey little sister, you're welcome," said Monica.

Bianca was quite taken aback to see her sister and her mum at home, instead of being by her sick dad's bedside in the hospital. "Where's dad? Let's go to the hospital," she said.

Monica stood up and held her by the hand and said their dad didn't make it. Things suddenly got sour, and the temperature in the room became fever-pitched as Bianca became feisty and threw herself on the floor and wept.

"What?" cried Bianca.

"Calm down, Bianca," said Monica.

"No, I can't, if you want me to calm down, then you'll have to bring dad back," Bianca protested.

Mariah who has been speechless cried the more, and asked Bianca to please beg her dad to come back to her. Bianca couldn't contain her grief she then stood up and headed for the back garden. Monica looked on in confusion and asked Bianca where it is she's going. Asking Bianca to calm down over her the news of her dad's shocking and sudden demise is a tree no one would want to climb.

"Leave me alone," said Bianca. She walked towards their back garden and continued to weep. Helping Bianca to manage this shocking news is now the focus. Arnold quickly interjected and asked Monica to go after her sister, while he stays with their mum. Monica then followed Bianca to the back garden and began to cry with her. Moments later Walter went to Bianca and Monica and said he knew how hard this is, but if there was any way he could bring their dad back he would. "Your mum would need you girls now, so she doesn't fall sick," said Walter.

Days later, Walter called the priest to inform him of Ron's death.

"Hello reverend," said Walter.

"Hello Walter, how're you?" replied the priest.

"I'm fine, reverend, just troubles," said Walter.

The Priest asked Walter about his wife and his boys.

Walter didn't reply the priest's question about his wife and children. He just went straight to tell the priest he isn't fine, and his sprit is low because he has just been faced with much more than the normal everyday troubles.

"Are you ok, Walter?" asked the priest.

"My friend Ron is dead," said Walter.

"Ooh Jesus, when did this happen?" asked the priest.

"Three days ago, Reverend," said Walter.

The Priest was shocked to hear of Ron's sudden demise, and asked how it happened. "Was he involved in an accident or what?" asked the priest.

"He died in a horse race accident. He won the competition but fell off his horse and died after crossing the finish line," said Walter.

The Priest was curious as to Ron's decision to return to the tracks after his insistence on not racing again. He then reminded Walter that the last time he spoke to him about Ron, he told him Ron wasn't willing to race with any other horse than Anvil.

"Yes, but we persuaded him, and thought it would help him move on," said Walter.

The Priest interjected and said Ron was a mystery, and maintained that they should've let him be. Walter seemed lost with the Priest's description of Ron as a mystery, he opened his mouth and told the Priest he doesn't get what he meant by Ron being a mystery.

"The last time I spoke with him, I knew there's some kind of strange bond between him and Anvil, it's more like a covenant," said the priest.

Walter laughed and became hysterical, the much he knew about Ron except during his dark moments is that he doesn't live his life like an unmade bed. "How can a person go into a covenant with a horse?" asked Walter.

"It isn't a covenant per say, but it's a strange bond, the horse has no hand in this, Ron put it on himself," said the priest.

"But Fanny is his horse as well?" asked Walter.

"Yes, but he bonded with Anvil in a strange way," said the priest.

"What a shame, this is on us then," Walter confessed.

The Priest tried calming Walter, as he told him it has happened and urged him to stop beating himself up over it. The Priest went ahead to give Walter information that sounds so surreal, as he told him Ron knew this would happen, that's why he didn't come for confession.

"Confession, what do you mean?" asked Walter.

The Priest informed Walter that Ron usually comes for confession before he enters into any race, and this isn't something that's common knowledge to those closest to Ron. Walter seem to have just been given a peek into Ron's horse racing mystery, and funnily, he remained open-mouthed and said he didn't know of this, and asked how long Ron has been doing this.

"According to Ron, that would be since he started horse racing, and each time he doesn't do that something strange happens," said the priest.

"Oh my God, why did Ron do this and why didn't he tell me about himself?" asked Walter.

"Because he didn't want to, though, I'm happy he started coming to church before this happened," said the priest.

"Ron didn't end badly then, but I'll miss him even though the guilt of feeling I failed him will continue to haunt me," said Walter.

For all it's worth, the Priest had to let Walter into Ron's mystery to provide him some latitude that will help him cope with this grief.

"Stop beating yourself up over this, Walter, you need to be strong for his family," the priest.

Walter then proceeded to inform the reverend he wants him to handle Ron's funeral.

"You want me to celebrate his funeral mass?" asked the reverend.

"Of course yes, you're the best person to do that," said Ron.

"When is it coming up?" asked the priest.

"I'll inform you of this, and maybe soonest," said Walter.

They concluded their conversation and said their good byes' the Priest then said he looks forward to hearing from Walter about the plans for Ron's funeral.

Two weeks after Ron's death, Bianca walked into the living room and was met with a surprise of an unusual guest. Interestingly, she walked in as Tommy Jones and Mariah were in a conversation. "Hello mum," said Bianca.

"Bianca, how did it go?" asked Mariah.

Bianca then turns to Tommy to see who the guest was and there's a flicker of recognition, yet she's still struggling to pin the face to a name. "Hello," she said to the guest. "Hello my dear, you've grown into a beautiful woman Bianca," said Tommy. Interestingly, Tommy's comment breaks the ice for her, and Bianca's face was suddenly wreathed in smiles as she turns to her mum. "Mum, I know this face, isn't this Tommy Jones?" Bianca asked as she points to a photograph of Tommy and Ron hanging on the wall.

"Yes, he is, your dad's death has given you another opportunity to meet the much talked about Tommy Jones," said Mariah.

Bianca fixed her gaze on Tommy. "Ooh my God, but why didn't you visit us all these years while dad was alive? I would've loved to see you and dad sitting side by side," she said.

Tommy smiled and said he's here now, and unfortunately Ron isn't, and hinted that Ron's death would have been avoided if he hadn't competed. Mariah continued Tommy's line of conversation and said Ron never wanted to compete with any other horse after Anvil's demise, and the mystery behind his decision amazes her even when Fanny was also his.

Bianca quickly interjected as she takes her seat. "Fanny is mine, not dad's horse," she said.

Tommy seemed to have opened a can of worms when he hinted Mariah that he almost fell off his seat, the moment he saw Ron on the tracks with a different horse even before the race started.

Tommy's remark leaves Mariah bewildered, because he has just painted a surreal picture of Ron's attachment to Anvil. Mariah thinks there's more than meets the eye, and queried further to know what could precipitate the kind of shock Tommy just expressed. "Why the shock! Is there something you knew about my husband that I don't?" asked Mariah.

Tommy is now beginning to choose his words carefully, particularly now that he has opened a can of worms, to avoid the warms swarming all over the place. Mariah's itchy ears listened keenly as Tommy laid it bare that the bond between Ron and Anvil is one that kept Ron bound and prevents him from racing with any other horse.

"What a mysterious bond, you just described!" exclaimed Mariah.

Bianca quickly interjected and asked Tommy, why he didn't act proactively if he knew something will go wrong if her dad races with Fanny.

Tommy had to explain himself more clearly as he sensed that there isn't a need for a barbed comment at this point, and said he knew Ron stopped racing after Anvil's demise and never knew he would ever return to the tracks. Seeing him on the tracks on the day of his death was a surprise to him.

Mariah confessed that Ron never wanted to race with any other horse other than Anvil, and he made that clear to her but she never knew encouraging him to return to the tracks could lead to a ghastly end.

"Where's Monica? I haven't seen her since I got here," said Tommy.

Bianca responded and said she went out to the funeral director and she'll soon be back. She then turned to Tommy and asked if he's leaving anytime soon.

"I'm still around; I'm lodged in a motel down town," said Tommy.

"I guess you will stay until Ron's funeral is over," asked Mariah.

"Of course, I'll be here until the funeral is over," replied Tommy.

Tommy stayed with Ron's family all day to keep them company, and unfortunately, Monica didn't return home on time as the day's activities took more of her time than necessary. By evening of the same day, Bianca walks into the stable while Tommy was giving Fanny a rub.

"You're here, I looked around the house and even the garden and couldn't find you," said Bianca.

"I felt like spending some time with Fanny, your horse, you said?" asked Tommy.

"Yes, of course! This horse gave me victory, are you aware I'm a jockey?" she asked.

"I know, and I can see it in you. I watched your race and you did great," said Tommy.

Bianca suddenly got emotional and began to sob, saying her dad was her trainer, and she doesn't think she can cope without her dad.

Tommy held Bianca to himself, as she lays her head on his shoulder, he then pats her back a few times and tells her everything will be fine.

"Will you be my trainer? I want to continue in dad's legacy," she asked.

Tommy reminded Bianca he's just a guest who travelled down from afar, and doesn't live in Dallas. Yet, he urged her not to worry because they would work something out.

"Don't let my mum know of our conversation, she doesn't want me on the tracks," said Bianca.

"Your mum's fears are justified," said Tommy.

"Err.., you worry about her fears, what about my career?" asked Bianca.

Tommy is now torn between dealing with Mariah's prejudice and Bianca's horse racing career, he then steered the conversation to the skills Ron passed on to her daughter. "Your dad must have introduced you to some of his rituals, I guess," said Tommy.

"Hmm, yeah, a few rituals I suppose, before my first race," said Bianca.

Tommy knew some of the rituals passed to Bianca must be kept as her secret, yet he's keen to know how safe these rituals are. He then asked Bianca what her relationship with Fanny was like. "Just a normal relationship, I like my horse and my horse likes me, or are you implying something else?" asked Bianca.

"Hmm…," said Tommy.

Bianca interjected and asked Tommy if he's implying the kind of relationship between Anvil and her dad that kept him bound.

"Of course, maybe, but I don't want you developing such bond with Fanny, because you can't handle it," said Tommy.

"Not that I can't handle it, I don't need it, and I don't want anything scary," said Bianca.

"Don't worry, Bianca, everything will be fine," said Tommy.

Bianca pleaded with Tommy to keep their conversation under wraps for now, and then looked straight into Tommy's eyes, and insists she wants this kept away from her mum, under wraps. Tommy had to be the adult in the room here, as he agreed to keep things away from Mariah, yet insists he'll need to speak to her mum at some point, before they commence training.

Tommy has been around as promised, and has always paid daily visits to Ron's family at least to comfort them. On the eve of Ron's funeral Tommy walks up to Mariah while she was seated alone in the back garden. "Err.., you're here, Mariah," he said.

"Hmm, Tommy! I'm just lost in thought reminiscing the wonderful life I'd with Ron, and also imagining life without my husband, going forward," exclaimed Mariah.

"Hmm, taking stock? That isn't a good place to be," replied Tommy.

Mariah chuckled, and then muttered. "How do you know?" she asked.

"I know that feeling, and it really hurts. Pain was what I felt when I lost Rochelle," he said. "Yours is long ago." She said and then looked straight into Tommy's eyes. "Do you still take stock of your life with Rochelle?" she asked.

"Yeah, I still do, because the pain doesn't go away," said Ron.

Mariah briskly rubbed her hands together, then placed her hands on her chin, and muttered, saying Ron should've stayed with her because she doesn't think she can cope without him.

"Don't worry, Mariah, you'll learn to live through the days without him. Though, with time," said Tommy.

Monica walks into the conversation.

"Ooh, you're back, Monica, and how did it go?" asked Mariah.

"It went well, and it's all set," said Monica. She then took a closer look at Tommy Jones, and there's a flicker of recognition, after all there's a photograph of Tommy and Ron hanging on the wall. "This is Tommy Jones, I guess?" asked Monica.

"Of course, yes, Monica! It's me Tommy Jones, and good to see you," replied Tommy.

"Oh my gosh! It's quite an age, where have you been all these years, and how's life treating you?" asked Monica.

"Life has been good! You girls were very young the last time your dad visited me in Pennsylvania," said Tommy.

Monica got chatty, and informed Tommy that her dad told them he later left Pennsylvania.

"Yeah, I left horse racing when my son became a Rodeo cowboy," said Tommy.

"What an irony! Life is full of tales, my dad used to be a Rodeo cowboy, he found love and became a Jockey," said Monica. It was quite a reunion as Monica shook hands with Tommy and said she was told of his visits days back, but she just doesn't know why they've serendipitously missed each other. After they exchanged pleasantries, Tommy steered the conversation into a contentious topic and for all it's worth, he thinks it's time they talk about Bianca.

"What about her? I think I know what this is about," said Mariah.

"Hmm, I guess this is about Bianca asking you to be her trainer," said Monica.

"Yes, and I think it worth's talking about," said Tommy.

Mariah got pissed, became quite incensed and described Bianca as incorrigible and she can't stomach this idiocy any longer. She immediately turned to Monica, and asked her to bring her sister here.

Tommy looked on as Mariah reacted brashly, with her squeaky voice that resulted from days of sobbing. Mariah have tried as much as she could to take the winds out of Bianca's sails, but Tommy had to caution Mariah by reminding her Bianca's already attached to horse racing, and advised her to handle this with caution.

Mariah didn't see any need for caution particularly when she thinks Bianca's daftness makes her as thick as a brush, and she'd rather put Bianca in her place. She turned to Tommy and asked why Bianca would want to continue with horse racing despite the too many strokes of bad luck her family has suffered.

Minutes later Bianca walked into the conversation "You called me, mum?" asked Bianca.

"Did you ask Tommy to be your trainer?" asked Mariah.

There's a need to unburden this family of the frenzy of the fear of what the future holds and Mariah felt her daughter just cynically gave her middle finger, in a casual but rude way. Bianca hasn't made the job any easy for her mum, who's obviously at a cross road. "Of course yes, dad is dead, and if fate brought Tommy my way, then should I just let him go," Bianca protested.

"**A**nd so, what? Tommy is here for your dad's funeral," insists Mariah.

Bianca insists her mind is made up and she's bent on continuing her horse racing career to keep her dad's legacy alive. Mariah looked on and was lost for words as Bianca took her stand, but since threats didn't work, maybe sending Bianca on a guilt trip will do the job of making her back down. "I guess you remembered how Edger died, and now, your dad has joined Edger," said Mariah.

Bianca didn't buy the threats as she picked her mum's argument apart, one after the other. She insists it was the doctor's error that killed Edger while dad's bond with anvil was responsible for his death, then wondered why her mum couldn't stomach her racing interest.

"Why can't you just be a lady! What's it with you and being a jockey?" exclaimed Mariah.

"My being a lady has got nothing to do with my sporting career," said Bianca.

"Why would you want to abandon being a Veterinary Doctor, for horse racing? Stop giving me the run around," said Mariah. Good things come in brightly coloured packages, they sometimes say, but this isn't it, as far as Mariah is concerned.

"Mum! Stop making this whole thing very difficult, I'm not leaving school," insists Bianca.

Mariah got tired of the back and forth with her daughter, she then felt the only way of making her snap out of this madness is to ask Tommy to stay away from Bianca because she doesn't want to see her hurt herself. Bianca shrugged off her mum's threat, and insists if her mum stands in her way, she'll get someone else to be her trainer, she then flounced off. Mariah then turns to Tommy. "What do you think?" she asked.

"Her mind is made up," said Tommy.

"How do I handle this foolishness?" asked Mariah.

"Give her a chance and I'll make sure she plays safe," said Tommy.

"Can I trust you with her?" asked Mariah.

"I'm old and grey, Mariah. I watched over her dad, and I think I can look after her," said Tommy.

"Let me take you for your word, at least for old time's sake," said Mariah.

After the conversation with Mariah, Tommy asked where Monica was, but Bianca interjected and said Monica just stepped out to get things ready for Megan.

"Is Megan here?" asked Mariah.

"She's on her way," said Bianca.

Tommy couldn't help but asked who Megan was.

"Megan is a friend of Monica, and she's coming down from New York," said Mariah.

CHAPTER

NINE

The Funeral

The funeral arrangements is all in place, and in less than twenty-four hours the legendary horse racing champion will be laid to rest. Later that evening, Megan arrives in Dallas and joins Monica who's already waiting to welcome her.

"Oh my God, Megan, you made it to Dallas just because of me?" said Monica.

"What are we friends for!" exclaimed Megan.

"Monica, how're you?" asked Megan.

Monica and Megan continued their catching-up as they take steps towards the house, but Monica seem to miss the office and was keen to know what's up in the office. Funnily, Megan isn't keen to discuss work as she passively told Monica work is good, yet steered the conversation away to the business at hand, which is her preparation for her dad's funeral service.

"The funeral preparation is all set, just that I won't get to see my dad again," Monica said as tears rolled down her cheeks.

"Stop crying, Monica, I understand how you feel," said Megan.

Interestingly, Bianca sensed Megan is around and walked to the balcony to meet up with them, and even before Bianca opened her mouth to say hello, Monica introduced her to Megan. "Meet my little sister; she's one of the greatest jockeys in this County," said Monica.

Bianca added to the banter as she told Megan not to mind Monica's description of her as a little sister, that they're actually age mates. "Whatever," said Monica.

Megan couldn't help herself, but laughed herself to tears as these sisters make jokes, and it didn't take long before Megan and Bianca began formal introduction. "How're you, Bianca?" asked Megan.

"I'm good, Megan, you're welcome, don't mind Monica she's my almighty big sister and I love her so much," said Bianca.

Megan burst into laughter again, and said it must be fun being around these sisters. After Bianca finished with asking Megan about her trip, she went on to flatter Megan as she hinted her that her sister has said a lot of nice things about her.

"Really, though we expected you to come around, but your sister said you changed your mind," said Megan.

Bianca liked Megan at first sight, and got all chatty with her, and said she actually wanted to come and impersonate her sister but the horse racing championship took over.

"Impersonate her, how do you mean?" asked Megan.

Monica then interjected and said her sister wants to come over to New York, put on her dresses, to make her look exactly like her and possibly steal her boyfriend.

"I thought I'm funny, I just realised I'm not, but we'll be expecting you in New York, Bianca. I hope you'll come," said Megan.

"Of course yes, I wouldn't want my sister to steal all the show," said Bianca.

Kenny Walter and Bill Shannon walked into their conversation, while the girls were still standing in the balcony. "Hello Monica," said Walter.

"Walter, you're welcome," said Monica.

Walter turned and pointed to Megan. "Is this your friend?" he asked.

"Yes, she's my work colleague who just came all the way from New York to comfort me," said Monica.

In his usual warm disposition, Walter welcomed Megan to Dallas, and after they dispensed with the pleasantries. Walter then turned to Monica and asked if they can have a moment with her, her sister and her mum.

"Sure, Megan, I'll join you in a moment," said Monica. She then stood up and went with them to the back garden where Mariah was seated. Mariah has found her serene green back garden more comforting of late, and this explains the reason she spends most of her time in the back garden.

Moments later, Mariah, Monica, and Bianca were all seated, and Walter started by saying Bill has something for them. Bill didn't just jump into the deep end of the conversation, he had to do the humane thing, starting with a formal exchange of pleasantries, and then commiserated with this family over their loss.

"Hello Mariah, how're you feeling?" asked Bill.

"You should know I'm not feeling great, and I'm just empty inside," said Mariah.

Bill apologised to Mariah and said he's sorry about her husband and then turned to the girls, then said he's sorry over their dad. He told them Ron will be greatly missed, and the likes of Ron are like a flash in the pan, after saying some nice things about Ron in his appreciation of his feat, Bill then handed Monica an envelope. Monica collected the envelope from Bill. "What's in it?" she asked.

"It's cash, though it's far more than I intend to give to your dad, the excess is my contribution towards his funeral," said Bill.

"Ooh, thank you, Bill," said Mariah.

"Thank you, Walter," said Bianca.

Walter then steered the conversation away from the Bill's business into a more personal stuff and asked Monica about her plans for her mum. Monica had it all planned out as she said her mum is coming with her to New York City immediately after the funeral.

"What about your sister, will she continue with the horse racing, or she's joining you in New York?" asked Walter.

"She'll stay with me in New York, but I'll discuss that with her," said Monica.

They spent time preparing for a future without Ron, Walter then promised he'll bring something for Mariah on behalf of the Dallas County horse racing Association.

"Thank you very much, Walter," said Monica.

After having a meeting with the family, it's now time for Bill Shannon and Kenny Walter to take their leave but Walter felt the need to discuss a needling concern. He then turned to Mariah and asked if he could speak to her privately.

"Ok, I'll be with you in a moment, wait for me at the balcony," said Mariah.

Moments later, Mariah joined Walter at the balcony while Bill waited for him by the car.

"Yes Mariah, I've been doing some thinking and there's something I want to ask you," said Walter.

Mariah listened keenly as she asked Walter what it was, and if everything is alright. Walter drew closer and using a low tone. "Yes, but the confessions, do you know about it?" asked Walter.

"What confessions, I don't get you?" asked Mariah.

Walter then said the Priest told him about Ron's confession before a race, and asked if she knew about that. Funnily, one among the too many mysteries surrounding Ron's horse racing career is now brought to the fore, and as far as Kenny Walter is concerned, nothing is off the table.

"I knew about that just two years ago, and it was a surprise to me," said Mariah.

"The priest finds it a mystery, and strange," said Walter.

Mariah's focus quickly shifted from Ron's horse racing mystery to platitudes and the morality of the priests' action. She then looked Walter in the eyes and asked if the Priest is supposed to discuss a person's confession with another.

"No, he isn't, and that's not how it happened, he's just surprised that Ron didn't come for confession before he ran his last race," said Walter.

"Does that mean anything?" asked Mariah.

"Maybe, and it's like Ron deliberately signed out of life," said Walter.

Mariah finds it hard to assimilate this punchy and shocking revelation. She looked at Walter, open-mouthed, and asked if he meant Ron deliberately killed himself. No matter how hard she has tried to dismiss insinuations about her husband, it keeps getting weirder by the day, and the mystery is now coming home.

"No, I think he knew this would happen if he raced with another horse, that was why he was refusing to do it," said Walter.

"Why then did he do it, if he knew this would happen?" asked Mariah.

There's no need second-guessing why he did, Walter have to admit, the pressure was too much, so Ron caved in. "Pressure from who?" asked Mariah.

"You and me, family and friends, and as so, he decided not to go for confession," said Walter.

"You mean he didn't go for confession?" said Walter.

"Yes, it's like he wanted this to happen, so he parked everything up," said Walter.

"Damn it, damn it Ron, why didn't you go for your confession and stay alive?" Mariah muttered.

Walter then held Mariah to calm her down as this new revelation seemed to rile her up the more, and said he just felt he should let her know. "Thank you for letting me know," said Mariah.

Walter then turned to Bill and said it's time to go, they said goodbyes and Bill urged Mariah to stay strong as they entered the car then left.

Later that night Monica and Bianca had to talk about the future, and funnily, when Kenny Walter asked Monica about her plans for her sister, Monica's response was sort of a guess. After all, taking the winds out of Bianca's sails has proved difficult. The sisters are now alone and away from everyone, and everything, Monica then told her sister she hopes she's coming with them to New York.

"Yes, I'm coming with you, though, that'll be for a short while," replied Bianca.

Monica looked on as Bianca set out her plans, yet she was keen to know why her visit to New York will be for a short while. She needed Bianca to unpack what's in her mind. Bianca perhaps has other plans wrapped under her sleeve, and this has already kept the family on the edge, she then looked away as she told Monica she intends to continue with their dad's legacy.

"Have you discussed that with mum? I know she wouldn't support the idea of horse racing?" said Monica.

"I know she wouldn't, but that's what I intend to do," insists Bianca.

Monica then asked her how she intends to cope, because staying in the house alone will make healing a bit difficult. They chatted about everything and anything, Monica then held Bianca's hand and advised it's best to leave for a while, and that will help them heal over the bad memories precipitated by their dad's and Anvil's demise. Funnily, that memory is what Bianca wants to preserve, she just doesn't want to forget, and she's also staying back for Fanny's sake, she insists.

"If this decision of staying behind is just for Fanny's sake, I can get you a stable in New York where Fanny will be well cared for," said Monica.

"Albert has promised to stay with me, to help me move past dad's loss," she said.

The conversation has taken a new turn. The mention of Albert is now a new twist in this conversation and Monica had to explore where her sister's heart lies. Monica looked at Bianca and asked if she's planning on living together with Albert. "You never told me you've accepted his proposal," said Monica.

"I decided to give him a try. Though, this decision was just about a month ago, and I intend to tell you about it," said Bianca.

Bianca admitted her relationship with Albert is in its budding stage, and they haven't been romantically involved so far, but they agreed to bring the conversation before their mum to formalise this relationship.

"That's good, but you need to take things slow," said Monica.

Bianca turned the conversation around and steered the focus on Monica's love life. She then asked Monica if she isn't settling down with somebody, and this shouldn't be about her and Albert alone. Monica smiled and said she'll do that soon, after all, a lot of good guys are coming around, and she's only taking her time.

Bianca interjected. "Mum's style, isn't it?" said Bianca.

"Yeah, you're right, but if you and Albert are moving in together, why hasn't he surfaced since dad's death?" asked Monica.

"Albert isn't in town, but he'll be here tomorrow for the funeral," said Bianca.

Monica quickly made a cursory assessment of Albert and asked if he's cutting his trip short just to be at the funeral. "Yes, of course," replied Bianca.

It's now two Weeks after Ron's death. His friends and fans, far and near, are all gathered once again, this time, not to watch him race on the racecourse or compete with him on the tracks, but for a funeral mass to send the legendary jockey off in style.

After the Priest finished with his sermon, Kenny Walter gave a short speech on behalf of the horse racing association.

Walter: One thing about death is its uncanny ability to remind us of how best we should make use of our time here on earth. Ron was facile, enthusiastic, and enjoyed horse racing, his amiable passion and ideology about horses and horse racing earned him his legendry title. He will be missed both by the Horse racing fans and the association. Therefore, on behalf of the Dallas County horse racing association, we say rest in peace, Ron.

Monica gives the Eulogy.

Monica: For many jockeys here, how they'll remember him is by reminiscing the horse racing championship they competed in together.

For me, he isn't just Ron Rogers the legendary jockey. He's my dad, my best friend, my confidante and my hero, who called me his Angel.

My sister Bianca is over there, and I know she misses him much more because to her, he isn't just the Ron Rogers you know. He's her dad, her friend, her lawyer who comes to her defence whenever she and mum disagrees, and most importantly her personal trainer who made her a famous jockey on her first racing attempt.

Finally, for my mum over there, Ron Rogers is her husband, her best friend, her soul mate and the man she was meant to grow old together with.

Dad, I love you, Bianca says she love you, mum says she loves you, and all your friends gathered here today say they love you. Good bye dad. (Tears rolled down her cheeks).

After Monica's eulogy, the funeral procession then continued to the graveside where Ron was to be interred.

At the cemetery, while Ron's casket was being covered with sand, most of the guests are beginning to return to their cars, leaving Kenny Walter, Mariah, and the girls by the graveside. Kenny Walter was standing by Mariah consoling her and strangely, Mariah, Monica and Bianca saw Ron's ghost waving them good-bye, and a White Chariot waiting for Ron. Ron then walked into the Chariot and the chariot rode off.

"Mum, mum look, look at dad," said Monica, as she points to the chariot.

Bianca was also open-mouthed, as she points to the same direction as Monica "Dad, dad, mum can't you see him?" said Bianca.

Kenny Walter finds the reaction of the girls quite bizarre and surreal as he looked around and didn't see what the girls are pointing at. Mariah immediately added her voice to her daughters claim. "I just saw Ron and Anvil," said Mariah. She pointed to the same direction as her daughters. "Look at them riding away into the sky," said Mariah.

"Mariah, what are you talking about? I didn't see anything," said Walter.

"Anvil just came to pick Ron up, you mean you didn't see them?" asked Mariah.

"I didn't see anything," he said and then turned to Monica and Bianca. "What did you see?" asked Walter.

"That's our dad going, he waved us good bye, you mean you didn't see him and Anvil?" asked Monica.

"I saw them," said Mariah. She began to wave into the sky. "Goodbye my good husband, have a safe trip, and I'll always love you," said Mariah.

Sadly Walter was left out in this one last mystery surrounding this legendary jockey, yet he can't deny them of what they have seen. "It's ok Mariah, please stop acting strange," said Walter.

Mariah was consumed by her husband's ride into the sky, and she continues to wave goodbye until the chariot fades out of sight.

Swing low, sweet chariot, coming for to carry me home.

Swing low, sweet chariot, coming for to carry me home.

Swing low, sweet chariot, coming for to carry me home.

Swing low, sweet chariot, coming for to carry me home.

Swing low, sweet chariot, coming for to carry me home.

Swing low, sweet chariot, coming for to carry me home.

Swing low, sweet chariot, coming for to carry me home.

Swing low, sweet chariot, coming for to carry me home.

Books by Boniface Ossai